Praise for
Second Chance Season,
book two in the Grand Valley series

"Sassy and sexy, featuring a hero and heroine whose playfulness and good, dirty fun are infectious. . . . Blake's city girl–country boy premise is nothing new, but Garrett's point of view as a very masculine man and Cara's endearingly fish-out-of-water reactions to country living are extremely well done, and their chemistry is off the charts. The author's exuberant writing makes a stock story line fresh, and her addition of just enough angst at the end gives it some substance."

—*Publishers Weekly*

"The second in the Grand Valley series delivers another fun and sexy story involving two complete opposites. When country meets city, the sparks fly and never let up. Blake is a master at developing chemistry between her characters. From their backstories to the natural dialogue and evolution of their relationship, it all works together to bring readers a realistic and enjoyable romance. Add in the hot and steamy sex scenes and you have a surefire winner."

—*RT Book Reviews* (4-star review)

First Step Forward,
book one in the Grand Valley series

"A sexy, smart romp that will appeal to both romance and sports fans."

—*RT Book Reviews* (4-star review)

"*First Step Forward* by Liora Blake is an entertaining read, filled with charming characters and plenty of humorous moments."

—*Harlequin Junkie*

"I loved this story! It's a football romance with actual football! But it's more than that. It's an epic opposites-attract love story that had me laughing out loud the entire time, from Cooper's filthy mouth to Whitney's granola view of life, I loved every second!"

—*Two Book Pushers*

"This book is funny, sweet, smart, and sexy. Being inside the heads of these two characters as they navigate the challenges in their own lives while moving toward each other is pure joy."

—*The Literary Gossip*

"I love books that when I finish reading them leave a smile on my face or a sigh escapes me. This is exactly what happened with this novel."

—*Mrs. Leif's Two Fangs About It*

"*First Step Forward* is a funny, witty, sexy, sweet, and just a bit quirky contemporary romance. It will make you smile, it will make you ache, and it will make you swoon."

—*Literati Literature Lovers*

"The author set up a fantastic series with this book. The only problem . . . it's going to be hard for her to go up from here. This was pretty much contemporary romance perfection in my opinion."

—*Smitten with Reading*

Praise for Liora Blake's True Series

True North
True Devotion
True Divide

Available from Pocket Star!

"Blake's debut is a heated, sexy romp that will entice readers to want more."

—*Library Journal*, starred review

"Highly recommend . . . adult romance full of love and forgiveness."

—*Harlequin Junkie*

"This series is amazing. . . . If you're looking for a hot read that will have you laughing out loud and falling for the hot guitarist, definitely pick this one up today."

—*Reading Past My Bedtime*

"Couldn't put it down."

—*Fresh Fiction*

"Simmering, smoldering, sensual."

—*The Love Junkee*

"Incredibly beautiful . . . entirely riveting, completely entertaining."

—*Smitten with Reading*

LIORA BLAKE

Ready for Wild

G

GALLERY BOOKS

New York   London   Toronto   Sydney   New Delhi

G

Gallery Books
An Imprint of Simon & Schuster, Inc.
1230 Avenue of the Americas
New York, NY 10020

First Gallery Books paperback edition October 2017

GALLERY and colophon are registered trademarks of Simon & Schuster, Inc.

For information about special discounts for bulk purchases, please contact Simon & Schuster Special Sales at 1-866-506-1949 or business@simonandschuster.com.

The Simon & Schuster Speakers Bureau can bring authors to your live event. For more information or to book an event, contact the Simon & Schuster Speakers Bureau at 1-866-248-3049 or visit our website at www.simonspeakers.com.

Interior design by Bryden Spevak

Manufactured in the United States of America

Library of Congress Cataloging-in-Publication Data

Names: Blake, Liora, author.
Title: Ready for wild / Liora Blake.
Description: First Gallery Books trade paperback edition. | New York : Gallery Books, 2017. | Series: The Grand Valley series ; 3
Identifiers: LCCN 2017021543| ISBN 9781501155178 (softcover) | ISBN 9781501155185 (ebook)
Subjects: | BISAC: FICTION / Romance / Contemporary. | FICTION / Contemporary Women. | FICTION / Romance / General. | GSAFD: Love stories.
Classification: LCC PS3602.L3458 R43 2017 | DDC 813/.6—dc23
LC record available at https://lccn.loc.gov/2017021543

10 9 8 7 6 5 4 3 2 1

ISBN 978-1-5011-5517-8
ISBN 978-1-5011-5518-5 (ebook)

Ready
for Wild

1

(Braden Montgomery)

> "The mission of men there seems to be, like so many busy
> demons, to drive the forest all out of the country . . ."
> —Henry David Thoreau, *The Maine Woods*

"*Forget it. Luck is with me today, I can feel it.*"

"*Luck? Take a look at this face. It was meant for television.*"

"*Age before beauty, you two. And pass the donuts.*"

The partially closed doorway to our conference room muffles the voices inside, yet I'm able to overhear just enough of my co-workers' conversation that I stop short outside the door. Luck? Television? Age before beauty? The donut talk, though, *is* familiar.

When I open the door and step inside, nothing in particular looks different. The small, stuffy room is windowless and always reeks of burnt coffee and something sickeningly sweet. Today's culprit is an open Dunkin' Donuts box in the middle of the conference table where my three game warden colleagues—Julia,

Drew, and Egan—have settled in, each wearing a khaki button-down uniform shirt embroidered with the Colorado Parks and Wildlife logo. Since the Dunkin' box is already half-empty, it's likely that everyone at the table is already working on their second artery-clogging snack of the morning, washing it down with their third cup of bad coffee.

All of this is what I expect to find in this room when I make the drive from my base in Hotchkiss to the main office in Grand Junction for staff meetings with our boss. And yet . . . something isn't right.

Today, the mood in the room is different. Instead of mumbled conversations and not-quite-awake expressions, everyone's energy is off. As in, wild-eyed-and-eager *off*—and it's making me twitchy.

I don't fucking like it.

Julia looks my way with a donut in her hand. A few flecks of granulated sugar fall from her chin when she pins me with a grin that's way too animated, even for her. With her short auburn hair in rumpled curls, a soft build, and the out-of-style eyeglasses she keeps on a chain around her neck, Julia always brings to mind my elementary school librarian—a woman I couldn't help but love with all of my little-kid heart because she was the keeper of the books. As a result, I find it nearly impossible to frown on anything about Julia, even when that grin makes me nervous.

"Morning, Braden!" Julia calls out.

"Morning," I answer flatly, warily taking in the equally jolly expression on Drew's face.

Drew is fresh out of college and probably too good-looking for his own sense. And this might be the seventy-five-year-old can-tankerous asshole who lives inside my thirty-two-year-old body talking, but with his precisely trimmed beard and his square-framed glasses he looks like every cliché hipster you meet in a craft brewery taproom. The kind of guys that *make* things in their spare time—like reclaimed-barn-wood cornhole boards or bottle openers fashioned out of recycled mountain-bike chains. Junk that only sounds ingenious to other bearded guys of his kind. I still haven't figured out how Drew ended up working as a game warden instead of doing something with, I don't know, websites. Or *apps*.

Even Egan, the seasoned veteran of our group, looks less like he's merely counting the days until retirement. The first thing he does each morning is draw a big red *X* through today's date on the calendar he has in his office for exactly this purpose, ticking one more day off of the two years remaining until he's eligible for his full pension. Today, though, he's smoothing the front of his shirt and sitting up straight in his chair, opening up a spiral notebook on the table as if he's planning to take notes.

Again, I don't fucking like it.

I keep my eyes shifted their way as I walk toward the coffee brewer, waiting to see if one of them is about to jump onto the tabletop and break out into song, or anything else just as bizarre.

When I step up to shove my travel mug under the pour spout of the coffee brewer, I nearly knock over a huge color photo that's been set up on an easel just off to one side. The photo wobbles, and I reach out quickly to keep from sending it to the ground. Once it's steady, I train my focus on figuring out what the hell it is and why it's here, in the goddam way.

I step back and scan the photo. A woman with a big smile, big curls of blonde hair, and bright blue eyes stares back at me. She's dressed in a hot pink camo-patterned tank top and a pair of impossibly short white denim cutoffs, while holding a compound bow in one hand. She's also wearing some sort of high-heeled sandals, one hip cocked out in a way I think must be an uncomfortable position to stand in for longer than ten seconds. All of this, while posing in the middle of a sagebrush-covered field, a ridgeline of snowcapped mountains in the background. Along with what I think are Photoshopped whitetail deer and some mountain squirrels lingering about behind her. At sunrise, of course. Like she's some half-dressed, witless Disney princess.

But, who cares, because an outfit like *that* obviously makes sense if you're headed out to do some shooting on what looks like a cold morning. Forget jeans, a sweatshirt, a ball cap, and some decent boots. Just throw on as little clothing as possible and bumble out there in some heels. I'm sure the wildlife won't notice when you fall down every other step and make enough noise to send them into the next county.

Ugly text is splashed across the top of the photo in varying shades of hot pink and carbon gray, in a garish, almost unreadable script font.

Watch RECORD RACKS *every Sunday*
Exclusively on the AFIELD CHANNEL

My nose wrinkles and my lip curls. I point my index finger accusingly at the photo, my gaze now frozen on certain areas of the blonde's tank top I feel a little pervy staring at but can't quite bring myself to look away from.

"What. Is. This." I growl.

Behind me, Julia claps her hands together like a seal cub and makes a strange chirping sound.

"You don't know? That's Amber Regan. She has a hunting show on the Afield Channel. Isn't she gorgeous?"

I grunt by way of answering the obvious. Even though she's dressed like a ridiculous, sexed-up advertising cliché of a sports-*woman*, I can't deny that something about the image hits me hard, and in ways I haven't felt in a long time. So much that if I hadn't decided a few years ago that my Chesapeake Bay retriever dog,

Charley, is the only female I'm interested in sharing my bed with, I'd consider making some room for Amber Regan.

Unfortunately, she has a hunting show. As if the killing of an animal should be both exploited and glossed over, edited until it looks like responsible hunting is something that happens in twenty-two minutes and includes obnoxious whispered voice-overs. And I don't say that because I'm antihunting—it's the opposite. It's because I *am* a hunter.

But I still hate hunting shows. Because they make all of us look like bloodthirsty morons hell-bent on nothing but a new mount for the living room wall. Those shows are just one of the many reasons I don't have cable and only rarely sit my ass in front of my crappy television to watch the one channel I pick up with an antenna. Even reading hunting magazines is sometimes more than I can stand, simply because they spend too much time writing about success and too little time on the reality of what happens in the field.

In reality, sometimes you don't get a shot, never see hide or hair of what you're looking for. Sometimes you take a shot and you miss. Even when it all goes as it should—good shot, clean kill—you still have to walk up to a dead animal, stand over its now-limp body and own what you've done. *That* is the truth of hunting. And if you don't feel that responsibility so intensely your heart hurts and your eyes water, then you shouldn't be a hunter. Just keep your hands clean and buy a steak at the grocery store if you're unwilling or unable to feel anything about the meat on your plate.

I peer at the photo and decide Amber does look vaguely familiar. Her bow is the same brand I shoot, so I must have come across her image before in a magazine ad. None of this, however, explains why she's on display here—in all of her poster-sized, sleek, high-res glory.

"Her being gorgeous and prancing around TV doesn't explain . . ." I swipe my hand through the air in front of the picture. "Whatever this is. Or why it's here. Blocking the coffee."

"Everybody here?" Our boss, Tobias, strides into the room before anyone can reply to my rant, taking quick inventory of the room and answering his question for himself.

Tobias drops a stack of folders on the table and drags out a chair, watching as I make my way over and drop into a seat across from him. He shoves up the reading glasses perched on his nose to sit atop his head, smoothing down his bushy *Magnum, P.I.* moustache with one hand.

"Let's get the obvious out of the way. I figure if we don't, none of you will pay attention to anything else I have to say."

His hand slips to the breast pocket on his uniform shirt, removes four skinny plastic straws that have been cut into varying lengths, and taps them on top of the file folders.

"As I think most of you already know, I received a call last week from the Denver office. Amber Regan, star of the show *Record Racks* on the Afield Channel, is interested in featuring an archery elk hunt in Colorado this season. She and her team will be out next month to scout locations, and they've asked that CPW provide some guidance on the area. I need *one* of you to spend the day with them, show off public lands in your units, and offer insights on herd population." He holds up the plastic segments. "Hence, the straws. It's the fairest way I could think of. Short straw wins."

Julia seal-claps again and leans forward, her hand already outstretched and reaching toward the straws. Drew and Egan follow her lead. I stay rooted in place, something near rage rising in my lungs, filling them so much I can't take a full breath. You have *got* to be shitting me. Amber Regan. Here. Bringing all of her TV-show bullshit to town and managing to somehow drag the state into the mix.

Tobias works the straws so that the tops are in a straight line, obscuring the bottoms from view. "OK, everybody in? Draw your straw and—"

"Wait," I bark.

All eyes cut my way and Tobias lets out a tortured sigh. My feelings about this sort of thing are nothing new to him, but the look on his face says he was secretly hoping I would play along this time. Not so much.

"Why do we have to play dog-and-pony show with her? And why is she even looking at units around here? Send her up north so they can show off their trophy bulls. Better yet, let whatever high-dollar outfitter she's in bed with do this for her. All she's supposed to do is show up and shoot, anyway. That's how this crap works."

Tobias pinches the bridge of his nose with his free hand, draws in a calming breath.

"She's supposedly taking a new tack this year. Going on DIY hunts that aren't a sure thing, getting her hands dirty and doing the work herself. But this comes from the top, so we don't have a choice either way. And she is hitting up other areas in the state, so who knows where she'll eventually end up. It's only February, so she has some time to think it over before her hunt this fall."

"But—"

Tobias cuts in. "No more discussion. Just draw. We have other things to cover today, and I'd like to get through it all sometime this century."

My chest clenches tight as if someone's attempting to wrestle my heart out of my rib cage. This—the way I can't gather enough breath to keep from feeling a little dizzy—must be the sensation that comes with selling your soul.

Not that anyone else seems to care. They've already each snagged up a straw and started comparing lengths. Egan's face falls when he sees he's out of the running, and all that bright-eyed light from five minutes ago goes dim with a harrumph. Julia thrusts a fist up when she beats out Drew, leaving him scowling at his straw.

"Not so fast." Tobias turns to me with the last straw still in his cupped hand. He jiggles it my way. I shake my head.

"No."

"Braden."

"No. Consider me a conscientious objector to this whole thing. I don't want anything to do with it."

"Just take the damn straw, Montgomery. This needs to be fair and square. I don't want you coming back later whining that you didn't get to play."

With a scoff, I narrow my eyes. "No chance of that. Trust me."

"Braden, come on. Don't worry about it, I'm destined to win. Luck is on my side," Julia crows.

Luck. Like that matters one bit. I don't believe in luck or fate or divine *anything.* Luck is for suckers and romantics, dreamers and believers.

I do believe in draw odds, however—the statistical factors that drive so much of my job. Only so many hunters who apply for certain tags to hunt are granted one, all based on how the population of whatever species they're after is thriving and what best serves long-term conservation. Part of my job as a game warden is to keep an eye on those hunters who do have tags and make sure they're playing by the rules.

As for my odds right now? Those aren't in my favor. Four people in the game, two of them already out. I'm at fifty–fifty. It's simple math. But Tobias is clearly running out of patience, and I like my job, so I'd prefer to keep it.

With a grunt, I snag the last straw from Tobias's hand and hold it up.

All measly two inches of it.

My jaw drops and Julia's does the same, all while Tobias tries to rein in the shit-eating look on his face. Fucker. Boss or not, that's what he is in this moment. Because he knew *exactly* what he was holding.

"Congratulations," Tobias deadpans, and a chorus of groans from the rest of the room follows.

I might believe that luck is for suckers, but right now one thing is for sure—today, *I'm* the sucker.

2

(Braden)

"Between every two pine trees there is a door
leading to a new way of life."
—John Muir

Maybe Tobias won't notice.

I could, theoretically, pull a disappearing act if I wanted to. Simply drop from sight in his rearview mirror, escaping what lies ahead. After all, his state-issued Ford truck is a good fifty yards ahead of mine, both of us driving slowly up the service road toward the trailhead, where we're supposed to, in the words of her producer, "rendezvous" with Amber Regan and her "team."

This road is surrounded by thick banks of spruce trees, which do great work of obscuring turnouts that snake down to basins littered with enormous aspen trees. Tobias is far enough away that next time his truck meets a curve in the road, I could make my move. I could drive down one, shut the truck off, and wait it out.

I even have two books sitting on the passenger seat, a Thomas McGuane novel and a memoir of a smoke jumper based in the North Cascades, a range I knew well back when I was fighting wildfires as a hotshot crew member in Oregon. These alone would keep me busy for hours, but even if they don't, I could grab the journal tucked away in the glove box and work on a letter to my parents.

That's right, a *letter*. And while I'm sure that sounds charming to some people, for us—a family with one eighteenth-century British lit professor (dad), one integrative biology professor (mom), and their happiest-outside-and-alone sole offspring (me)—letters are simply the way we communicate best. All the words, none of the talk.

No matter how I while away my time, it would leave Tobias to coddle the blonde bombshell currently waiting at the end of the road. He has four grown daughters and an amazing wife, and he's patient enough to put up with all of my crap, so he's far better equipped for this situation than I am.

Just as I spy one of those turnoffs I've been fantasizing about, the brake lights on Tobias's truck come on and he slows to a stop. His driver's window rolls down, and he flops his arm out the opening, gesturing up the road with a sharp jab of his index finger, indicating that he's somehow cottoned onto my plan.

So much for my disappearing act.

We drive another mile or so, past a sign for the Grand Mesa National Forest, and pull into a small parking area. I yank a knit beanie on over my hair and tug on a pair of fingerless gloves, then take a deep breath before getting out of my truck. The cold midmorning air of early March means I can see my breath when I let out a resigned exhale.

This trailhead offers a decent view of *the* Grand Mesa, a beautiful and distinctive ridge of low-lying buttes. Not to be confused with the *town* of Grand Mesa which is about thirty minutes away, nestled in what locals call the Grand *Valley*. You'd think the whole area was inhabited by egomaniacs, with all the grandness going on, but instead it's mostly ranchers and farmers, with a few hippies and artists tossed into the mix, not unlike where I grew up in Oregon. The mountains might be bigger back home, but I could never claim they're prettier. Big or small, covered in snow or sage, mountains remain the best sight I can imagine.

Speaking of sights, the *worst* sight I can imagine is currently clouding my view of the mesa. At the other end of the parking lot sits a brand-new Dodge truck, jacked up with a lift kit, and decked out with brush guards and a roof-mounted LED light bar. I have no idea what color the truck is because it's been wrapped from bumper-to-bumper in a camo-patterned vinyl decal, broken up only by the logo for the Afield Channel splashed across the truck's doors. Hooked behind the truck is an enclosed trailer, also decaled to the hilt with the same terrible design. Behind that is another truck, same decals but no trailer—instead there's a shiny fifth-wheel RV hooked to it.

And behind that? A third truck. This one is black, absent of any Afield decals, but both of the crew-cab windows are plastered with stickers for various brands of hunting gear, archery equipment, and optics manufacturers. The back glass has a large Lone Star State decal on it, which means this is more than likely Amber Regan's personal rig. She's a Texas girl to the bone, something I couldn't miss the first time I looked up her social media—and every other time since when I've found myself pointlessly scrolling through her posts.

It should be noted that each time I do, I clear my search history afterward. In the unlikely event I go missing, when the local Keystone Kops comb my laptop trying to piece together my last days, it's possible that cookies from certain not-for–prime time videos I've streamed will pop up like dirty little whack-a-moles— which I'm fine with. But a digital footprint that leads to images of Amber Regan sunbathing on a boat or sweating it out in her workout gear? Please don't let some potbellied detective discover *that*. I'd probably stay missing just to avoid explaining why I'd wasted so much time in the last month Googling her, mostly because I can't quite figure it out for myself.

But no matter how diverting her posts and pics may be, all those trucks simply reinforce every notion I have about people like Amber. Instead of venturing into the woods with one iota of humility, they bully their way there with big trucks, too much gear, and a conquer-and-destroy mentality. Zero respect for the natural world and their teeny-tiny place in it.

Tobias makes his way over to the camo carnival, greeting a tall, willowy woman who's bundled up in a down coat with a fur-lined hood. Her dark, almost black hair has bright pink and purple hunks dyed into it, contrasting dramatically with her porcelain complexion. She and Tobias share a few words before he sends a glare my way that's enough to get my feet moving.

"Braden, this is Teagan King, Amber's producer." Tobias waves me forward. "I think you two have talked on the phone over the last few weeks."

Teagan offers a look that says she remembers all of our phone conversations and exactly how one-sided they were. She slips off a mitten to extend a hand, and I spy the tattoos on the back of her hand, a riot of color that runs nearly to the tips of her fingers. Add in the tease of ink I can see on her neckline and the dime-sized onyx earrings that have distended her ears unnaturally, and you have someone I can't picture doing a lot of hunting.

Like it or not, there is a *type* when it comes to hunting—and Teagan isn't it. The demographics might be evolving away from exclusively white, male, and middle-aged, but it's a slow tide. We're still a long way from filling the forest with women who would look more at home in a dive bar nursing a pint of oatmeal stout while watching some singer-songwriter do his best impression of Johnny Cash.

"Braden. So nice to put a face with a voice. I can't tell you how grateful we are for your time and expertise."

I take her hand while casting a look around for someone more . . . blonde.

Huh. Maybe Amber stayed home to shoot her bow in heels.

"Nice to meet you." I drop Teagan's hand. "Are you ready to get going? The climb isn't long, but it's tough, so it's smart to start up the hill sooner rather than later."

Teagan laughs. "You *are* to the point, aren't you? I like that." She drops her head to the right and calls out behind her, directing her voice to the other side of the trailer. "Amber?"

"Yeah?"

Out of nowhere, my entire body starts to hum. The sound of Amber's voice, entirely feminine but with a faint whiskey-smoke edge, turns my usual buzz of impatience into something anticipatory and eager—like I'm one syllable away from barreling toward the sound. It all feels base and irrational, trumping how I can't stand what Amber Regan represents. Brought on by her uttering one word. Great. My brain and my body are already at odds with each other, which I'm sure does not bode well for whatever comes next.

"You decent?"

A short laugh from Amber. "Pretty much."

The inference that she was naked or sort of naked, or somehow *indecent*, just a few feet away drives my thoughts straight into the gutter. I ball my hands into fists and drag my mind back where it belongs.

Teagan tips her head to invite us around the trailer. When I fall in line behind her, Tobias locks his eyes on mine with an evil gleam, like he is convinced he's about to watch the beginning of the world's most fucked-up blind date.

Between him and my buddy Garrett, I'm at no loss for people who think the situation I've found myself in is hilarious. Garrett is a redneck with no filter for his mouth, who always defaults to a joke when he can. He's done nothing but yell, "Rolling!" and, "Cut!" when I walk into a room for the last three weeks, and that's only when he's not calling me George Clooney. Last week, I came out of the local grocery store in Hotchkiss to find a torn-out article from some women's magazine stuffed under the windshield wiper on my truck.

Posers Unite! 10 Tips for Better Selfies and Viral-Worthy Vids

Fucking kid needs a hobby.

When we round the corner, my first real-life glimpse of Amber Regan is almost more than I can take. It's also not of her face.

Instead, I'm greeted with her bent over at the waist, her perfectly rounded backside pointed our way, hopping around on one foot as she tugs on a wool sock. She's dressed in formfitting base layer gear, black pants, and a long-sleeve top. Her blonde hair is spilling down around her face, and when she turns her downcast head so she can see us, she blows out a sharp exhale to urge a few stray pieces out of the way. Her blue eyes pick me out and don't shift, even as she continues to hop, then loses her balance, careening directly toward me.

My arms shoot out on instinct, but she rights herself before I have to touch her, which feels like the best possible turn of events. Because no matter what I imagined or what I ogled of her on the internet, I'm not prepared for the entirety of her. Her shape, those blue eyes, the tumble of shiny hair—or how she's a little thing, nowhere near as tall as I thought. Whether it was the heels or the larger-than-life persona, I expected someone who might at least clear my shoulders. Instead, when she unfolds upright, I realize the top of her head would just barely meet my bicep.

"Sorry about that. Great first impression, right? I'm Amber. And I swear my balance is generally better than that."

Her eyes are still on mine, sheepish as she acknowledges her near tumble, and I'm caught off guard enough to counter her embarrassment by offering up my own.

"Braden Montgomery. Once I fell on my face trying to crawl out of a layout blind. No real reason why, just hit the ground."

My random confession surprises us both, and Amber lets out a chuckle, sticking her hand out when she does. I take it, and her tiny hand clasped in my boorishly big one means I reflexively loosen my grip. She responds by firming up her own, making it known that, petite packaging or not, she's not interested in being seen as fragile. I give my full strength back and catch a slip of approval in her expression before she drops my hand. I step back to give her some room, watching as she walks toward the rear door on her truck while working valiantly to keep my eyes aboveboard.

Because all that time I spent *researching* her also revealed something about Amber's fans. Mostly that lots of them think about Amber Regan naked, and more than a few of them post fucked-up and inappropriate comments about it, too. Whether it's on a hunting forum, the message boards on the Afield website, or her Instagram account, the contingent of asshole guys who think they can say anything on the internet is strong. It's as if their one-dimensional experience of her—on television and lap-top screens—means they can't understand that she is real. Flesh and blood, three-dimensional, and, perhaps, not OK with some creeper declaring she's *bang-worthy*. So no matter how much my body reacts to hers, the last thing I want is to be anything like those guys.

Amber opens the truck door and pulls out a pair of camo brush pants and a matching pullover. She puts the top on, draws her long hair out from underneath the collar, and starts to braid it to hang over one shoulder.

"So the Hagerman Draw looks like it's the best way to access the high ridges," she says. "We can glass a bit, plus get some nice footage for our cameraman, Colin, to work with while we're at it."

Once she pulls on her brush pants, she dusts off the bottoms of her feet before slipping them into a pair of boots. Then she cuts her gaze to me, rolls her shoulders back as if she's intent on adding a few inches to her height, and her expression changes, becoming all business.

"Hopefully, you'll be able to show us what we need to see. I'm not here for a nature hike. And I hate having my time wasted."

Behind me, I swear I can hear Tobias snicker under his breath. She's not here for a nature walk? She expects me to show her what she needs to see? And she's implying I might not be up to the task? Try again, *Amber*. This is my unit, and I've spent more time here than she's spent getting her hair done. I grind my jaw together, using the time to temper my words.

"Good. I'm only here because I drew the short straw."

Her lips twist into a smug sneer. "Sounds like you have shit for luck, then, Braden Montgomery."

"Luck is for suckers," I volley back. "Hard work gets you what you want, even when bad odds get in the way. You just have to work for it."

We fix each other with narrowed eyes, and around us there's nothing but slow breathing from Teagan and Tobias, prime viewers of our little showdown at the O.K. Corral. Tobias breaks in before either one of us draws a sidearm.

"OK. I think everyone here is good to go, so I'll head out." He and Teagan exchange goodbyes, then Tobias calls my name.

I drag my eyes from Amber, cutting over to Tobias, who mouths a caution before making for his truck. *"Play nice."*

Fuck that. He's the one who threw me to the wolves in the first place. Might be a pint-sized wolf—one that my dick is all too interested in—but she's a killer nonetheless. She doesn't want her time wasted? I can help her with that. I return my focus to Amber, who is currently yanking a wool hat on over her hair a little forcefully.

"Since you're so worried about your time being wasted, using the Hagerman Draw to access the high ridge points is the wrong choice. The Sawtooth Trail will get you there in half the time."

"It also bypasses at least three watering holes we saw on Google Earth." She grabs a tablet off of the backseat of the truck and starts to poke at the face with the tip of her index finger. "Sawtooth gives us nothing in the way of spotting game on the way in, so we'll be stuck with whatever we find at the top."

While I'm impressed that she's done some research on the area, I'm not impressed that she thinks looking at some crap on a tablet replaces boots on the ground. When you spend time putting miles on your boots, you see what no satellite can. Scouting trips in advance of a hunt are invaluable because, excepting outside disruptions—human- or weather-related—big game animals like routines. The same watering holes, the same game trails, day after day after day. Effective scouting is about discerning those routines without creating a disturbance. And I'm damn good at both. I level my gaze on the smart-ass disturbance in front of me.

"Those watering holes are nearly dry these days. I was in here a month ago, and I didn't cut a single track down there. But I didn't use Google Earth. I just used my eyeballs."

She shoots me a death glare. I launch the damn thing right back at her. Another round of her poking at the tablet while muttering under her breath. Teagan steps to the space between us, taking a referee-type stance.

Amber's eyes scan the tablet while she calls out behind her, "Hey, Colin?"

A male voice replies from somewhere on the other side of the trucks, "One sec."

Amber keeps talking, ignoring his answer because she's apparently too fucking impatient to even give him the "one sec" he asked for.

"Can you come check out this map with me again? We *might*"—she shoots another death glare my way—"need to switch up our original plan."

A twentysomething kid saunters out from between the first two trucks, humping a full backpack onto his tall and lean frame, while holding a video camera in his right hand. He pauses to settle the pack on his shoulders and cinches down the pack's waist belt. And while Teagan might not fit the type when it comes to the typical hunter, this kid does. He might not be middle-aged, but he's white and male, and that backpack he's carrying happens to be a custom brand preferred by hunters who value performance over everything else. It's built to be lightweight and strong, using military-grade materials.

Colin stops near Amber and tips his chin to me as a greeting, then squints down at the tablet. He pushes back the bill of his ball cap to scratch the top of his head, revealing a buzz cut on his blond hair, and then puts the hat back in place.

"I heard some of what you two were saying, but not the details. What's the problem with Hagerman Draw?"

Amber and I start to talk over each other, then both clamp our jaws tight. Colin raises his brows, sending a *what the hell* look Teagan's way. I wait to see if Amber's going to grant me the distinct pleasure of being able to speak without her interrupting. She flicks a wrist my way.

Fucking pint-sized pain in the ass.

I turn to face Colin. "Hagerman will take at least three hours. The satellite images you saw those watering holes on must be out of date; drought conditions have dried up everything along that route. If we take Sawtooth, we can cut our hike time in half."

Colin nods then opens his palms for Amber to give up her tablet. She proceeds to cross her arms over her chest and kick her hip out, just like she did in that poster picture, except this time there's certainly no smile on her face. Just her pink lips pressed into an angry pout.

"Looks steep," Colin offers absently, still studying.

"It is. I didn't say it was an easy climb, but it is efficient and direct. And the ridge leads to a prime spot to see the valley below. The game trails are heavy down in there."

Colin's eyes move over to Teagan, assessing her. "How are your joints feeling today?"

Teagan doesn't return his gaze, just bends her knees a little and bounces lightly on the balls of her feet. "I'm good."

"You sure?"

She bounces again, seemingly to prove her point. "I'm fine, Colin. Stop babying me."

"I'm not babying you, I just give a shit if you . . ." He stops short when she snorts, grumbling a quiet curse under his breath. He hands the tablet back to Amber.

"It's already ten. If we take Hagerman, we'll be lucky to hit the ridge by one. Weather's supposed to come in this afternoon, which means we need to be back to the trucks well before dark, and that doesn't leave us much time. I think the straight shot is a better plan. He's right."

Amber groans. Actually full-on groans. Colin ignores it and starts toward Teagan, taking the water bottle she has in one hand and strapping it to his already-full pack. She sort of waves her hands around helplessly until he bats them down gently.

"You two can set your own pace. Teagan and I will bring up the rear. If we drop off and disappear, don't worry about it, just keep going. We'll catch up."

Amber drags her own pack out from the backseat of the truck, muttering, "If I worried every time you two disappear on me, I'd have an ulcer."

Ten minutes later, I have my own pack on and we're all assembled at the trailhead. Teagan has nothing but a pair of walking sticks, while Colin looks like a weighted packhorse. Either being a cameraman requires way more gear than I assumed or he's one of those guys who spends the off-season walking around with a fully loaded pack, just to be sure he's conditioned when it comes to hunt big game in the fall.

I point from the trailhead toward the narrow path that ascends.

"The grade is pretty unforgiving, so it's a hump. But the trail is clean; there isn't much to trip you up." I direct my eyes to Amber.

"Just holler if you need me to stop or slow down. No shame in needing to catch your breath."

She grinds her jaw together hard enough I can see her cheeks flex under the strain.

"Don't worry about me." Her brows tick up and a wry light flashes in her eyes. "I *love* a challenge."

3

(Amber Regan)

> "So that was the way. No fair play. Once down,
> that was the end of you."
> —JACK LONDON, *THE CALL OF THE WILD*

Braden Montgomery is a beast.

A huge, broad-shouldered, thick-thighed beast who can eat up a trail with a ten percent grade in the same way normal people take a midday stroll in a city park. While we've been in Colorado long enough that my body has acclimated to the altitude and my VO_2 max is nothing to scoff at, Braden evidently operates on another level.

Honestly, I don't think I've heard the man take a single unsteady breath this entire time, let alone huff or wheeze as if he was feeling anything but easy-peasy about scaling this trail. But my endorsement deals with performance gear companies, muscle recovery supplements, and protein powders did not come by way of the sort of *luck* Braden claims not to believe in. Those companies came calling because I'm in damn good shape.

Braden though, is built like a power lifter while performing like a triathlete—showing off an enviable combo of brawny strength and nimble agility with every step he takes. Even when he should stomp about from his sheer size alone, he doesn't. And, after much visual examination, I've determined his glutes do most of the work to drag that beast of a body around.

In my defense, I had no choice but to notice. You try spending an hour and a half hiking behind that *behind* while it flexes away, right in front of you. Good luck trying to keep from noticing—or appreciating—it.

Unfortunately, he's also a complete pain in *my* ass.

The moment we crest the top of the ridge, he pauses for all of ten seconds, enough time to glance back and verify I'm still alive. And seeing that I *am*, I'm not sure he views it as a success. He starts to loosen the waist belt on his pack, motioning toward the east.

"I'm going to set up over on that rock outcropping. You do what you want. Try not to fall off the mesa or anything."

Fall? Off of what? This top is huge. Compared to the damn ice-covered scree fields I picked my way over while hunting stone sheep in British Columbia and the razor-edged ridgeline I tiptoed over while chasing ibex in Kyrgyzstan, this mesa is the equivalent of an empty football field.

I go to work on my own pack, pulling it off and setting it on the ground to retrieve my water bottle, taking a slug before replying.

"Like I said before we started up this trail, don't you worry your pretty head about me. I'm more than capable of taking care of myself."

He strides off. "I've seen you try to put on your socks."

Re-capping the water bottle, I slam it to the dirt and resist the urge to lob it at his head. But he and those glutes of his are already a good twenty yards away, deftly scaling the rocks to sit atop the tallest boulder.

In the last ten days I have been introduced to no fewer than twenty different Colorado Parks and Wildlife staff members. *Twenty.* And Braden is the only one who didn't act like I was interesting, important, or exciting—or some combination of the three.

While being fawned over can sometimes be overwhelming, for the most part, it's pretty damn gratifying. The fact that anyone recognizes me at all is a triumph over the tomboy I once was, trying to find my way in a tiny Texas dust town. That little girl couldn't have dreamed of this life, the one where I have my own television show and enough social media followers that companies pay me to endorse their products. Not to mention they keep me in all the right swag. I haven't purchased a single piece of hunting equipment, outdoor clothing, optics, or a freaking energy bar, in years. Back in the day, I was turning in aluminum cans at the recycler for six months just to earn enough to buy my first fishing pole. These days I take a selfie with an aluminum beer can and a couple thousand people will comment on it.

So running into the brick wall that is Braden Montgomery is unexpected—and it's also throwing me off my game.

First, I almost fell into him, or very nearly *onto* him. But I was bent over, perched on one foot, hair in my face, and trying to extend the courtesy of looking him in the eye, and when I did, the sight was more than I'd planned on. I expected another game warden like those I'd already met: middle-aged, a little doughy, and not my type. Instead, I looked up to find six foot five and two hundred plus pounds of brawn. Along with a pair of terribly pretty green eyes, messy dark brown hair, and a scruffy beard with just a tinge of salt fleck to it. He was glowering and somehow eating me up with those eyes, and nothing about his intense gaze was off-putting. Braden was looking without leering, and I liked it so much I lost my balance.

But I didn't want him to know how much he was throwing me, so I bucked up and went into control mode. Braden responded with the same, along with an extra large side serving of *surly*.

After unzipping my pack, I drag out my binoculars and scan the area to see where I'll have the best view of the basin below. Time scouting in the field is what will make or break this hunt for me, because I won't have the benefit of an outfitter like I usually do. It's been a while since I've done my own scouting, because unfortunately, having a popular hunting show sometimes means you become a glorified shooter, not a hunter.

By this last season, my fourth one on the air, every episode we filmed was a luxury hunt on a high-fence ranch, where we spent more time doing my makeup than we did outdoors. While it looked good on camera, it was also boring. For me *and* the viewers, it seems, because it showed in our ratings—enough that next season is in limbo.

And that is why I'm here. To get back to the roots of how I was raised to hunt: no outfitter and no luxury digs, just me and my bow on the lookout for a nice bull elk in Colorado. My livelihood depends on making it happen, because I don't have a fallback *anything*. I've got no college degree, no skills beyond what I'm already doing, and my body can't be a meal ticket forever. Before I was Amber Regan of *Record Racks*, I was Amber Regan of the local Dollar General. Not exactly a life I want to go back to.

So if Braden Montgomery wants to make my life difficult, fine. But I'm not just going to scuttle off somewhere. Despite being a glowering pain in the ass, Braden clearly knows what he's doing, which means if he's over there you can be damn sure that's the best place to be.

I grab my water bottle in one hand and pull on the harness for my binoculars. When I start toward the rock outcropping, Braden's head casts in my direction, and I swear I can hear him sigh all the way over here. God, he shouldn't strain himself like that. All those overwrought noises can't be good for a person.

Up close, the boulders are taller than I expected. Watching Braden mount them with so little effort was deceptive, likely because his height and leg length give him the advantage. The rocks are also relatively smooth, and there are few places where my short legs might find their first foothold. I circle around to see if there's a better access point on the other side but find nothing other than a rock face that goes straight up.

Braden appears above me, face as stony as the rocks. "Come back around. I'll give you a hand."

I set my hands on my hips and take another look at the rocks, mentally willing an obvious handhold to reveal itself so I can do this on my own.

"I don't need your help. It's just that not all of us are built like the Jolly Green Giant."

"Well, Jolly Green Giants aren't exactly built to outrun mountain sprites. But that didn't stop you from basically running me over trying to get up this trail. You didn't hear me complaining about you breathing down my neck the whole way, did you? So let my overgrown ass give you a hand up here."

I train my eyes up to where he's standing in the glare of the noonday sun, casting a shadow with the breadth of his body. In the distance, voices and laughter carry our way, growing louder. Braden turns and points his binoculars toward the trail.

"Teagan and Colin. About fifteen minutes away." His head tips forward a few inches, as if he's squinting their way. "Maybe more, because unless my 'nocs are screwed up, I think Colin is carrying her. Jesus. That kid's an animal, isn't he?"

I roll my eyes. Colin *is* an animal, freakishly strong for a guy his size and build, with the endurance of a Wyoming antelope—so there's no question that with one peep of discomfort from Teagan, the Prince Charming of Pig Farmers probably gathered her up before she could protest. It might also explain how they ended up twenty minutes behind us. Either that or they kept pace just fine but found themselves off trail with certain parts of their clothing strategically unbuttoned. It wouldn't be the first time their weird-ass mating rituals delayed their arrival somewhere. What's wild is that the second we cross the state line into Texas, they'll act like strangers. But when we're on the road? They can't keep away from each other. I love them both like family, but why two people who are that into each other work so hard to keep from being together is beyond me.

After making my way around the rock cropping, I stick my arm straight up and wait for Braden to extend his. Almost before I can get my footing, he's pulling me toward him. I let out a surprised yelp and scramble to find my balance, nearly toppling into him—again. His hands are suddenly at my waist, spanning the width with his grip, his body pressed to mine, and my face buried in his chest. Without thinking, I draw in a long, steadying breath, and . . . well, *shit*.

This in an unfortunate discovery.

He smells good. Really good. Like the strangest combination of nutmeg and sweat. And, because the world isn't already unfair enough, he *feels* better than good.

"Got it?" Braden's voice is a cautious rumble, spoken near the crown of my head.

I pull my hands back from his chest, hovering over the wall of muscle I just groped, my eyes fixed on the space between my fingers.

"Yes. I've got it. All of it."

His fingers grip my waist a touch harder. "You sure?"

I have no idea if he's goading me or groping me now, but either one is a bad idea. The first would piss me off, and the second might turn me on, so I need to clear some space between us. I wriggle my hips a bit as a prompt.

Bad choice. Bad, bad choice. Because his fingers dig in. He grunts. And my heart starts to thump—in the best way.

Finally, he loosens each of his fingers and steps back, quickly dropping into a crouch on the rock. I steel my nerves, watching as he shimmies out of his coat and tosses it next to him, then points at it.

"You can use that to cushion your mountain-sprite ass."

I flop down on it without protest, because I'm already tired of the bickering. Plus, I know how much your butt hurts after a few hours sitting on a rock. Braden brings up his binos and aims them off to the east.

"There are a couple of cows in this draw to the east. See the cluster of dead pines? Go straight down from there. They're bedded in that opening."

Immediately, I draw my binos up, working to find the dead pines he mentioned. "How many?" I ask.

"Four. Maybe five. There's something off to the left, but I can't tell what."

I find the cow elk, four ladies sunning themselves leisurely and noshing on grasses occasionally. After working my focus to the left, the dark brown clump he can't identify comes clearly into view for me. Another cow.

"Five. And this last one, she's big."

"How can you see that? All I get is a blob."

He leans back and stares at me. I tug my arms free from the harness strap that holds my binoculars and hand it all his way.

"Swarovskis. From their EL line, new this year. The built-in range finder is top-notch, and you can't beat the angle adjustment features. Might burn your freaking retinas out if you use them too much, but you can see *everything*."

Braden brings them up to his face, adjusts the fit, and then I see his jaw drop.

"Holy shit."

I tamp down a snort. *Welcome to the world of free swag, Braden.*

After a few minutes, he reluctantly hands them back and watches as I slip the harness back on, both arms and my chest pushed out like I'm pulling on a vest. With most guys, I'd consider the longing look on his face might be a reflection on the way my boobs are currently thrust forward, but with Braden, I'm ninety-five percent sure it's all about the optics. Once everything is in place, I cast a look his way and he immediately flicks his eyes up to meet mine.

"I hate hunting shows," he blurts out.

"*No*," I scoff, drawing the word out. "Really? Because you've been so warm and welcoming, I just can't imagine how that's possible."

Braden gives up an exasperated sigh and turns away to scan the hillside below.

"But here's the question: Is it just *my* show? Is it seeing me and my ovaries out there that pisses you off?"

Braden shakes his head. "I hate all of them. Your gender-specific organs have nothing to do with it. Although I really hate all those hot pink camo outfits with high heels that someone is sticking you in."

"No one *sticks me* in anything. I decide if I'm wearing heels, or hot pink, or whatever the hell I want."

He continues to peer out to the distance. I tilt my head, studying the side of his face.

"So why do you hate them? Not the outfits—I don't care what

you think about that—but the hunting shows. You're a game warden, so you probably aren't morally opposed to hunting. I'm guessing you hunt yourself. Archery, right? Probably traditional. You give off that self-righteous vibe."

He ignores my jab about the superiority complex some archery hunters have and lazily gestures with one hand at the wide expanse ahead of us.

"I hate hunting shows because of that." His chin juts out to emphasize his point. "Going out there, with the express purpose of taking an animal's life. That shit is sacred. It's not entertainment, so you shouldn't film it, package it, and broadcast it, then sell ads to go along with it. You should respect it."

A laugh bubbles up before I can stop it, and Braden jerks his head my way, eyes narrowed into slits that would pin me to the ground if possible.

"That's funny? Fucking unbelievable. I take it back. I hate all hunting shows, but yours is at the top of my list."

I let my laugh taper. "You sound exactly like my uncle Cal. Practically word for word. Only he usually ended his speech with some quote from Aldo Leopold."

A grunt from beside me. "Your uncle Cal and I would get along."

My uncle Cal has been gone for three years now. Aggressive lung cancer took him swiftly, but his odd hillbilly-meets-conservationist teachings are still with me. He was one of the few people in this world—although I wouldn't be surprised if Braden might be counted among them—who believed a little moonshine and a little Muir made for a perfect night.

"You probably would have."

Braden's eyes soften, curious suddenly. When I note there's no judgment in his expression, I let out a tired sigh.

"Cal raised me after my parents died. Once he figured out

I had a knack for staying quiet in the field and a good eye for targets, he had me out behind the house shooting arrows until I could land a group damn near with my eyes closed. And that's when I wasn't wading in the crick that ran through his property, working out how to cast a line just right. All of this before I had boobs."

Credit to Braden, his eyes don't drop below mine. He keeps his face neutral and his tone flat. "And after?"

I give up a quiet chuckle. "Same plan, different objective. He figured if I was in a tree stand, it made it a hell of a lot harder for the boys to find me. Only worked so well. Turns out lots of guys like girls in camo."

Braden looks perplexed. I shrug a shoulder and crack a half grin, wordlessly owning up to the obviousness of my brand. I know why the camo works, why advertisers want me showing skin. And my body is mine to do with what I choose, even if that means I'm sometimes the target of many a hateful shaming comment on my Twitter and Instagram. Add in the fact that I'm a hunter and it's open season on me. Pun intended. Lots of folks believe in girl power, sure. But some of them also believe that feminism should look and sound only the way they want it to— meaning it doesn't wear short shorts or carry a shotgun.

When Braden's brow crinkles just a bit, I consider how much I might be screwing with all his preconceived notions about me. That no, I'm not some dress-up doll or a mindless bimbo who is being pushed around or exploited by some moustache-twirling puppeteer who keeps me in line by making me feel worthless. Instead, I was raised by a true conservationist, I've been in the field since I was eight, and I wear the pink camo and the heels because *I* want to.

"Why?" Braden suddenly asks.

My brow wrinkles. "*Why?* Why what?"

"Why do guys like girls in camo?"

I tilt my head and think. I've never tried to put the concept into words; I simply know it works. But when I consider his question for a bit, I find my answer.

"Because I'm not supposed to be wearing it."

Braden looks more confused than ever. "I don't get it."

I sigh and turn toward the hillside, drawing my binoculars up to scan the bottom as I try to explain.

"You know how some guys love the image of a woman prancing around in a men's white dress shirt? Her hair's all tousled, so she looks easy and hot? Same concept, just a different demo. To these guys, it's like I snuck into their closet and slipped on their favorite Realtree T-shirt. Now their manly shirt smells like me and that taps into the whole weird caveman *you're mine* thing."

"'You're mine'? Like you're a *possession*? All because of a stupid pattern that was designed for function, not fashion? That's asinine."

Hiding a grin, I continue to work my optics over the shady draw at the bottom of the basin, eventually landing on a yearling cow bedded down behind a clump of pinons. "So you're a white-button-down guy, then. Got it."

Braden lets out a choked-off sound, part growl and part cough. "I didn't say that. I'm not a white-button-down guy."

"A trench-coat-with-nothing-on-underneath guy?"

Another growl. "No."

"A pencil-skirt, hair-in-a-bun, naughty-librarian guy?"

"Jesus. *No.*"

"Really? I thought I might have nailed it with that one. Come on, everyone has a thing, Braden. Women *and* men. The fantasy they're into. The look that gets them going."

He groans quietly, the sound of him asking me to shut up, I suspect. But now, no matter how inappropriate this entire conversation is, I have to know—what turns Braden Montgomery's crank?

I reel through a few more stereotypical concepts in my head, eliminating each until a very specific image comes to mind and I give into a sly smile, thinking I may have just figured it out. Slowly, I start to paint a picture.

"Wait. I know what it is. You're all about a tight dress with heels, the all-dressed-up-for-dinner-with-her-man look. A bandage minidress. In red." I labor over that detail for a moment. I'm off base there—red is far too bold for this one.

"Nope, *blue*—cobalt blue. Not too short, no crazy patterns or cleavage showing. She's covered but still showing it off. Simple heels, bare legs, no big jewelry. Just sophisticated and sexy."

I pause, trying to decide if it's a good idea to voice what else just ran through my mind. Ah, hell. Screw it. The guy hates my show and is at the very least irritated with me as a human being, so I'm rather enjoying giving this big bear a poke.

I lower my voice. "That is, until they get home. Then all bets are off. Along with the dress."

I crane my head his way, intent on giving him a smug smirk, but Braden's expression—the set of his jaw loose and his mouth relaxed—is entirely neutral.

All except for his eyes.

His eyes tell me that I just nailed it, identified exactly what redlines his motor. Heated and glimmering, those green eyes stay fixed on me, his eyelids hooded just enough to melt my smug intentions into something else entirely. Like wondering what his big body would feel like pinned beneath mine. Not that I'd have any hope of keeping him there if he didn't want to be, but Good freaking Friday, those eyes of his mean business right now—and the business in question may be that Braden's mentally undressed me from my current ensemble and now redressed me in that blue dress and heels.

And, quite possibly, is *nailing me* in it.

He blinks once, deliberately. Then simply turns away, raises his binos, and starts to glass. No denial. No scathing retort. No "fuck off" or "fuck you." Just *nothing*. And all that nothing says more than he ever could have had he opened his mouth.

I realize that my face, my cheeks, even the back of my neck are heated and a touch damp—enough that a sudden gust of wind raises a shiver across my skin. Everything from my heart down to the senselessly base space between my thighs is either trembling or clenching or otherwise reacting to what just went down, and . . . oh, hell.

Really? Now?

Unbelievable. This is when my body decides to perk up and take real, carnal notice of a man? And for this guy? Mr. Jolly Green Giant with a bad attitude?

What. A. Fucking. Joke.

In general, guys are my indulgence. Some people watch bad TV or read trashy books when they get bored or lonely and nothing else will fix their mood. I happen to prefer my indulgences a bit more tactile. As in hands and lips and skin, all tangled up together in sweat and release.

And because I live in a city like Austin, Texas—where the weather stays warm, the downtown scene is never boring, and the average resident is young and single—I'm not at a loss for a tactile fix when I want one. I don't do it often, but the simplicity of keeping men as an indulgence does have its merits. While I've been happily single for years now, before that I was a notorious three-month girl. Relationships that were just long enough to enjoy the newness but never so long as to end up discussing things I find exhausting—like whether to spend the holidays with his family or mine, debating the exchange of house keys, or the requisite-but-tiresome conversation about where our relationship is headed.

I'm just fine going solo in life; I have everything an established twenty-eight-year-old woman needs: my own house, a legit career, friends and family, and a decent bank account. I also have a healthy imagination and two hands.

So I'm *all* good on my own.

But those hands of mine are currently shaking, tiny tremors I'm determined to chalk up to hunger pangs. Entirely unrelated to the potently male being sitting next to me and instead, low blood sugar–induced. Understandable, given that I just humped it up a steep-grade trail, fueled only by the whole-wheat tortilla slathered with cashew butter that I ate this morning.

I slip one hand into the inside pocket on my coat and attempt to extract the protein bar I have stashed there as quietly as possible. A learned habit from years spent hunting, because every sound you make is amplified in nature and even the quietest snap draws attention your way—in direct opposition of what you're trying to do, which is be invisible. Today, it's a good thing we aren't actually hunting, because the wrapper doesn't do me any favors, making a crinkling sound that's almost deafening given our surroundings.

Braden lets out a short gust of air—a huff, really—a split-second snort that makes it clear, yet again, how put out he is by this whole ordeal. The ordeal being *me*.

And that trembling in my body that I was just fussing about? The involuntary *oh, look, a pretty man with pretty eyes* reaction I didn't want to deal with?

Poof.

All gone.

One obnoxious little snort from him is all it takes to huff and puff my appreciation into oblivion. I pluck the still-wrapped bar up with a flourish, hold it right in front of me, and proceed to yank on one edge to tear it open, then give it a good rip to see if

I can get him to groan again, all because I have the audacity to eat a snack.

He does me one better. Groans *and* huffs. I take a huge bite of the bar, enjoying the mushy pecan pie flavor, then do my best to chew loudly while still keeping my jaw shut. No need to gross him out, just irritate him.

"You shouldn't eat that."

Silently, I finish chewing. Braden exhales sharply through his nose. I take another bite, doing all I can to draw it out.

"You're eating a candy bar. You realize that, right? It's a candy bar masquerading as a protein source. Same calories, same sugars. It's just those things are made with brown rice sugar instead of high fructose corn syrup. All those shitty things will do is spike your blood sugar and give you a stomachache."

Oh, goody. Now he's going to get all sanctimonious about nutrition. The fact that my belly does sometimes rumble unhappily after I eat these is not for him to know. Any bellyaching I might experience is easily dealt with by using some of the endorsement money I make from this company to buy some antacids. I open my mouth and lean forward exaggeratedly to take another bite. But a big man paw appears before my face, snatching the bar clean from my hand so quickly I instead end up sucking in a mouthful of clean Colorado air, like a big-mouth bass surfacing to make for some bait.

I stare slack-jawed at the place where my bar used to be. Are you kidding me? In what universe is it OK to do what he just did? We've known each other for a few hours, for God's sake. In no universe is two hours enough time to yank anything out of my hand. Anything. Only the fact that I'm speechless saves him from me letting him have it.

Braden snags the bar out of the wrapper and proceeds to chuck it into the forest with the force, speed, and accuracy of an MLB pitcher. OK, now he's littering. For someone who's all about being right and righteous, and is employed as a steward of state lands, that's not exactly a cool thing to do. He flattens the wrapper out so he can point accusingly at the ingredient list.

"Organic brown rice syrup, organic cane syrup, organic *dried* cane syrup, organic date paste. Just fancy ways to cover up the fact they're all sugar. Fucking thing has twenty grams of sugar. Don't get me started on soy protein isolate. It's like the Twinkie equivalent of soy, stripped down and fucked up. Do you know there's research connecting too much processed soy to breast cancer?"

I yank the wrapper back into my possession. "Thank you for your concern about my breasts. But they're fine. And these 'shitty things' help pay my mortgage, thank you very much."

To prove my point, I grab my phone and hold it up at the perfect selfie angle while clutching the empty wrapper in my other hand, making sure the company logos on my knit hat, the protein bar, and my camo coat are all clearly visible in the shot.

"What are you doing?" Braden barks.

"My job," I mutter. I turn my head and tip my chin, checking my hair and giving my best smile before snapping the pic.

Lowering the phone, I review the picture and spot Braden's face peeking in from the corner of the screen, scowling a little and looking appropriately broody. A quick internal debate as to whether I should crop him out or not. Leave him in, I decide; he looks hot, scowl and all.

I start to tap a few keys, reading aloud as I do. "'Can't beat the view. Or my midday power up snack. #ColoradoElk #scouting #RecordRacks #fulldrawlife #womenwhohunt.'"

My eyes stay glued to the screen, fingers tapping away as I add the names of the endorsers. I can feel Braden leaning in, his head craning toward my phone.

"Are you posting that? Right now? Out here?"

"Yup. You want in? Give me your handle."

"My *what*? No. Whatever you're doing, the answer is no. Jesus Christ."

I shrug. "Suit yourself."

The signal up here is weak, but one bar is enough to post the picture. I turn my attention to Braden, who's clearly so horrified he looks close to either screaming or sucker punching his backpack, just to get some frustration out.

I'm feeling nearly the same, with an added dose of *hangry*. There are three other energy bars stashed in my pack, but they would probably meet the same fate as the first, so going for those will be a waste of time. I'm relatively sure there's a small baggie of trail mix buried somewhere in there, but I'm guessing it's stale and not worth the effort of digging it out.

My stomach growls. Loudly—like it's cussing out Braden with the sound. I sigh and take a drink of my water. Best to stay hydrated at the least.

"Are you hungry?"

This freaking guy.

"Are you insane?" I snap. "Yes, I'm hungry! I had a tortilla with cashew butter hours ago, long before I had to chase the Jolly Green Giant up a steep grade. All those calories are burnt off. That's why I was eating that bar. Because I'm *hungry*."

Braden curses under his breath while jamming his hands into his coat pockets, pulling out what look like small pale yellow dish towels with a honeycomb pattern printed on them. He dumps them in my lap where I'm sitting cross-legged. I draw my hands up, palms out—*yes, Officer*—and stare down at the packages.

"Eat those."

"Dish towels? No thank you. While I'm sure they are very low in sugar, I'm guessing they don't taste too good."

"Those are reusable cloth wrappers lined in beeswax, not dishtowels. Saves on plastic bags—and bonus, unlike the wrappers on those crap bars, it doesn't sound like a herd of buffalo crashing through a field full of tinfoil when you open them." He flicks the top of one of the wrappers. "Homemade fig millet energy bars in this one and some snack mix in the other. Like Chex Mix, but without the additives that will kill you."

I continue to stare down at the wrappers, hands still up, now feeling as if this is some version of your crazy house cat leaving a dead mouse on the doorstep in offering, or a wolf who leaves a half-eaten carcass for the taking as some weird-ass sign of submission.

"Look, I'm sorry." He lets out a long exhale, resigned. "That was a dick thing to do. I just reacted. I didn't want you to eat that junk, OK? You obviously take care of yourself, and that stuff is terrible for you. I mean, your body is . . ."

My eyes immediately cut his way at mention of my body, and his jaw snaps shut before I get the distinct pleasure of hearing him finish that sentence. My body is *what*? I can't even explain how badly I want to know what he was about to say. So much that I'm two breaths away from egging him on, pushing him somehow, getting him to crack. But my sanity dictates that I let this go and just take the Jolly Green Giant's dead-mouse offering without comment.

Plus, I'm so hungry. Starving. *Hangry*.

Silently, I work on unwrapping the first cloth. Three energy bars are inside, cut to the same size as my prepackaged ones and chock-full of dried cherries, pumpkin seeds, and big quinoa-like nuggets of what must be the millet, and flecked with what I think are chia seeds and orange zest. My mouth waters, and despite wanting to hate these things on sight, after one bite I can taste the difference between this and what Braden previously heaved into the forest. This tastes like real food, a cross between the granola my mom made when I was a kid and a Fig Newton. I almost say so out loud, but given that Braden would likely lose his sanctimonious shit over the latter comparison, I keep it to myself.

"Thank you. These are good. Great, actually."

He nods and I work on opening the other bundle, revealing a mix of popcorn, almonds, and pretzel pieces, all dusted in a spicy herb blend. I toss a piece of popcorn in my mouth.

"And I appreciate you acknowledging that you're a dick. I didn't want to have to point it out myself."

Braden snorts quietly. Behind us, Colin and Teagan have finally crested the top, voices carrying as they head our way. When they arrive, Colin looks smug and Teagan looks sheepish, cheeks flushed and her wild-child hairstyle even more mussed than usual. They *so* got off trail on the way up here.

I crook a brow and give Teagan a knowing look. "You two get lost?"

She thrusts her arm out and points in Colin's direction but doesn't look his way, barely stifling the guilty grin that threatens to break free.

"He made us stop every ten steps so he could ask about my knees. No exaggeration. Every. Ten. Steps."

A year ago, at the ripe old age of thirty, Teagan couldn't shake a few nagging aches in her joints, but chalked it up to an aftereffect of a bout with the flu. A few weeks later, she blamed it on her new kettlebell workout regimen. Two months after that, she claimed it had to be a sudden onset of gluten intolerance. Then it was nightshade vegetables. Then a mineral deficiency. Then she decided there was mold in her house. She gave up wheat, dairy, peppers, tomatoes, wine, coffee, and air-conditioning. Nothing helped.

Six doctors and a million self-diagnoses later, a specialist finally landed on a real answer: rheumatoid arthritis. A shit diagnosis for a woman who works as a freelance producer to help pay the bills (and only works on my show as a favor to me) but is a different type of artist at heart—a painter and mixed-media designer whose hands are everything to her and which she may eventually end up unable to use the way she wants.

Despite her remaining as active as ever and having more good days than bad, Colin can't help hovering over Teagan's every move. Yes, Colin is a God-fearing army vet who now works part-time as an outdoor sports cameraman and full-time as a pig farmer in the tiny town of Harper, where he grew up. And yes, Teagan is a heavily tattooed agnostic who is part of progressive Austin's modern art elite. So on the face of it, the two of them together is almost impossible to fathom. But no matter how unexplainable their mutual adoration is, it's there.

"So stopping that often must mean there was plenty of time to film b-roll on the way up?" I ask.

B-roll footage is what fills in the blanks for viewers on shows like ours; it gilds the lily so we can tell the whole story: panned shots of the land and the game, early moments at the truck and trailhead, and anything else that might set the tone for the final cut. Even if I don't end up back here for my hunt, it's best to gather what we can now, because, on average, every hour of raw b-roll captured yields only a few minutes worth of usable show content.

Colin fiddles with his camera.

"Still need a little more," he mumbles, finally working up the courage to peer up at me. "How did it go for you two? You guys spot anything good while you were glassing?"

Too bad for Colin, but his face owns everything. He looks happy—like he always does when he and Teagan are together, no matter how temporarily.

Maybe that's why my body is intrigued by the Jolly Green

Giant and his bad attitude. Maybe because as much as my indulgences with men are uncomplicated, they're also fleeting, and
maybe I miss the happy buzz of chasing someone around—just
one specific someone—then enjoying all the good stuff that
comes when you finally have them. Because even if they routinely
seem to make a mess of it, Colin and Teagan get the good stuff
when they're together. And maybe I'm just a little bit jealous of
that. *Maybe.*

Darting a glance in Braden's direction, I try to figure out how
to answer Colin's question. How did things go for us? There's no
easy answer to that.

"She didn't push me off this rock ledge or fall off of it herself,"
Braden finally offers.

He stands up and makes his way off the rock with a nimble jump down to the ground. I'm now expected to dismount
the rock myself—straight into his awaiting arms, apparently—
because he turns back to extend his hands in my direction.

"So we're both still alive." Braden flicks his wrists to encourage
me. "I think we can agree that's a win."

4

(Amber)

"Range after range of mountains. Year after year
after year. I am still in love."
—GARY SNYDER

A few hours later, Braden and I descend the trail under the cover
of heavy clouds. Our trip down was predictably slower because
the steep grade would have made it easy to turn an ankle—and
because it seems Braden and I have reached a silent agreement
that there is nothing to prove by racing each other down the hill.
Either that or we're both just too tired for any more antagonistic
hijinks today.

Once we reach the parking area, Braden continues walking
without even a slight pause, evidently hell-bent on getting to his
truck. He doesn't bother with a goodbye, a handshake, or even a
parting grumble.

With an eye roll for my benefit only, I walk to my truck and promptly off-load my pack into the backseat, then return to the trailhead. Hopefully, Colin and Teagan resist the urge for any more off-trail shenanigans and get down here before those darkening clouds decide to do more than just hover ominously. I take a peek at my phone for the time—almost four o'clock. Given Teagan's knees, I'm guessing they're at least thirty minutes out. If they aren't here in an hour, I'll head back up the trail to make sure they're OK.

"They'll be fine."

I nearly jump out of my skin at Braden's voice behind me. Jesus. He truly should crash around like a pissed-off grizzly bear given all that mass, making himself impossible to miss—but instead, he's stealthy. And given how close he is now, I also can't miss how he still smells pretty good.

I probably smell like I've been sautéing onions in my armpits, with a bonus layer of whatever aggravation smells like. I'm a woman, for Christ's sake. *I'm* supposed to smell like sunshine and snickerdoodles, not him. There is such a perverse amount of injustice in our long-day aromas, I can't even stand it.

I tip my head back to see him. He's taken off his pack and traded his midweight camo coat for a black puffer. He gives his knit hat an adjustment, tugging it low enough on his forehead so only a few stray locks of dark hair around his ears peek out.

"Pretty sure Colin wouldn't let anything happen to her, even if that means he ditches his pack, carries her out on his back, and goes up again to get his stuff."

I breathe a sigh of relief. Braden's put words to what I already know, but it's nice to hear anyway. *They will be fine.* But even if I know that Colin's a hell of an outdoorsman and Teagan's as tough as they come, they're also part of my family by design. And after losing my parents and Uncle Cal, I'm prone to doing whatever it takes to keep the rest of my family from disappearing on me.

"I just want them down here before any weather rolls in. I'm guessing that trail is dicey if it gets wet."

I close the short distance back to my truck and drop the tailgate, hopping up on it and loosening the laces on my boots, allowing my tired feet some relief. Being able to wiggle one's toes after a few hard miles is a wicked pleasure intimately understood by both hikers and hunters.

Braden follows, leans on the bedside of my truck, forearms resting on the top so he can drum his fingers on the metal. My brow furrows up.

Braden reads the confusion on my face. "What?"

I crook a brow. "You're free to go. You've served your sentence, so consider yourself a free man. You can go back to your warren or your Grinch-esque off-the-grid compound. Wherever it is you lay that enormous head of yours at night."

"I'll wait with you."

"Not necessary."

"I'll. Wait."

We lock eyes until Braden gives in and drops his head to rest on his forearms. I silently congratulate myself on the victory before reaching for a cooler in the bed, dragging it forward to tip the lid up.

"I have water, peach Snapple, and beer. Pick your poison."

Braden begins to roll his forehead across his arms. "Who drinks Snapple? I didn't even think they made that crap anymore."

"*I* drink it. Water, then? I'm sure beer conflicts with your high-minded ethics about what people should and shouldn't consume."

Head still cradled in his arms, he exhales slowly. "Don't compare beer to your shitty energy bars and Snapple. Beer is different; it's practically a whole grain. I want a beer so badly right now, you have no fucking idea. But I'm driving my work truck and wearing my uniform." He lifts his head incrementally. "Water, please."

Well, well, *well*. Was that politeness I just heard? And he's insistent on waiting with me until Colin and Teagan get down the trail? Interesting.

I hand him a water and open my own, taking a long drink. The cold water combined with the cooling temps prompts a full-body shiver.

"Your truck or mine?" Braden asks quietly.

Try as I might, when I peer his way, I can't find even the tiniest bit of contempt in his expression. If anything, he looks concerned. Like he genuinely gives a shit if I'm cold.

That does it. He's exhausted or something. Dog-tired and too beat down to sneer or mock. He *must* be.

I tip my head toward the cab of my truck. "I'm closer."

What I'd much rather do is unlock the fifth-wheel RV we've been staying in and snuggle down in my bunk, but since Braden's decided to play minder, that isn't an option. Leaving him outside to wait seems rude, but inviting him in isn't happening. He's just demonstrated the ability to care, the quarters are too cozy, and he smells like a big, just-sweaty-enough *man*. God knows what state Colin and Teagan might find us in if we're left unattended too long.

We each make our way to the truck, and I start the motor so the heater will kick on, watching as Braden slumps down, taking up the entire seat and then some. His presence overwhelms the cab with far too much virility for such a small space. Maybe the RV, bigger by a stretch, would have been a better choice.

Braden scans the dash of my truck, strewn with topographical maps and big game brochures. My truck looks like a command center because I've voluntarily sequestered myself here more than once on this trip, desperate for some quiet time to study my maps. Although it was nice of Colin's parents to let us use their RV for this trip, it's definitely made for close quarters, and all of us are used to living alone. Colin also managed to use his pull over at Afield to borrow two of their decaled trucks, one we could hook the RV to and another to carry our remaining gear. Given that *I* don't seem to have pull anymore, I need every favor Colin can garner on my behalf.

Braden's gaze lands on the map at the top of the pile, detailing the Routt National Forest hunting unit near Steamboat Springs. Before we made our way to Hotchkiss, we spent time there and near Aspen, scouting those as possibilities for my hunt as well. When we leave here, we'll make one more stop down south in Durango to check out a unit in the San Juan Mountains. Braden attempts to get a better look at the map by tilting his head and skimming what he can see, but he doesn't reach for it.

"Unit fourteen," I offer. "We were up there last week. Nice herd, but I think there are too many roads in and out of that area. Might feel like Grand Central Station come season. Horse and foot traffic I can deal with, but the last thing I need is a bunch of guys roaring around on their ATVs like idiots because they're too out of shape or too lazy to walk anywhere."

Admiration flickers in his expression, like he's pleasantly surprised to discover I've given my hunt some actual thought. That I understand why less motorized traffic in the area is best, especially when archery hunting demands a closer range to your target and if some joker on an ATV spends too much time barreling up access roads, that will spook the elk. Inside, I grouse a little. *Of course* I understand that. I may have spent the last few years on luxury ranches with expert outfitters, but I went on my first deer hunt when I was twelve, which makes this my sixteenth season hunting big game.

Hunting 101: Don't make a bunch of noise. Fucking *duh*.

Braden points to the map, asking for permission. I give him a nod and he drags it into his lap, hunches over, and begins to trace the tip of his index finger across the map. After a few moments of silent study, he sets the map on the center console between us and circles his finger on a small section.

"What about this basin? I've never hunted here, but I've camped near Mt. Zirkel. If I remember correctly, this area takes you east enough that you'll have some breathing room from high-traffic areas."

I lean closer to the map, but doing so puts our faces nearer to each other, from where I can hear him breathing steadily and feel the heat from his body. He also just spoke to me like he might if he was planning a hunt with one of his buddies—assuming he has any—instead of the way he would if I was just a blonde with a hunting show.

Unfortunately, the respectful camaraderie he just offered up doesn't make me want to have a beer with him. Nope. It makes me want to crawl over the console, straddle his big body, and kiss him.

I lock every muscle in my body to keep from doing exactly that and force my brain to focus clearly on the spot he's pointed out, eventually recalling the area in my mind.

I nod. "We spent a little time glassing from a ridge up above there. And that basin is a honey hole, for sure. But it's also steep. If I fill my tag down in there, I also have to get him out on my own, and I can only carry so much weight at a time. No way am I risking losing any meat because I can't get him out fast enough."

Braden immediately gives me the same look he did a moment ago. Again, the fact that I know a bull elk will yield hundreds of pounds of meat and require multiple treks in and out of the wilderness to pack it all out seems to blow his mind. And when our eyes meet, I think he might be considering how best to drag me over the console and into his lap. He takes a labored swallow.

"Then hire a packer with horses to haul the meat out."

I tip my head back and forth loosely, suggesting that I'm not sold on the idea—because that might feel a little like cheating. Braden shakes his head, replies to my hesitation without my even having to say it aloud.

"No shame in that, Amber. Especially when it's at the cost of possibly losing meat. It's a practical, responsible solution."

I sigh. "I know. I just want to do it all myself. One hundred percent. Not to mention, then I have to find the right packer to hire. One who won't take my money and then flake out. Or expect that by working with me, he'll automatically cash in on big exposure for his company."

Braden tosses the map back on the dash. "I'll help you with that part. I can make some calls to the wardens in that unit, find a reputable company, and send you the info—"

A sharp knock against my door glass interrupts us, Colin's cold-reddened face on the other side. Teagan is a few steps behind, already taking advantage of the signal strength by peering down at her phone. I roll down my window.

"That sucked," Colin announces. "The snow's already starting up there and I need to get Teagan warmed up as quickly as possible."

My lips curl wryly. "I'll just wait out here, then. Let me know when you're done and it's safe to come in the RV."

Colin blushes. "I didn't mean it like that. Let's just get cleaned up and then go find ourselves some food and some beer."

Teagan sidles up behind him with a grin, pointing her phone my direction. My post from earlier is up on her screen.

"Braden's practically trending. Even Trey's chimed in."

I pull my phone out and open the app to scan the comments. My followers are split about sixty–forty between men and women, but broody Braden has driven the female contingent to the forefront—and they're feeling chatty.

Who's the hottie in the corner?

Grrr. Somebody looks grumpy. And yummy.

IS HE A GUIDE? I'd follow him anywhere!!! #hotguysincamo

And from my little brother, Trey, one of his dry-witted gems.

@amberregan, are you aware that you've been photobombed by an angry yeti?

A near psychotic laugh bubbles up before I can stop it. Braden immediately begins to launch a series of irritated questions at us.

"Why are you laughing? And why in the hell are 'trending' and my name being uttered in the same sentence? Someone tell me what the fuck is going on. *Now.*"

I finish my giggle-fest with a satisfied sigh and slump into my seat, turning lazily to point my phone his way. "The picture I posted earlier. Part of your handsome frowning face is in the shot, and chicks are getting lady boners over you."

His face screws up. "That's a sign of some sort. I'm going home. I have shit to do later, and Charley will pout if I hold up dinner—and I hate it when she pouts."

My grin starts to fade. Not that he owed me a relationship status disclosure, but who is this pouting "she" he's talking about? What sort of woman does Braden go home to? She pouts? I can't picture him putting up with much drama of any kind, let alone female drama. What does she look like? Is she pretty?

Oh, hell, who am I kidding? Look at him. The dark hair and the scruff, the serious sage eyes, and a sourpuss attitude many a woman would love to claim she single-handedly charmed into submission. All of that and he's built like the caricature of a lusty lumberjack. So yeah, she's probably gorgeous.

My phone beeps with a text, interrupting my internal ramble. Bless my little brother's heart, because he probably just saved me from making a fool of myself had any of the ramblings become external.

> Where is your extra laundry detergent? I know you have some. You're my laundry whisperer. Better yet, come home, laundry whisperer. WHITES! COLORS! MY DELICATES! THIS IS TOO HARD!!!

Sigh. The kid is twenty-five going on twelve. His adulting skills are especially weak when it comes to laundry, and since I find laundry to be the most relaxing chore in the world, I'm content to be his enabler when it comes to his aversion to washing machines.

Plus, he's my kid brother. We lost our parents in a fire when I was ten and he was seven, and despite Uncle Cal taking us in and loving us the best he could, the two of us still became a little codependent unit. I mothered him and he protected me—and we do the same today. If I were home, he would have shown up with his laundry basket like a college kid, dumped it next to the washing machine, and then concocted a bullshit story about a sudden work emergency. But given that he's part owner of a burgeoning custom furniture company and runs the design portion of the business, most of his job involves him hunched over a sketch pad. Not exactly a job fraught with crises.

Another text lights the screen.

> You'll need to buy more peanut butter when you get back. And eggs. And milk. Toothpaste. TP. I'll make a list. You're welcome.

I snort. He also struggles mightily with grocery shopping, so I've been known to stock up on extras of the things he likes. I tap out a quick reply.

Stop *shopping* in my pantry and take your lazy ass to the grocery store. IT'S THAT HUGE BUILDING NEXT TO THE STRIP-MALL DIVE BAR YOU FREQUENT.

Teagan peers toward my phone. "Trey?"

"Yeah," I answer, clicking the lock on my phone. "I can't leave him alone. His laundry won't do itself, and I'm not there to make it magically disappear, then reappear clean and folded."

Braden clears his throat and my eyes shoot to his. We're both holding our phones awkwardly, somehow quizzing each other without so much as a word.

"Well, I'm sure your *brother*," Teagan offers, "will figure it out. Either that or I'm sure he can just brush off the sawdust and make do."

Visible relief works across Braden's features. Suddenly, he thrusts his phone in my face. My eyes drop to his home screen, where there's a picture of a dark toffee-colored Chesapeake Bay retriever zonked out in a layout blind, her head resting on what I'm assuming is one of Braden's manly thighs.

"Charley," he declares.

A smile spreads across my face. Braden returns my smile with his own.

OK, calling it a *smile* might be pushing it. But he isn't glaring or frowning, and the left side of his mouth is curved up ever so slightly, enough to send a zing of satisfaction through my body. We stay that way until Colin's stage whisper absolutely kills the moment.

"Jesus. Is that what we look like?"

An *oof* follows, likely the back of Teagan's hand whacking against Colin's abs. Teagan then chimes in with an invitation.

"Come to dinner with us, Braden. We need you to tell us where to go anyway—you're the local."

His eyes drift over to Teagan before opening the truck door to get out. "I can't. I wasn't bullshitting about having a thing to be at tonight. Your choices for dinner are limited in Hotchkiss, but there's a barbeque place called True Grit. It's pretty good. Give that a try."

The door shuts, and he disappears into the low light of a late afternoon creeping toward sunset. We wait until his truck starts before turning to give one another the same skeptical expression.

"Did he just recommend a *barbeque* joint to us?" Colin asks.

"He did," Teagan replies.

We all go silent for a few beats. Dumbfounded by what Braden has just so innocently proposed.

Shocked by the nerve of it.

Entirely confused.

"Was he joking? He knows where we're from, right?" Colin continues, prompting only a shrug from Teagan and a questioning headshake from me.

Because if there's one thing we Texans readily unite behind, it's our barbeque—the belief that no matter how you smoke it, baste it, or slather it, no one else does it the way we do. We do it right. Everyone else does it wrong.

And to claim otherwise is blasphemy.

5

(Amber)

"When a man hits a target, they call him a marksman.
When I hit a target, they call it a trick.
Never did like that much."
—ANNIE OAKLEY

True Grit BBQ does not disappoint. At least not in the way the three of us expect, because we're snobs. Total barbeque snobs.

Snobs who pulled into the parking lot and sat in the truck, took a good look at the outside of the restaurant Braden recommended and groaned in unison, then shook our heads sadly when we stepped out and sniffed the air like bloodhounds. Not a trace in the air of post oak, or mesquite, or pecan wood. And a joint that has *barbeque* or *barbecue* or *BBQ*—I don't care how you spell it—in its name should reek of wood smoke because there should be multiple offset smokers out back, perfuming the air for miles.

Still, we went inside. Curiosity and all. The sort that killed the cat—and his taste buds.

"There should be a law," Colin grumbles, giving the pile of sauce-drenched brisket in his Styrofoam container another accusing poke with his fork.

Teagan nudges her plate Colin's way when he continues to grouse, claiming he's going to write his congressman about this supposed law he wants.

"I told you not to order that, but you didn't listen. Here. Stop torturing yourself and just eat some of mine."

Teagan proved herself the smartest of our bunch, ordering a mixed plate of sides. Her container is piled full of cheesy corn, smashed red potatoes drizzled with an almost obscene amount of melted butter, some braised greens, and a very respectable-looking sweet potato casserole.

I give my container of pulled pork another sad look and think longingly of getting back home, where I can hit up Franklin Barbecue for a proper fix. Hopefully, no one else standing in line there will be able to smell the oversauced scent of my disloyalty.

If only people like Braden understood the religious experience that proper barbeque can bring about. We're talking about not-too-thin-not-too-thick slices of beef brisket with a beautiful smoke ring, encased in a near-black crust of salt and pepper, still tender and moist despite hours on a smoker. Served on an old-school lunch tray lined with a humble sheet of brown waxed paper, with nothing but a few pickle slices and rounds of raw onion on the side. Maybe a slice or two of white bread. No sauce needed or recommended.

Such a pity. Braden looks like he can put away the groceries, and he's all for making sure it's quality stuff. And he's been eating this. Poor Jolly Green Giant doesn't know any better.

My phone vibrates in my back pocket, distracting me from the decision whether to go hungry tonight or consume what's left of the so-called barbeque on my plate. A quick glance at the display and any appetite I had disappears, replaced by a ball of nerves. I stand up with the phone in one hand, grabbing my coat in the other.

"It's Jaxon. I should get this."

Colin doesn't offer any reaction, still busy glowering at his brisket. But Teagan's brows rise a bit, because she knows that every call from my manager these days has been either bad news or what feels like impending bad news.

I make it outside just before the call rings over to voicemail. I answer on a huff, my breath visible in the cold night air.

"Hey, Jaxon."

"Hello, Annie Oakley. How are you, doll? Is the state of Colorado treating you right?"

Jaxon calls me Annie Oakley, and has since the day when we met four years ago at an invite-only party for the new Filson store in Austin. I was trying to decide if a seven-hundred-dollar field coat could possibly perform in any way that would justify the price, when Jaxon sidled up next to me.

He was barely my height, with features chiseled and strong in a way that seemed out of place on a man his size, but with his pale blue eyes and gingersnap hair it all made sense somehow. He was decked out in an unapologetically green tweed suit and using the toothpick in his hand to gesture at the field coat with a sneer.

"*Only Tom Hardy could make that coat attractive.*"

Then he gave me a once-over and, from around the toothpick, asked who I was. I introduced myself, then offered my recently crafted pitch about starring in a new show on the Afield Channel. He listened, advised that my spiel needed some work, and handed me his card. *"Call me if you ever need a professional who will always tell you the truth, Annie Oakley."*

Since then, Jaxon Metcalf has become my friend, my lawyer, and my manager. I've also tried to explain to him all the ways in which I'm not like Annie Oakley, how what I do as a hunter has nothing in common with a trick shooter from the 1900s. But he thinks it's charming and adorable, and I think *he's* charming and adorable—which is the main reason he gets away with continuing to call me Annie Oakley.

I work to tug my coat on as I answer.

"Well, let's see. I spent the day with a game warden who hates hunting shows, called me a mountain sprite, and declared the fact we both survived the day alive, to be the only redeeming quality of our time together. He then recommended a fine local barbeque joint to us for dinner. I'm now standing outside said restaurant, which is named True Grit, I kid you not. And I'd much rather eat grit. Not grits, mind you. Grit. Like dirt. I'd rather eat dirt."

Jaxon is quiet, but I can hear him typing away on his laptop. After a few more keystrokes, he makes a sharp sound of discovery.

"John Hickenlooper. He's the governor there in Colorado. I'll call his office in the morning and demand this game warden's head on stick. And a formal apology. Otherwise we'll sic the Rangers on him. Send you to a barbeque joint? These are the sort of grievances that demand *action*."

I let out a laugh at what I know is his trumped-up, lawyerly attempt to put me at ease.

"All right, let's calm down. I don't feel the need to lawyer up; it wasn't that bad. And the game warden's head is too pretty to end up on a stick. Not to mention it would be a waste of a very fine body, all headless and such."

"Yeah? Would I like him?"

I consider Jaxon's preferences when it comes to guys. He likes his men more on the featherweight side, lean forms earned by way of barre classes and strict Paleo diets. The sort of guys whose smiles are blindingly white, whose artfully disheveled haircuts cost hundreds of dollars, and whose shoes cost twice as much. Braden, with his lumbering, glowering form and his rough-edged everything, simply wouldn't tick any boxes for Jaxon.

"Nope," I offer casually. "He's too big."

"Oh, doll, be serious." He lets out an appreciative sigh. "We both know there's no such thing. But I'll assume you mean that he's just not for me. Does that mean he's for you? Were you two playing the hating game, but what you really want is to play the *let's get naked* game?"

I return his sigh with my own, but far more frustrated in comparison. Is Braden Montgomery for me? No. He can't be.

At least I don't think so.

"I'm taking the fifth on that one. But it's Friday night, which means there's a Weather Up old-fashioned waiting for you, and I'm out here standing in the cold. So why don't you tell me why you really called. Did you hear back from Smeltzer?"

The head of programming at the Afield Channel, Bud Smeltzer, was my biggest ally for years. By "ally," I mean he practically has his nose up my back end for all his efforts to keep me happy. He also insinuated how happy it would make him if our working relationship included me in his bed. That did not happen and will not. Because, among other reasons, he's old enough to be my father.

Regardless, his admiration for me and *Record Racks* was steadfast—right up until my ratings stalled out. And when they started to slide, he was suddenly nowhere to be found. Now I'm without a contract for next year, filming episodes on spec and crossing my fingers it will all work out once Smeltzer sees this Colorado elk hunt come together.

"No. Smeltzer is still incommunicado." Jaxon lets out an irritated grumble. "I'm giving him another week, and if he hasn't called me back I'm going to show up at the Afield offices dressed in a Speedo, crooning a very inappropriate singing telegram. That should get his attention." He pauses. "But I do have other news."

" 'Other news'? Care to be more vague?"

"I got a call from Bona Fide Media in LA. They produce adventure reality shows. You know, beautiful people stranded somewhere they shouldn't be. A remote island, the Alaskan bush, Area 51, the Ozarks, the fucking North Pole. Think *Surviving Santa's Sexy Workshop* or, like, *Seven Amish Brides for Seven Hipster Brothers: The Iditarod Edition*." He snorts. "Those aren't real shows. Not yet, at least. But you get my drift, right?"

Of course I get his drift. I own a television and I don't live under a rock, so I've sometimes landed on a show like what he's describing. What's more is that I don't need Jaxon to tell me *why* these cats at Bona Fide called, because offers for reality shows have come my way before. Usually, it's for a glorified dating show, one where securing a D-lister like myself might help garner a green light. I always pass, but the offers do provide material for the two of us to mock relentlessly over drinks and tapas.

"Am I going to be the gun-toting Amish bride? Or perhaps I'm one of Santa's scantily clad elves?"

"Neither. The concept is a reality show set in a boutique resort down in Los Cabos. You'd come on as the sport fishing guide for the guests. The staff will be the focus, partying hard and looking hot. Insert a bar fight here, a cat fight there, plus plenty of time on the beach, and you've got yourself a show."

My initial reaction isn't a word—it's a sound. *Blech*.

Jaxon keeps on, doing his best to highlight the positives.

"The pay sounds promising. You'd be the big name and they're willing to offer all the money because of it. Six weeks in sunny Mexico, nice digs, surrounded by guys who look good in board shorts and flip-flops."

My answer sound rises again when I picture those sorts of guys. The tans they spend far too much time on, the big white sunglasses, the puka-shell necklaces. And the flip-flops. That non-stop thwack-thwack-thwack as they shuffle around looking for their surf wax.

Blech.

Jaxon registers that I'm unmoved by the potentially lucrative payday or the notion that I'd be the big *pescado* in the house. His tone turns wry.

"Now, yes, you may be prompted to yank out someone's hair extensions while you call her out as a supposed slut. Likely because whatever flip-flopped dude manages to catch your attention on the first night will then stick his tongue down her throat on the second night."

Double *blech*.

"You may also be asked to do something topless. Sunbathe, fish, vacuum, or cartwheel down the beach."

All the *blechs*. All. Of. Them.

I decide to add a few words, just so we're both clear on exactly how much I hate this idea.

"What about hijacking a yacht in order to escape this whacked-out *Fantasy Island* nightmare? Would the studio execs be into that? I mean, I'd be topless, obviously."

"They would *so* be into that," Jaxon deadpans, then sighs. "Let's not slam the door on these guys just yet. Keep our options open, yeah?"

I focus my eyes on the already quiet Main Street of downtown

Hotchkiss, doing my best to steady a rise of anxiety inside. Jaxon doesn't speak the hard truth, but I hear it nonetheless. That I don't have the luxury of casting off these offers so callously as I once did. If I do, I might regret it.

"Sure. Keeping the door open. Topless as I do," I mutter.

My gaze tracks up and down the empty street corridor, on the lookout for anything that might distract me from this unnamed feeling, the one I want to shake off before it takes root.

"Smeltzer is playing possum for a reason, doll. But you just need to keep your head down, get your Annie Oakley on out there in Colorado, and come home ready to make things happen, no matter what."

Standard Jaxon—no pep talks with reassurances he can't back up, just a candid directive before we say goodbye. I tuck my phone into my back pocket and stare straight ahead. As much as I'd known my brand needed a reboot, losing my show still felt like a far-off and unlikely disaster, and one I had time to elude. Like a tornado watch that suggested I keep an eye on the sky, but didn't yet require bolting the cellar door. Now it felt like the skies were too dark, the air was too dense, and it was time to seek shelter in something sturdy.

I scan the area again, looking for anything that I might use as an escape, but there's nothing. No neon lights of a bar, no drifting smoke from the doorway to a club, not even a movie theater or a pool hall.

One more deep breath before giving up my search, only to catch sight of a figure across the street, lumbering toward a truck parked in front of a liquor store. And as much as I shouldn't know that shadowed sight at such a distance—I do.

My lips curve up. If I walk over there, he might very well cuss up a storm at the sight of me or grumble like the enormous grouch that he is.

He may also be just what I need tonight.

I head that way almost without thinking, a sudden spring in my step, rounding the side of his truck and stopping just shy of my target.

"*Hello*, Braden."

6

(Braden)

"Praise her endlessly. It's wonderful what a compliment does to hearten us girls."
—*The Sierra Club Wilderness Handbook*,
"Especially for Men," c. 1971

This is what I get.

I should have known better. You can't obsess over a woman like a fucking teenager and expect that shit to go without consequences.

You also cannot have a seriously insane conversation with your dog about the object of your obsession, complete with you showing your dog a picture of her on the internet, then blathering on about how in person she's pint-sized, but her hair is even shinier, and she smells like strawberries. Fresh strawberries muddled up with honey and oranges and . . . just other things I want to suck, lick, taste, and otherwise make use of my mouth on.

All of this happened; all of this was discussed. In detail. With. My. Dog.

It was weird and pathetic, and inappropriate, really.

And I may not believe in luck or fate, but I do believe in willing what you want. So spending the last few hours rehashing every detail of my day with Amber must have sent a siren call out into the universe, only to conjure her up in front of me. Right here, standing near enough that her strawberry scent is impossible to ignore. I dare myself to look her way, completely, to take her in without accidentally owning up to that earlier conversation with my dog.

She's traded in her gear from earlier for an entirely new outfit: dark jeans the color of red wine that hug her every curve, some little boots with heels, and a sweater that's oversized but cropped, revealing how low those jeans sit on her hips. Her hair is down, loose and wavy around her face. When she flips it back over one shoulder, I get hit with a strong wave of strawberry. It's her shampoo, I realize. Which may mean she's showered since I last saw her.

Either that or I'm just like all those other guys who drool over her and we all like thinking about her naked. And wet. And soapy.

Fucking hell. I'm *such* an asshole.

"What's with all the ice, Superman? Doing some renovations on your broody little ice castle in space?"

I swing the two bags of ice in my left hand into the bed of my truck, then follow with the two over my right shoulder, and start to stack them with the others.

"It wasn't an ice *castle*. That makes it sound like the Superman version of a Barbie Dreamhouse." I slam the tailgate shut. "It was his Fortress of Solitude. And it's not in space, it's in the Arctic. But it's not always made of ice—depends on what incarnation of Superman you're talking about."

Amber lets her lips quirk up on one side.

"I don't like the way you just implied that a Barbie Dreamhouse is somehow inferior to your little Superman Ice Capades Wonderland or whatever. Also, serious nerd alert there, Braden." She lowers her voice, growls a little. "'But it's not always made of ice—depends on what incarnation of Superman you're talking about.'"

Another pathetic growling sound. I crook an eyebrow.

"Let me get this straight. I don't give the right props to some plastic piece of crap that looks like a Pepto-Bismol factory exploded on it—and I'm an asshole. But you can mock me and that's OK?"

"Yes." She steps closer, lazily dragging her fingertips across the top of my tailgate before she tips her head. "Haven't you noticed? I play by my own rules."

Reflexively, I lean back. When I realize what I've done, I can't decide if I'm losing my mind or if I'm just rusty when it comes to this stuff. Because I haven't done this in a while. The flirting, chasing, wanting, and craving. Any of it.

But when you come home one day to find all of your fiancée's belongings packed up and loaded into the back of some other guy's pickup, it's easy to end up shell-shocked when it comes to women. No man in their right mind should want to go through that again, which made it simple for me to settle on a life alone. And this is the first time in three years that I've wanted anything different—with Amber Regan, of all people. A woman I was convinced couldn't possibly hold her own in the field, only to figure out quickly that she knows her stuff. Once I acknowledged that, I realized how easy it is to typecast people into roles they don't necessarily belong in. This—seeing Amber as more than an obnoxious trophy hunter clad in hot pink camo—takes more thought.

Hours of thought, if my afternoon is any indication.

Amber's phone beeps and she pulls it from her back pocket to scan the face. Then she rises up on her tiptoes and gawks across the street toward the True Grit parking lot, giving a wolf whistle in that direction. Colin and Teagan emerge from behind one of those God-awful decaled trucks and head our way, Colin taking Teagan's hand when they start to cross Main Street. Safety first, kid. Because the traffic here is *so* treacherous.

They stroll over to us, and Colin immediately sends me a glare.

"I need to find some liquid amnesia after that dining debacle. Tequila, maybe. Seriously, man. What were you thinking?"

I return his glare, confused by the attitude he's tossing around. "What?"

"It's like sending ol' Giuseppe from Rome to the freezer case for a Red Baron when he wants a pizza. Or swinging by Taco Bell with the *abuela* who wants a burrito. It's—"

Teagan cuts Colin off, yanking her hand from his with an eye roll. "Ignore him." Her eyes move to Amber. "How bad do *you* need a drink? Everything OK?"

Amber's shoulders sag as if a weight has been placed there, shrinking her in a way I don't like. That and the obvious concern in Teagan's tone puts my body on edge, and not just in the way I've felt since the moment I met Amber. Instead, I want to know exactly what Teagan is angling at and wrestle that weight from Amber's shoulders. But Amber cuts a glance my way, then straightens her spine and pulls her shoulders back, making it crystal clear that she isn't interested in sharing.

"I'm fine. But I could go for a drink." Amber looks to me again and her eyes take on a teasing gleam. "In fact, Braden is headed back to his Fortress of Barbie Dreamhouse Solitude and I think we should join him." She steps closer, near enough that her thigh brushes mine.

"Do you have drinks at the Fortress, Braden? I bet you do. I bet you have lots of pink drinks and fruity cocktails there—look at all this ice. Take us, Braden. Take us to your Fortress of Frosty Doom."

Jesus Christ. Why do I want to smack her ass and kiss the fuck out of her when she talks to me like that? Why am I fighting a laugh, a growl, and a hard-on all at the same time? My entire reality has been turned on its ear, and even when I should be doing everything in my power to turn things the right way around, my body refuses to get on board.

"It's called a Fortress of *Solitude* for a reason," I grumble, then gesture down the street with a jut of my chin. "There are no bars in town except for the Elks Lodge. So unless Colin's an Elk, you'd better stock up here before old man Carl closes up for the night."

I start toward the front of my truck, but Amber stops me with a palm to my chest. My jacket is unzipped, so her warm hand rests over what now feels like the flimsiest, most threadbare T-shirt I own. Fucking great. Now she's touching me. Tame, yes, but she's the first woman in forever who's made my dick ache, and now she's touching me. My heart starts to work overtime, beating too hard and too fast.

Amber's eyes meet mine. "But where are *you* going? With all this ice?"

The heat of her, so close and so good, means any hope I had to walk away without a second glance becomes impossible. I swallow thickly.

"It's a local thing. You guys wouldn't enjoy it."

Her hand starts to trail down my chest. "Is it a party?"

"Kind of."

"Are there drinks? Entertainment of some sort?" Her nails scrape lightly over my abs and each one contracts until her fingers meet my belt. Only when her hand drops away am I finally able to breathe properly again.

"Yes." I nod my head toward the bags of ice. "My buddy Garrett and I are in charge of the drinks. Needed more ice than we planned on."

"Sounds like a real fiesta," she offers. "But now I'm curious— do you and this Garrett fellow do the whole *Cocktail* bottle-tossing tomfoolery? Or anything else that would earn you status as a beefcake bartender? Bare-chested body shots, bar-top dance acts, or something a Coyote Ugly gal would wholeheartedly endorse?"

There it is again, the urge to lay my palm across her ass— *hard*—as a reprimand, and then kiss her until we both can't breathe. I give up and lean in just a few inches, but it's nowhere near where I truly want to be.

"*No*," I answer.

"Oh, for Christ's sake. Either tell us where this party is or you two need to just get a room."

Amber and I both snap our heads up and jerk our attention to an exasperated Colin and a ridiculously entertained Teagan.

"I vote for disclosure of the party's location. Because, honestly, dude?" He points an accusing finger my way. "After sending us to that so-called barbeque joint, where the ketchup they call 'sauce' did nothing to fix that brisket nightmare, you owe us a drink."

Amber and Teagan try to stifle their snickering and I finally figure out what has Colin's dander up. Apparently, True Grit did not meet their expectations. Too bad. Even so, there is no way Amber and I are getting a room, leaving only option A.

"It's over at the fire station. Our annual fundraiser for the Hotchkiss Volunteer Fire Department. Twenty-five bucks a head, but that includes all the drinks and desserts you want, plus some crappy carnival games, and there's a band playing."

Teagan's eyes go wide with a grin, and she starts to clap her hands like an overexcited tween girl. "Dessert!"

Amber does the same for a moment, then goes still suddenly.

Pointedly, she puts both of her hands to my chest, and I peer down at her. A smirk curls across her mouth.

"Oh my God. Are you a *firefighter*, Braden? Or do you just play one in a calendar?"

There's something new in her eyes. Appreciation mixed with curiosity, but tempered by that ever-present sass. Why, I'm not sure. I'll bet it's more complicated than some overblown fantasy about firefighters, though. One I ran helmet-first into more often than I care to remember when I was a hotshot. But I'm not buying the idea that Amber is the sort who is keen on that crap, or likes those charity calendars she referred to—the ones that apparently require a drum of canola oil and a rucksack of docile kittens on set.

I scan her face when I reply, "I'm on the volunteer squad, yes."

My answer earns a full smile from her. A real, genuine, not for the camera or the internet, smile. And it's like sunshine I can feel, warming my entire body, in my bones and my every nerve ending.

Amber's smile tapers slowly. "Well, let's go, then."

Her lips then ease into a soft pucker—one that she's a smart remark or another smile away from having kissed or nipped. Or both.

"And I'm riding with you, Mr. December."

7

(Amber)

"The sweetest hunts are stolen."
—ALDO LEOPOLD, *A SAND COUNTY ALMANAC*

The Hotchkiss firehouse sits near town limits, a gray cement-block building with large red bay doors spanning the front. Tonight the bay doors are raised, music pours out, and based on the size of the crowd, the entire town is in attendance.

We pull into the parking lot and Braden slows to glance in the rearview mirror for Teagan and Colin, then drives around back to park. He sets the gearshift in park with a shove and shuts off the truck.

"You guys can go in through the front there. I'm going in the back way with this ice. Have fun."

Then he just gets out.

Maybe I wasn't sure exactly what to expect when we arrived

here, but based on what was happening back at the liquor store, being treated like some fare he's delivered to her destination, was not what I had in mind. There was touching and lingering looks just a few minutes ago, after all. Lingering looks where his hooded eyes were on my mouth and I wanted him to keep staring—just like that—because the whole scene made my head swim pleasantly.

I watch Braden disappear around to the back of the truck before shoving open my own door and following. He slings two bags of ice up to rest on his shoulder and tips his head toward the far side of the building.

"Just walk around the side there, but stay on the asphalt. The grass has big holes in it because we had a few sprinkler heads start leaking this summer. We dug them out but haven't replaced them yet. Need the ground to thaw before we can put in the new ones."

"Thank you for the landscaping update. Fascinating."

Braden lets out a tired sigh as he bends his knees slightly, then lurches up to seat the bags of ice on his shoulder where he wants them. He gathers two more in his free hand, letting them hang at his side. And for a moment, my corrupt mind takes up a fantasy where I'm over his shoulder and he's tossing me about so I'm exactly where he wants me, before dragging me inside his Fortress of Solitude.

Braden clears his throat and my eyes shoot up to his pointed gaze. He tilts his head toward the side of the building again. No words, just a silent order for me to get moving.

Has he not figured this out yet? The worst way to get me to do what you want is to order me around—with or without words. You want to tell me what to do? Go ahead, knock yourself out. I'll be sure to do the opposite.

I grab a bag of ice in each hand. "How about I help you with the drinks?"

All I hear is a groan as I walk away, headed for the back of the building, where a door is propped open with a sandbag. Braden catches up easily, muttering under his breath. He lets me go through the doorway first then immediately cuts in front to lead the way. The band is playing a George Strait cover about getting carried away, every note bouncing off the unforgiving cement-block walls and floors, but no one seems to care about the poor acoustics. Braden moves through the crowd to a far corner of the room, where two folding tables are set up. One table holds ice-filled metal tubs stocked with a variety of beers and the other has three large glass dispensers of what look like sangria, a lemonade, and something with apples floating in it.

Braden shimmies behind the tables and lets the bags of ice drop to a third table near the wall, where there is a large clear bin that looks low on ice, surrounded by endless bags of Solo cups. Garrett, I assume, is busy busting open a case of Coors Light.

"Ice," Braden says. "And no, I did not get you any cough drops. I got waylaid."

Garrett's head falls forward weightily. "I thought we were friends. I thought you *cared*, Braden. My throat is on fire, and it's like you don't fucking care. Waylaid by what? What could waylay you from my comfort, my well-being, my goddam health?"

"Well, you were incorrect. I don't care about your comfort. Comfort is what girlfriends and moms provide. My only job is to point out that you're acting like a fucking pussy." Braden thumbs in my direction. "Amber, Garrett Strickland. Garrett, Amber Regan. The waylayer in question."

Garrett immediately cranes his head to track Braden's gesture. And despite being really good-looking—in a redneck, hide-all-the-farmers'-daughters way—he also looks worn-out, sporting the same bedraggled expression that my brother does when he has a cold. When he spies me, his eyes light with surprise.

"Amber Regan. As I live and breathe." He coughs a little, covering his mouth with the crook of one arm while sending Braden a weary glare. "I'd shake your hand while I tell you I like your show, but I'm ninety percent sure I'm brewing the world's worst head cold. I may also have pneumonia. Bronchitis. And SARS. And the bird flu. In short, I may not live to see another day. Now, if I had the cough drops I requested, I might at least enjoy the small comfort they provide before this affliction finally takes me."

Braden pretends he's deaf, ignoring Garrett completely, and sets about tugging his coat off, revealing a dark blue pocket T-shirt underneath. Every contour of Braden's chest is highlighted by the perfect fit of the shirt and my eyes drift shamelessly over his body for a moment. But my inspection comes to a halt when I zero in on the left side, where one word is printed in large block letters over the pocket.

HOT.

My eyes go comically wide. "Oh my God. Please tell me why your shirt has 'hot' printed on it. I mean, other than the obvious."

Braden looks down at his shirt as if he'd forgotten what he was wearing. With a throaty chuckle, Garrett pulls back the placket on the flannel he's wearing over his own T-shirt, revealing a matching design.

"They're the shirts our captain's wife had done up for tonight. We all have them." He makes a little twirling motion near Braden's head. "Show her the back."

Braden locks his eyes on mine, half-pitiful and half-challenging, and then turns slowly.

When he's completely turned around, I don't know what to do first. Laugh? Sigh appreciatively? Go over there and rub my hands all over the expanse of his broad shoulders?

Because printed across Braden's back is the image of a cheesy cartoon-style woman fanning herself, surrounded by similarly silly cartoon flames. At the bottom is another cartoon, this one a fire-fighter aiming his hose toward the overheated gal with a toothy grin. And sandwiched between are words I'm sure it pains the ever-uptight Braden to know are printed—loudly and proudly—on his back.

IS IT HOT IN HERE?
SUPPORT THE HOTCHKISS VOLUNTEER FIRE DEPT.
WE FIND 'EM HOT—AND LEAVE 'EM WET!

I drop the two bags of ice I've been holding awkwardly this entire time, letting them hit the floor with a theatrical thud. Braden faces me again, shoulders slouching as his expression quirks, all but saying *go ahead, I'm waiting* with his body language.

"Introduce me to the woman who designed those shirts. And somehow wrangled *you* into wearing one. I want to shake her hand."

Garrett lets out a croaking laugh while Braden merely goes about tearing open a bag of ice. I gather the bags I'd dropped dramatically and shimmy behind the tables to put them with the others. Braden continues filling the ice bins as Garrett hauls the case of Coors Light onto the front table, leaving me with nothing obvious to do—which means the Jolly Green Giant is about two seconds away from shooing me out of here. But I note that the beer tubs are sorely low on Budweiser products and—*ta-da*—I suddenly have a task. I spot a case of Bud Select, heft it into my arms, and head toward the bins. Braden cuts me off by stepping directly into my path.

"What are you doing?" he gripes, simultaneously moving to swipe the beer from my arms.

"Helping." I swivel myself out of reach in one smooth move.

"You don't need to do—"

Garrett interjects and unknowingly buys me just enough time to skirt around Braden.

"So, Amber, given that I'm dying, I have to know now how your day with Braden went. Was he a camera hog? A diva on set? Did he demand you only shoot his good side?"

I barely stifle a laugh, catching Braden shaking his head out the corner of my eye.

"No, no diva moves today." Dropping the case onto the folding table, I tear the top open. "Although he did make a bit of a splash on my Instagram."

Garrett freezes, his hands clasping the last few beers from his case in midair. "Details, please."

I decide to let my app do the talking by pulling up the post so Garrett can see for himself. A few new comments have come in, all with hashtags that have nothing to do with me.

#hottieswithbeards #camochasersunite #luckygirl #ihearttheyeti

Garrett leans in and scans the comments with a smirk on his face, then clicks his tongue a little.

"I told you all that scowling would look bad on camera, George Clooney. And here you are for all the world to see, with crow's-feet and those wrinkles between your eyebrows. Hashtag *no filter*."

Braden steps up next to me and elbows his way in to unpack the case I brought over.

"Stop talking, Strickland. An hour ago you were whining about losing your voice, so why don't you prove it?"

Garrett shakes his head thoughtfully. "Someday, Braden, when we're old and gray, you're going to ask me to tell you a story about some duck hunt we went on, or every time I kicked your ass shooting sporting clays. You'll *want* to hear me talk."

Braden scoffs as a reply and Garrett laughs until the sound

becomes a cough. Once the cough dissipates, his eyes turn unfocused and his face pales a shade.

I tilt my head just enough to find his line of sight. "You OK?"

Garrett meets my eyes then ticks them toward Braden.

"See that? Compassion, Braden. Florence Nightingale and I have known each other for ten minutes, and she's expressed *concern* for me." He ignores a loud snort from Braden. "In fact, do me a favor, Amber. Feel my forehead, will you? I think I'm—"

Just as Garrett closes his eyes and starts to bend at the waist to lean toward me, his forehead hits the heel of Braden's big palm, now thrust between the two of us.

"No. She will not feel your forehead. Christ."

At the same time, Braden starts to do exactly that. He pats Garrett's cheeks a few times, then returns his hand to Garrett's forehead. I check the urge to coo, because it's the sweetest, funniest, most endearing act ever, between this yeti and his redneck.

"And, yes, you're hot. Really hot," Braden says.

A loopy grin covers Garrett's face. "Thank you for finally acknowledging that. Cara agrees, though, so you two are going to have to fight it out to win my heart. Fair warning, she's stronger than she looks."

Braden uses the hand on Garrett's forehead to give him a stiff-armed shove backward. "She can have your dumb ass. Go home. I can handle this."

"No way," Garrett insists. "That's not happening, there's too much work to do and the clean up is a bitch, so just forget about it, I'll be—"

"I can help," I blurt out.

Both men look my way, clearly taken aback. I narrow my eyes on Braden, who looks especially suspicious. "I'm more than capable of doling out ice and refreshments."

They continue to look at me as if I've just offered to rewire a nuke rather than help hand out beer and party punch, so I turn on my heel and go to work. Granted, most of what happens is that I start to fiddle with the plastic cups, gathering them into stacks and lining each up evenly, like good little plastic soldiers. Behind me, a man conference is under way, Braden griping and Garrett protesting, all while I attempt to look indispensable.

"May I have a cup of that cider punch, sweetheart?"

I look up to find a sixtysomething woman gesturing to the large glass carafes.

"Coming up," I answer, all confidence as I fill a cup with ice, only to stride over to the dispensers and hit a stumbling block. The lemonade is obvious, but the other two are less so. I volley my gaze between them trying to decide what looks more like cider.

Before I finish my analysis, Braden's body is behind mine—my back grazing his chest, my ass brushing the front of his pants—reaching around with both arms to gesture at each carafe as he ticks off their descriptions.

"Red wine sangria. Lemonade. Cider rum punch."

His arms drop out of sight, only for his hands to find a home on my hips. A loose grip at first, but when a measured exhale leaves me, I swear he urges my body backward. Only an inch, maybe less. Even so, it's enough to shorten my breath and turn my heart beat erratic. I let a curve settle in my low back, naturally shifting my lower body closer to his. Braden's fingertips meet the bare skin above my jeans and just under the hem of my sweater, then he slides his hand forward so that more of my bare skin is now under his touch. My mind goes blank.

Shit. I definitely need him to point out which one is the cider again.

8

(Amber)

"But when you poured out your heart I didn't waste it,
'cause there's nothing like your love to get me high."
—Chris Stapleton, "Tennessee Whiskey"

Only two hours in and I've mastered my newfound gig. Bantering with everyone who stops by, including those who recognize me and ask for a picture. I also enacted a workflow system to better serve our parched patrons. The system is simple: I greet them with a smile, help determine what drink best suits them, and then direct them to the beer bin as needed. If they want one of our other concoctions, Braden is to fill a cup with ice, handing the cup off to *me* so I can fill it up with their preferred swill and complete the transaction—with a smile.

In this kick-ass system of mine, Braden has one job. Unfortunately, he refuses to get on board with the system.

"Because it's stupid. I'm already holding the cup. It has ice in it and I'm standing right here, next to the dispensers. Your little system is inefficient as hell."

Braden steps in front of me to thrust a not-full cup at the old man in overalls who's waiting for it. That's another thing: he's stingy.

I interrupt his hand off and grab the cup before it's too late, filling it up to the brim.

"Here you go, sir. Enjoy." I smile and the man gives me a bushy-browed wink.

Behind me, Braden lets out a careful exhale. I grab my own cup and take a sip of the cider rum punch I poured for myself once I paid my twenty-five bucks to properly support the Hotchkiss Volunteer Fire Department. I turn back to Braden and cock one hip out.

"My system isn't based solely on efficiency. This isn't a fast-food joint, it's a fundraiser. A little sparkle goes a long way at these things, trust me. You do not sparkle. Whereas I am all sparkle." I gesture toward myself with an open hand, fingers wiggling as I circle my face, batting my eyelashes for added effect.

"That's the cider rum punch talking. How many cups have you had?"

"Two. Why?"

He shakes his head. "Because that punch is potent. We make it every year and the rum-to-cider ratio favors rum, so it will sneak up on you. Half the kids in this town were probably conceived in some sort of cider punch haze."

"Well, I like it. I think it's just right."

I give Braden a grin, not for any particular reason, merely because I want to. And while I'm certainly not drunk, or even buzzed, I am pleasantly warm inside, enough that it's easy to imagine how another cup of this stuff might lead to your clothes coming off in a rush.

Braden makes a show of looking in my cup to assess the contents, then raises his brows. I set the cup down and back away with my hands palms out, playacting as if I'm trying to keep a mountain lion at bay. Colin and Teagan come walking up just as I clear a few steps, each holding plates in their hands.

"Amber, you have to try this." Teagan gestures at her plate where a hand pie sits, dusted in heaps of powdered sugar. I break off a piece and the dough flakes beautifully. Inside, the still-warm peach filling is sweet without being sugary, and the fruit is more flavorful than I've tasted before. I give up a satisfied moan.

"Right?" Teagan grins. "Imagine that, with your ice cream. The toasted almond one you make?"

While no one would call me Martha Stewart, I'm not a complete slouch in the kitchen, and homemade ice cream happens to be my thing. Don't ask me to bring the seven-layer dip or the veggie platter, because in our circle, no barbeque or summer party is considered complete until one of my creamy frozen creations is dished up.

I nod and snag another bite, considering all the options. "Or the salted caramel. Oh, the gingersnap praline."

Colin snags a beer from the metal bin and cracks it open. Passing off his plate to Teagan, he takes a long drink of the beer and swallows. "Your pistachio would kick ass with this pear thing."

Teagan extends the other plate and a fork so I can sample the pear torte with a chocolate crust, making sure to sneak a sizable dollop of the whipped cream. Another long moan emerges when the concoction hits my taste buds, and I drop my eyes closed, murmuring as I try to savor the flavor.

"So. Good."

I open my eyes and find Braden's hooded gaze fixed on me.

"You have whipped cream on your lip," he rumbles, his darkened gaze dropping to my mouth.

My heart starts to beat wildly as I consider how best to handle this situation. Use the heel of my hand to wipe the whipped cream away, recalling the grubby tomboy I once was? Perhaps. I could also find a napkin to dab it away properly. Or I could use my tongue. Peek it out and tick the tip across that spot, watching Braden as I do. With his rapt attention on my mouth, my decision is nearly made, right up until Braden's eyes rise to meet mine, cautioning us both as if he knows what I'm considering. He's as aware as I am that we're in the middle of a crowded room, there's an obvious attraction between us, and we're both a little too tired to think rationally.

Which is why I pull my sweater down to cover the heel of my hand and use the sleeve just as I used to do when I was eight. Despite my going that route, Braden's intense stare doesn't let up.

Teagan clears her throat. "We're fading fast here, Amber. Are you ready?"

Her pointed question snaps the spell, and Braden answers before I can, glancing at his watch.

"The band is about to finish up their set. We'll be kicking everybody out to clean up right after, so you aren't going to miss much."

With that the band begins to play what may be their last song of the night, and the three of us recognize the opening bars immediately. It's a country song that's been covered more than once, but its latest incarnation these days is bluesy and raw, and *fabulous*. Colin shoots Teagan a grin, extends his hand, and they disappear into the crowd. My insides tumble unexpectedly. The good stuff, right there—so close, and a million miles away.

Without hesitation, without even looking at him, I take a deep breath and ask for my own little taste of the good stuff. "Dance with me, Braden."

"I don't dance."

"I'm sure you don't. But I love this song." I turn to crook my finger at him. "Let's go."

To my surprise, Braden doesn't put up one syllable of further protest. He simply sweeps his hand forward toward the dance floor with a deceptively neutral expression on his face. When we find a spot on the dance floor, he holds his hands up, fox-trot-style. I drop my head and chuckle.

"Come on. Stop that. You know where to put your hands."

I grab his hands and pull them down, set them on my hips, then reach up to clasp my fingers together at the back his neck, teasing a few unruly curls of his dark hair at the nape.

Braden relaxes and draws me closer. "Thank you for your help."

I glance up with a smile. "You're welcome. I had fun. Even if you can't follow my system." He cracks a grin but stows it away before I have much of a chance to enjoy it.

The band starts in on the song's chorus, lyrics that always make me think of my parents, a misty childhood memory of the two of them sitting on the front porch and sharing a glass of whiskey at our cabin in West Texas. The place we spent a few weeks every summer, the same place they went away to every year for their anniversary, and the same place they died when a forest fire trapped them in the house they loved. The song, the memory, the fundraiser—the freaking cider rum punch—all come together, and before I can stop myself, I'm *sharing*.

"The whole firefighting fundraiser thing hits me in a soft spot."

Braden tips his head, listening carefully. I give an offhanded shrug before continuing, not because I feel offhanded, but because my heart demands I keep it safe from eyes that suddenly seem too prying.

"My parents died in a wildfire. We had a cabin in the mountains outside Fort Davis, and they were up there for their anniversary when a fire started. The cabin was remote, no phones, no communication. The fire was on them before they could get out."

Braden's entire face slackens in a sweep, from his forehead to the downturn of his mouth.

"Jesus." He scans my expression for more, waiting. My heart locks tight on itself and I look down, watching as our feet barely move. "I'm so sorry, Amber."

I shake my head. "It was years ago. I was ten, my brother was seven."

Braden's grip at my waist tightens. "Doesn't much matter how long ago it happened, does it? You lost them. That sticks with you."

The simplicity of that statement—the way he highlighted what I've always known—is what makes it almost too much to hear. We sway in silence for a few beats, then Braden pauses us and he moves one of his hands up my back, my eyes drawing up his body in time. He takes a labored swallow.

"I was a hotshot before this. Back in Oregon. So I've seen forest fires up close, the way they move and what's left in their path. The destruction they can cause. So, I . . . fuck, I don't know . . . I just . . ."

He pauses, fumbling for the words he wants. I want to tell him not to bother. No one ever has the right words, not exactly. Plus, the two of us barely know each other, and we seem to work best when we're antagonizing each other, so this moment—no matter how real it feels—is nothing but a mirage. Courtesy of the contents of a Solo cup and hastened along by my memories and the right song. What he says next won't make or break us, because there is no "us." Braden takes a deep breath before speaking plainly.

"I hate that this happened to you."

A few spare, sincere words—from a man who I'm still not sure knows what he thinks of me—that were somehow just enough. Just right, just enough, just shy of flawless. My heart hears every one, and suddenly I'm beyond exhausted. Not only from the whirlwind travel of the last few weeks and the mounting pressures with my show, but because it was overwhelming to hear someone say that they wished for something better for you. That you deserved more than what life may have handed you in a small, dark moment of fate.

Braden sweeps a lock of my hair away from my forehead, and then presses his hand to the back of my neck, urging my head to his chest with an impossibly gentle nudge. I tell myself to shore up and sober up, and most important, keep my head off of his chest. But when he exhales and speaks, my body has other ideas.

"I love this song, too. Just so you know."

My head flops forward. Not gracefully or daintily. Not swoonily or softly. Nope. My forehead just thumps right into his sternum like it weighs three times what it should, and I groan, loudly enough that I feel Braden's chest shaking beneath me on what I think is a silent chuckle.

"No more talking, Braden," I mumble through the press of my face to his chest. His chest quakes again. I sigh, long and slow. "That punch has done snuck up on me, just like you said it would. And if you say one more nice, thoughtful, insightful, not-rude thing to me, I'm going to let the rum haze start doing the thinking here."

Braden's body goes taut. I know why, too. Because he knows how good a hazy night between us would be. And so do I.

9

(Braden)

"Infinite patience and practice are needed to make a hunter."
—Saxton Pope, *Hunting with the Bow and Arrow*

Much of my career choices have come down to one thing: avoiding offices. Because you know what they have in offices? Desks, computers, and—worst of all—printers. More specifically, they have desks that are not properly sized for my body, computers that run molasses-slow, and printers that jam five sheets for every ten they actually print.

Also, offices have this tricky way of being indoors, and I prefer to spend as much time as I can anywhere but. Outside is always my first choice, but my truck is the next best thing. Turns out that even if I came to this job as a game warden simply because I was looking for an excuse to put a few states between me and my ex-fiancée, it's nearly the perfect job for me.

Thank you for that, Laurel. Thank you for deciding that you were tired of waiting for me to get home from fighting some new forest fire in another state and that the dreamy, newly divorced dad of one of your preschool students—good old *Brad*, with his safe, stable, home-for-dinner job at the tire store—was a much better fit for that picket fence life you wanted. Not that I was blameless in the demise of our relationship, but I'm claiming the moral high ground because *I didn't cheat*. I might have put my job as a hotshot firefighter ahead of everything else, I might have taken you and your easy temperament for granted, but still.

I. Didn't. Cheat.

But thank you for your infidelity being the worst of it, and most of all, thank you for not trying to keep Charley from me. I need her and she needs me, and in her eyes, I'm perfect. In turn, I try damn hard to be home on time for dinner. Just like *Brad*.

Now I spend ninety percent of my time in the Colorado sunshine. And even if most people wouldn't believe it, all that sunshine has been good for my disposition. The satellite CPW office I'm responsible for in Hotchkiss has limited public hours, which means I can keep my time here to only those required, plus a few extra at the end of the month, when certain reports I have to turn in are due.

Today is one of those days. Month-end reports are due ASAP, and as expected, given the scrap IT monies allotted to offices like mine, the computer has crashed twice and the printer has jammed one too many times to count. That alone puts me in a bad mood. Add in the fact that I'm also tense in other ways, and you have a recipe for office equipment disaster.

I take a deep breath and stare at the computer screen. I swear, if I hit print this time and that results in anything other than the prompt production of the ten pages I want printed out, then this hunk of crap and I are going to have it out in the parking lot, because I'm about to go Michael Bolton from *Office Space* on this thing.

Ten seconds later, the printer beeps loudly. And stops.

Calmly, I turn my attention to the LED display on the shitty piece of office equipment that's about to end up in pieces.

OUT OF PAPER

OK, that I can deal with. You've been granted a pardon, Lexmark E460.

Shoving away from the desk, I sidestep out from behind it and do the same to clear the doorway in my so-called office, which was once a storage closet. Down the hallway, the main public area is only slightly bigger than my office. A large reception desk takes up half of the space, and display racks holding game regulation booklets clutter up the rest. I grab a ream of paper from the open shelving in the reception station and start back to my office, only to have a knock at the front door stop me.

Can't people read? Office hours—not now—are clearly marked on the front door. I let out a heavy sigh, knowing I could ignore the knock, easily and without a guilty conscience. But being available to answer questions or field concerns from the public is a big part of my job. Even if I'm not one for a bunch of chitchat, for the most part, people who take the time to seek out a game warden are smart and interested in following the rules, and value the outdoors as much as I do.

Which is why I stride over to the front door and take a look out the sidelight window adjacent to it.

Well, I was right—sort of. Because the woman smiling at me from the other side of the glass is smart, yes. She also values the outdoors as much as I do. As for following the rules? That depends.

Amber makes a twisting motion with her hand, gesturing for me to unlock the door. Blank-faced, I point to the "CLOSED" sign next to my head. She kicks one hip out, sets her hand there, and tilts her head.

"Open the door, Braden." Her voice is slightly muffled, but her antagonistic singsong delivery comes through loud and clear.

I twist the lock on the door and open it a few feet. I raise my arm up and brace my hand to the door edge while tucking the ream of paper under my other arm.

"Office hours are clearly marked. Come back tomorrow."

Amber cuts her gaze to the hours posted on the door. "You aren't open tomorrow."

"Exactly."

"Stop it," she scolds, then darts under my arm before I can do anything to stop her.

Fucking mountain sprites. Too damn wily for their own good—or mine.

Amber turns on her heel slowly, taking in the room, then stops when she's facing me. She's dressed in comfy-casual workout gear: yoga pants and a long-sleeve top that's oversized but cropped like her sweater from last night, except this top also falls off of one shoulder to expose a spaghetti-thin bra strap. A good two inches of her belly are on display, and her toned abs rouse my first-ever desire to take part in a body shot, regressing my emotional age a good decade or so. Her hair is up in a messy knot on the top of her head, and her skin is free of anything that looks like makeup. And she still smells like strawberries.

I've spent the hours since we parted ways at the fundraiser trying to forget everything about last night, especially how much I wanted to kiss her. Just kiss her. Not only because I imagine her body is kissable everywhere, but because for those moments when she was in my arms, a great song playing in the background while she shared something real about herself with me, it felt like the beginning of something.

Full disclosure: I also thought about tossing her over my shoulder, dragging her out to my truck, and taking her home with me, where we could kiss without an audience and fuck without thinking about tomorrow. Because I'm not noble enough to keep those thoughts at bay, and the depraved areas of my mind are obsessed with her. Here's hoping that Amber can't see the growing evidence of that depravity right now, inspired by her bare belly and an imagined tequila shot in my hand.

"I'm glad I caught you here. I wanted say thank you properly before I head out. I tried to catch up with you at the grocery store, but I didn't want to interrupt while you were talking to that girl. Then the next thing I know, you're gone."

She stumbles distastefully over the word "girl," and a flicker of interrogation crosses her expression.

When she and Teagan strolled into the local grocery store earlier today, I was minding my own business, trying to find a damn avocado to purchase that wasn't already rotten, while reminding myself, yet again, to stop thinking about Amber because she was likely already gone from town. Then midrant, there she was. Waving, smiling, and looking at me like she knew exactly how to get my blood boiling without breaking a sweat. I was also attempting to hold a civil conversation with Garrett's girlfriend, Cara, about how he's an enormous pussy who believes he's knocking at death's door with his case of the sniffles. In short, the whole situation made my fucking head feel like it was about to explode.

"I had places to be," I mumble.

Like my truck. Followed by my house, where I punished my body with a long workout in the makeshift gym I have set up in a shed out back. It helped. Until now.

Amber widens her eyes to near saucers, raises her brows to

match, goading me for the info she really wants. I count to five, making her wait. Because I'll be damned if I'm going to be the only one in the room feeling frustrated, even if I know I'll eventually grant her anything she asks for—all she'd have to do is flash one more centimeter of bare belly and I'd cave to whatever. Hell, if she put a lemon wedge in one hand and a saltshaker in the other, I'd probably commit a felony if she asked me to.

"I was talking to Garrett's girlfriend. She just got back into town and was unaware that her crybaby boyfriend had contracted what he thinks is some version of the Black Death. So I was attempting to be sociable while allaying her concerns and reminding her that giving a shit about any of it falls under the heading of 'girlfriend.'"

Amber gives up a relieved laugh. "How is he? Still alive?" She tips up one side of her mouth. "And don't stand there and say you don't know, or don't care. We both know neither is true."

"He's alive and still a pain in the ass. I dropped off a jar of my sauerkraut earlier, which should help."

Her entire face squishes up. "You took him *sauerkraut*? Who the hell wants sauerkraut when they're sick?"

"My sauerkraut kicks ass. So Garrett, and anyone with taste, would want to eat it every day. And it's full of good bacteria. The kind that help kick your immune system into gear."

"Of course," she mutters, craning her head to gawk down the hallway. "Is that your office?"

She heads in that direction without waiting for an answer, disappearing inside before I'm able to claim it's not my office but a top secret, no-Ambers-allowed safe room—or something equally as pathetic and unbelievable. I follow her anyway, cussing under my breath as I do. I don't need this in my life; I'm far too on edge as it is. What I do need is for my mountain sprite to flit her way back to Texas and leave me be, with nothing but her goddam Instagram and my memories to slobber over.

When I round the corner into my office, I find her where I least expect: sitting on top of my desk.

Christ, now what am I supposed to do with her? A hundred filthy answers come to mind, swimming forward in a rush. Most of which involve her staying put while I take advantage of her position, plopped right atop my desk calendar with her legs spread just so.

She glances around the office, taking in the fact it probably looks like it's my first day here. No mementos, no pictures on the wall. No potted plants or coat trees. Nothing on the desk but the computer, the printer, my water bottle—and that desk calendar she's currently impressing her fine ass upon. In her defense, along with the lack of other decor in here, there aren't any chairs for visitors, either.

"Cozy setup you have here." She takes a gander at the computer screen and taps a few keys. "Is this a herd ratio report? Can I have a copy?"

I'm around the desk in a flash, bumping into her legs with mine and grabbing her hand, hoping she hasn't managed to screw up or delete the last three hours of my work life.

"*That* is proprietary information belonging to the state of Colorado. So no, you cannot have a copy. And stop poking buttons— this fucking computer is touchy."

Amber, noting the limited space, spreads her knees to make room for me. Right between her legs—the place I've spent far too much time thinking about. Her hand is still in mine, and when I give a little tug to release my grip, she twists our fingers together and sets them on her thigh.

"*You* are touchy." She urges her knees inward until they meet my legs. Amber ticks her gaze up to mine and worries her bottom lip. "Why so tense, Braden?"

The already-small room seems to shrink in half, and my chest starts to work roughly over each breath I take, seizing every bit of oxygen I can. All because I'm fighting the instinct to tell her exactly why I'm so tense.

Because I've expended a tremendous amount of effort and willpower over the last few days resisting the urge to jerk off, that's why. Knowing if I give in, Amber will fuel every moment of that experience—the feel of her, the scent of her, the way her mind works, the way her voice sounds when she says something that should irritate me but doesn't. All of it, every single element of what makes her frustrating and sexy, fascinating and demanding.

But I won't go there. Not this way, not when it feels like that would reduce me to one of the countless assholes who get off thinking about her, or imagine fucking her every way they can just to get their rocks off. If she and I could somehow be more to each other, things might be different. But they aren't. So yes, I *am* touchy.

I grind my jaw together and try to remove my hand from hers again. Amber tightens her grip.

"I think I know why." A sly smirk from her. "And I'm right there with you. I can't even do anything about it, either, staying in an RV with two other people. Maybe if we'd stayed in a hotel, I'd have a room to myself, and then I could—"

A pained sound leaves my mouth, and I jerk my free hand up between us, palm out in warning. I close my eyes.

"I swear to God, Amber, if you say one more word that nears you talking about getting yourself off, I will lose my mind." I let my eyes open, fixing a steady gaze on her. "Either that, or you will find yourself laid out on this desk."

We stare each other down for what feels like minutes. Then her eyes light with challenge and she leans closer. She drops her voice to a near whisper.

"It wouldn't take much. I'm so keyed up, all I'd have to do is slip my hand down and—"

I sink my hands into her hair, pulling her close, and crash my mouth to hers. Amber's lips part and our tongues tangle in the hottest way I've ever experienced, breaking our kiss only to breathe because we have to. I pull my hands from her hair, set them to her ass, and yank her forward as Amber fists my shirt in her hands, grinding her pussy to the fly of my pants. Urging her body backward, she slithers one of her legs up around my hip. I immediately latch one hand behind her knee, sliding my grip up her thigh and across her hip, pausing only when my hand meets the waist of her yoga pants and the bare skin of her belly is under my touch.

Amber sighs into our continuing kiss, and I take the sound as her permission, her demand, for more. Slipping my hand higher, the thin silk of her bra meets my fingertips, her soft flesh beneath, a hard-tipped peak under my palm. One quick yank and her full, bare breast is in my hand. I moan into her mouth. Loudly. Embarrassingly. Amber mutters a soft curse.

We pause only long enough to catch up with this moment, how good it feels, and then we're back at it. Nipping and kissing, teasing and tasting, fueled on by the way she's arching her back into my grip and the way I'm grinding my body to hers as best I can without crushing her.

Amber gives up a long moan when I slip her nipple between my thumb and two fingers, hard enough to be sure she feels it, but not so much that she gets everything she truly needs. I could give her more—I could give her everything. So much she wouldn't fucking know what to do with it all. I could. If she wants me to.

I work my mouth across her neck and over her jawline, pausing near her ear, taking a moment to inhale her strawberry scent.

"Do you want more?" I rasp.

Amber stills, and I do the same, frozen in place with my hand up her shirt, still copping a feel like a horny teenager. Suddenly, I'm just a stupid sixteen-year-old again, one who just got caught in his girlfriend's bedroom doing exactly what he thought he would never get to.

Finally, Amber lets out a trembling exhale, one that ends in a breathy laugh.

"More? Are you proposing we have sex on your desk? Right here next to the proprietary information on your computer?"

Holy shit. Am I? Is that what I think should happen here? What I want to happen?

I fumble over the debate in my head, still trying to catch my breath while I do. Amber weaves her arms around my waist, drawing her nails gently across the back of my T-shirt as if she knows my mind is working overtime, and I relax into her hold. I give up my own unsteady exhale.

"I have no idea. Maybe. My fucking brain is scrambled."

I'm rewarded with her lips pressed against my neck, followed by a teasing nip of her teeth to the same spot, then another kiss to ease the sting. Every hair on my body stands on end.

I grant myself the last few seconds of whatever the hell this is, soaking up the satisfaction that comes with, before rising up to brace my outstretched arms on either side of her. Amber stays put, looking pleased with herself. Her cheeks are flushed, her eyes are bright, and her lips are reddened and plumped, enough to send a new pulse of need straight south. She grins, coy but knowing.

"Did that help or make it worse? Your eyes look all drunk and relaxed, but I can see the bones in your jaw flexing. It looks uncomfortable. Loosen that thing up, Braden. Smile, maybe."

I can't hold back a grin, snorting when she wiggles her brows playfully. I drop my head wearily and sigh when Amber threads her fingers into my hair, scratching lightly along my scalp.

"Right now, it's helping. But now I know how hot you kiss, how good you taste, and how fucking amazing you feel. So later, when you're long gone, that's gonna suck."

Amber blushes, a sweet bloom across her cheeks that's the last thing I expect to see. She feels the heat and throws one arm over her face, flopping the other out and across my desk. Her hand whacks into my water bottle and it nearly topples, but I grab it just in time. She yanks her arm away and flips her eyes open.

"Got it." I hold up the bottle. "Don't want you getting wet."

She raises her brows and drawls, "Too. Late."

I drop my eyes shut, my jaw flexing tight again. She laughs and whispers a teasing apology.

"Sorry. I like it when you do that. Get all frustrated."

My eyes drift open when she tugs on my shirt, using it and my weight as leverage so she can sit up. Automatically, I slip one arm around her back to help, knowing she doesn't need it but wanting to anyway. Once she's upright, she fiddles with her hair a little and somehow manages to make the messy bun look even cuter than it did before. I step back, giving her room to slip off my desk. She makes her way to the doorway, and just when I'm positive she's about to leave without another word, she pauses and turns to glance over her shoulder.

"I don't know about you, but that was even better than I imagined. I needed this." Amber tilts her head and sends a sated smile my way. "Thank you, Braden. For everything."

She disappears down the hallway. I stay rooted in place until I hear the front door shut, then I flop into my desk chair and stare at the empty doorway.

There is one upside here, no matter how depressing it might be. My first taste of Amber Regan also happens to be my last. We both know that my unit isn't where she'll end up for her hunt in a few months—not if she wants footage that's worthy of TV time—

which is a saving grace to my sanity. Wanting more, obsessing over her, or craving her: all of it is pointless. And I don't waste my time on shit that's pointless.

I cast my eyes down to the desk pad I never much noticed before. Now I'll never be able to look at it without thinking of what just happened.

Maybe it's time for a new one, imprinted with something banal and stupid, like palm trees, or an ugly floral pattern, the kind best left on Grandma's curtains. Maybe some little playful, frisky kittens.

Nope. Not kittens. Especially not frisky ones. Because a mere hop, skip, and a jump will put my mind where it doesn't belong: on *pussy*cats.

Screw it. I'll toss this one out and leave it at that.

She's leaving.

Thank fuck for small favors.

⌒⌒

Ten days and one new desk pad later, I'm in the office again for public hours. We're between hunting seasons, so I expect a quiet morning. I'll keep myself busy by restocking hunting brochures and preparing for what is sure to be a lively afternoon. One that involves *me* giving a presentation at a local Girl Scout troop meeting.

Fifteen giggling little girls vs. one grumpy game warden. I don't stand a chance. I'll be outnumbered and potentially outwitted. Even so, I'd take this over dealing with a poacher or a bear wreaking havoc in town any day.

I grab an empty box from under the reception station and start to fill it with a stack of Parks and Wildlife coloring books, crayon sets, and the Bear Aware educational DVD I'll need for my presentation. My phone rings just as I spot a long-forgotten bag of

Jolly Ranchers. I toss the bag of candy in the box. Kids like sugary crap, and a couple of these won't stunt their growth too much. As an added benefit, if they're sucking on Jolly Ranchers, that may keep the squealing and giggling to a minimum.

I dig my phone out of my pocket, glancing at the display to see Tobias's name as I answer.

Tobias offers a snort first, followed by a long exhale. "Brace yourself, Montgomery. I have no idea what you did, but you somehow managed to convince Amber Regan that a unit managed for elk hunting opportunity over trophy bulls would be the perfect place to film her hunt. Must have been your friendly and agreeable nature."

My body seizes up, prompting exactly what Tobias first cautioned: to brace myself. I grip the edge of the flimsy shelf where I found the Jolly Ranchers, trying to keep from breaking it in two.

This can't be happening. Amber chose one of *my* units? Can't be. Maybe she said unit 201—one of the trophy units in Colorado—but the line was garbled. She was in a tunnel, a car wash, something, and they thought she said 421, one of my units. We have elk, sure. But we do not have *big* elk. We have a unit that's managed for those hunters who want to fill the freezer far more than find rack worthy of mounting on the wall.

"Are you sure? This has to be a mistake. Maybe you misheard her."

Tobias scoffs. "My hearing is just fine. I heard her tell me all about how excited she is for her hunt, how the Hotchkiss community was so welcoming. How *you* were especially helpful." He pauses. "Is that true? Were you *helpful*, Montgomery? Because if that statement has a subtext, let me advise you what a bad idea that is."

I swallow hard. "Just a bad idea? Or a direct violation of something in my five-hundred-page employee manual?"

Tobias curses under his breath. "No direct violation that I can think of. But let me say it again. Bad idea."

Relief ripples through me. I might be dangerously close to losing my mind over Amber, but at least my job is safe. Tobias doesn't let me enjoy the feeling for long.

"That being said, prepare yourself, regardless. Since she's going solo for this hunt, she's determined to show up prepared, and she has all your contact info. I suspect she plans to wear out your cell with any questions she might have. Good luck continuing to be so . . . *helpful.*"

When Tobias hangs up, I take stock of the time I have left. It's nearly April, and archery elk season doesn't open until August. I have months. Months to tether up my lust and bury it deep inside.

Months. No problem. That's *more* than enough time.

10

(Braden)

Tobias, oracle and sage that he is, was right. His claim that Amber might wear out my cell phone was not only correct, but an understatement. Her texts are constant, her emails are incessant, and her phone messages are long-winded. She's apparently short on an attention span and entirely lacking in impulse control, at least when it comes to contacting me, which is fucking my strategy *all up*.

Best laid plans and all that shit.

What's worse is I've become Pavlovian in my response, salivating at the sound of my phone alerts. Her messages are equally funny, frustrating, and interesting—which means I look forward to every one of them. I've taken to turning my phone off before I go to bed because she's up at all hours, it seems, and I can easily wake up to a stream of texts, just as I did this morning:

(1:30 a.m. Amber Regan text)

Muzzleloader season starts when?

(1:52 a.m. Amber Regan text)

Are lighted knocks legal?

(1:57 a.m. Amber Regan text)

Bear canister—yes or no?

(1:58 a.m. Amber Regan text)

Any grouse up there?

(2:25 a.m. Amber Regan text)

Doing all my own filming for the hunt. Any restrictions I need to know about?

Each message also includes a bunch of obnoxious emojis— most of which I don't recognize or understand. Stupid little animated images of everything from bears and pieces of pizza, to vibrating hearts and winky faces. At least the winking one I get. I've considered searching out the perfect way to communicate how badly I want her to stop using them when she messages me, but instead I ignore them, keeping my replies to words.

(5:45 a.m. Braden Montgomery text)

Do you sleep? Ever?
Answers in the order these insomniac txt were rec'd:
Sept 2. No. Don't bother. Yes. No.
FYI: CPW has a handy website with all this info. Use it.

(11:47 a.m. Amber Regan text)

I sleep when I'm tired. I just woke up from a solid eight hours. CPW website is SLOW & lacks your sarcasm. I prefer the personal service you provide.

And now, seven hours later? She wants more personal service.

(6:45 p.m. Amber Regan text)

How likely is snow in early Sept? Dry snow? Wet snow? Will Leroux Creek run high? Trying to decide if gaiters are worth the pack space.

My head drops heavily onto the back of my armchair as I let out a sigh. I set the book I'm reading down on the side table.

(6:46 p.m. Braden Montgomery text)

Hold on a second. Just polishing up my crystal ball. Needs to be really clean if I want to PREDICT THE FUTURE accurately. How am I supposed to know if it's going to snow? Buy a Farmer's Almanac.

(6:48 p.m. Amber Regan text)

Polishing your crystal ball? Sounds dirty. Please describe to me, in detail, this polishing process. Is there a special polishing *cream* involved?

Followed by emojis. Lots of them. All of which I have no trouble interpreting. And here I was, doing so well to keep my mind out of the gutter. I should just turn off my phone, refocus my attention on the night I had planned.

It's a Sunday night in early June, and in Hotchkiss that means it's warm enough to open a few windows during the day but when evening comes, the air turns cool and calm, all part of the strange microclimate that makes the Grand Valley an unexpected banana belt, perfect for growing the stone fruits and grapevines this place is well-known for.

There's a maple-whiskey-glazed turkey breast roasting in my oven, some asparagus from a wild patch in my backyard that's ready for a quick poach, plus a bottle of Pinot from a local vineyard in need of only a corkscrew. My favorite Jason Isbell LP is playing, Charley is conked out on her bed and snoring softly, and I'm a few chapters into a reread of Saxton Pope's *Hunting with the Bow and Arrow*. All in all, a damn near perfect night for me—and I'm not sure if a little banter with Amber makes it more or less so.

My phone rings before I can decide. I know who it is without even looking at the display. I raise it to my ear and answer without so much as a greeting.

"You and I both know that gaiters are rarely worth the pack space. Colorado's practically a high desert climate. Leave that shit at home."

Amber laughs, a soft, genuine sound. My eyes drop closed. As insane as it seems—especially since our relationship amounts to a few hours of bickering, one dance, and one hot make-out session on my desk—I missed her laugh. Fuck. That's not a good sign.

"True. I think I've used them once, on a moose hunt in Canada. But I've packed them fifty other times when I didn't need them."

"There you go."

Neither of us continues, and when the line goes silent, things immediately begin to feel awkward. Another laugh from her, nervous this time.

"God. Are you still polishing your crystal ball? The way you're breathing into the phone all steady and slow, it sounds like—"

I cut her off with one word. *"Amber."*

Same nervous laugh.

"Sorry. I can't help going there with you, even when I shouldn't." She breathes a steadying sigh. "I'm surprised you actually answered the phone. I thought you'd send me to voicemail like you usually do. Then I would have been forced to leave you one of my rambling messages."

"I'm sure you would have," I say, working to sound put-out, even when I'm not.

There's no need for her to know that I listen to her messages at least twice. The first go-around is to hear what she wants, and the second time through is because I *like* the way she rambles and sometimes loses her train of thought.

"Although it's a little too early for you to ramble. You seem to be at your best at two in the morning."

Amber snorts. "Well, since you answered, I'm assuming you have time to talk. Are you busy? Am I interrupting anything?"

Other than my quiet, easy, uncomplicated life? In a way I'm not sure if I hate or love? No. Feel free to keep at it. Because I missed your laugh.

I give myself a quick lecture on self-preservation and stupidity—and it does absolutely *nothing*.

"Nope. Go ahead."

I hear the sound of papers shuffling and Amber's tone turns purposeful.

"OK, I'm down to the little things, detail stuff. I'm planning on ten days camping in the backcountry for my hunt, but I'm thinking I'll want to come into town halfway through. Get water and a decent meal, fuel my truck, and stock up on anything I might be running low on. I'd also love to get a shower if there's a motel around that will rent to a hunter for a few hours. Give me some leads on the best places to do all that."

As I listen to her, I'm vaguely dumbstruck by the way her mind works. Mostly because it works a little too much like mine. She plots and plans in the same way I do, working through the details to be sure she's setting herself up for success. And if we were both honest, she could probably find all the answers for herself, too. She's plenty resourceful and completely driven, which means these texts and calls are as much about us keeping in touch as they are about anything else.

"Fuel up at the Crossroads station; they have the cheapest gas in town. You're stuck with the local A&P for water and supplies, and everything is priced like a small-town store, which means it's overpriced. For a good meal, I've already told you about True Grit. But based on all of Colin's shit-talk, it sounds like you guys weren't impressed."

She doesn't laugh, yet her tone tells me there's a smile on her face.

"It's a Texas thing. Barbeque is practically our religion, and we worship at one altar. You don't know any better, so it's not your fault. Come to Austin someday and I'll prove it to you."

The invitation there is nothing but a sidebar to her speech on barbeque, I know that, but that doesn't mean I don't then picture myself in Austin, with Amber playing my tour guide. My very friendly, welcoming, *personal* tour guide.

Austin's always been on my to-visit list, but with all my stalking of Amber online, it's risen from "maybe someday" to "how about next week?" Because if the local tourism board isn't paying her, they should be—she's a standout ambassador for the city, because every landmark, restaurant, and attraction looks like a place you want to go, so long as she's standing in front of it.

Amber rambles softly, talking through whatever she's now writing down, and I force my focus back on our conversation when I hear more paper shuffling on her end.

"OK. What about a motel? Not to stay the night, just a place that will let me pay for a few hours' time to grab a shower, maybe a nap."

My grip on the phone tightens. The closest motel is halfway between Hotchkiss and Paonia, and it's a dump. Its name—the Empire Ambassador Motel—in no way suits it. I know this because they do cater to hunters, and my job routinely takes me through their parking lot, on the lookout for anything out of place, like antler tips peeking out of a truck bed the day *before* elk season opens, or a trailer full of goose decoys a week *after* that season is over. When I've had cause to knock on a door or two, I've also caught a glimpse of the inside of those rooms, enough to know I hate the idea of Amber anywhere near one. They're dirty and dingy, and I'm guessing the door locks are about as sturdy as a tuna can.

"The nearest motel is a shit hole," I grit out. "You shouldn't go there, even for a shower."

She casts off my caution with a snort. "I can guarantee you it's no worse than anywhere else I've showered while on the road. So long as the water is reasonably warm and it comes out of a shower-head, I'll be happy."

"It's a *dump*."

"I'm sure it is. But that's part of the experience, isn't it?"

I try to keep my reaction in check, but fail when an image of Amber stripping down in the craptastic Empire Ambassador Motel comes to mind. A protective streak I didn't know I possessed rushes forth—and right out of my stupid mouth.

"I don't want you to go there. The carpets are disgusting, the doors locks aren't secure enough, and come elk season there will be too much testosterone prowling around. Not safe. Not for you. *Don't*, you hear me?"

Amber says nothing. She's silent, only the sound of her breathing evenly. I drop my head and consider how best to extract my foot from my mouth. I've earned whatever wrath is headed my way, because what I just said wasn't merely an overreach, it was unwarranted.

Still nothing but silence. Charley lifts her head from the dog bed, locks eyes with me, and then lets out a long, dramatic doggy sigh as if she's disappointed with me, too.

Amber finally speaks. Calmly. Almost too calmly.

"I'm smart enough to read between the lines and hear what I think was genuine, non-controlling-asshole concern for my safety. But I hope you're smart enough to pay attention when I tell you to stop acting like some chest-thumping boyfriend I'm about to break up with."

Fuck. Fuck, fuck, *fuck*. I let out a long exhale.

"I have no idea where all that shit came from. Doesn't matter. I'm sorry. Not OK and I know that."

"Apology accepted. Now give me the name of the damn motel. I'll do a little research and decide for myself."

"The Empire Ambassador Motel."

"Sounds classy."

"It isn't. And you really shouldn't, because—"

"Braden," she warns. "Do not start again."

I clamp my mouth shut and try to think. A thin shaft of light appears in my foxhole, inspired by an idea she might shoot down—or I might regret bringing up.

"Permission to offer an alternative?"

She sighs. "Granted."

"Use my place. Shower. Eat something that isn't freeze-dried. Wash your gear if you need to and catch some sleep up off the ground."

She doesn't immediately tell me to fuck off, so I add a critical piece of information. "I won't be here, so you'll have the place to yourself."

"What? Why?"

I won't lie, her obvious disappointment makes my chest swell. I know the feeling, because when Amber gave me the dates for her hunt in one of her first texts, my heart sank straight into my gut. Whether it was the universe working with me or against me, I'm not sure, but the dates overlapped almost exactly with the time I'd put in for to hunt deer back home.

"I'll be at my parents' cabin in Oregon."

"Oh." More disappointment, and my chest swells again. I clear my throat.

"I've got a deer tag and a score to settle with a wily buck that I've been chasing for three seasons now. Even a chance to piss you off in person won't change my plans. So you'll have plenty of alone time in my house to plot some prank in retaliation for everything I've ever done to irritate the shit out of you."

Amber hums, scheming mischievously. "Like Scotch tape on your sink sprayer? You're bound to turn the faucet on at some point. Woosh. *Waterworks.*" Amber then full-on laughs, I'm sure because she's picturing that scene playing out in her mind.

Side A on the LP I've had playing comes to an end, making her laughter all there is for a moment, and I settle into the sound as I push myself out of my chair and cross the room. Tucking the phone between my ear and shoulder, I flip the record over. Side B starts, and Amber's now soft laughter goes quiet.

"Jason Isbell?" she asks.

Slowly, I twist the volume knob up. "Yup."

"*Southeastern*?"

I answer quietly, only a little surprised that she knows the album. At this point I'm more apt to notice the things we have in common, than not. If I were prone to indulging in the sunshiny sort of optimism that romantics believe in, I might find myself considering *exactly* how much we truly share.

But even if I did, a cloud cover of pessimism reminds me that not only do we live states apart, but Amber also happens to star in her own TV show. I've been known to go months without so much as even turning my television on. We live our lives in entirely different ways and neither of us seem interested in trying on a new way.

Amber lets out an almost resigned exhale, as if she's battling against the same realizations I am. "Let's say I take you up on your offer. Give me an idea of what I should expect."

A little confused, I try to determine what it is she wants to know. "What you should *expect*?"

"Tell me what your place is like. A bachelor pad with black leather couches and a bitchin' media system that you don't want me to touch? A frat-boy den with stained recliners and a futon for a bed?"

I roll my eyes. "Neither. I'm a thirty-two-year-old game warden. I don't live like a college kid or a bachelor with a hard-on for surround sound."

"But what *do* you live like? Pretend I'm on my way to your

place tonight. Tell me what I would find when I walk through the front door."

My entire body soaks up the idea of that. Amber back here in Hotchkiss, on her way over to my place—all of her sass in tow, along with her strawberry scent and her soft skin, those blue eyes, and the curves I've had the momentary pleasure of reading with my fingertips. I step toward my front door and stop on the threshold, right where Amber might be if this were truth instead of fantasy.

Charley eases off her dog bed and makes her way over me, then plops down to lean all of her weight on my leg. When she does, I imagine Amber leaning down to pet her, making friends with the only female companion in my life these last few years. I reach down and ruffle the fur behind Charley's ears.

"You'd find a renovated miner's cabin crafted out of cottonwood timbers. Inside, there are a lot of books, a decent number of records, a TV that picks up one channel not worth watching. Furniture that's old but not shabby, including a bed that's sized to fit a guy like me. Although on nights when a bed hog like Charley is determined to take more than her fair share, it doesn't feel near big enough."

Amber sighs, soft and almost needy, the way I'd want her to if she were here and I had her in that bed of mine. I tamp down a groan at the thought, only so I can tell her more and hopefully draw another sigh out of her when I do.

"And tonight? You'd hear the rest of that *Southeastern* LP playing in the background, on the old record player I stole from my parents' house. A maple-whiskey-glazed turkey breast in the oven, off the Merriam's jake I shot this spring. A bottle of local wine on the table that puts most Napa shit to shame, ready to crack open. And outside, there's a damn nice Hotchkiss sunset."

I take a beat, pausing so she can soak it all in. "*That's* what you'd find."

She trumps my pause with her own. I hold my breath.

"Jesus," she breathes. "I can't tell you how much I'd love to walk through that front door, Braden. Right now."

When she's finished, I hear it—that sigh I wanted to draw out of her. The unsteady sound of Amber Regan wanting more.

11

(Amber)

"Your restless ways and your solitude,
I see you leaning your lanky frame just inside the door,
a figure behind the kitchen screen staring down at the floor,
little angel, little brother."
—LUCINDA WILLIAMS, "LITTLE ANGEL, LITTLE BROTHER"

"That's beautiful, Amber. Now shoulders down and chest out. Smile."

Oh, if only I had a dollar for every time I've heard those words.

I do as instructed while keeping a firm grip on the twelve-gauge shotgun that's slung over my left shoulder, my arm smarting a little from holding this pose for the last ten minutes. The photographer—a silver fox with a reputation in Austin for often blurring the line between personal and professional—continues to cajole and compliment, making that reputation of his seem well earned. I give the camera another smile without suggesting anything with my eyes that might mean I'm smiling at the man *behind* the camera. Here's hoping the silver fox can tell the difference. Even if he can't, the Lucinda Williams mix I chose is blaring from speakers behind me, which boosts my bravado. Nothing like a little "Changed the Locks" to erect an emotional barricade when needed.

He stops shooting, concentrating on the camera's viewfinder as he flicks through the images, absently tracing the tip of his tongue to the center of his upper lip as he does.

Blech.

"OK, I think that's good for this setup. Let's take a quick break, and then we'll move on to the Sunday supper scene."

He wanders off and a timid, waiflike assistant appears in an instant, extending a bottled water with a straw in it my way. Then she awkwardly mimes with her hands as if to take the shotgun from me. With a smooth twist of the barrel in my palm, I shift the gun from my shoulder into the crook of my opposite arm, and accept the water bottle with my free hand.

"My gun. I'll put it away."

Her big brown eyes widen as she blinks rapidly, trying to process what I just said. Perhaps no one clued her in as to the premise of this photo shoot, or the backstory on the woman posing for it, because she looks entirely baffled by the idea that this shotgun belongs to me, and is also not a prop. She continues to look bewildered until I gently shoo her off with a patient smile.

My outfit surely isn't helping matters, seeing as I look like I just stepped out of a men's magazine from the 1950s. I'm wearing a vintage shirtwaist dress in mint-green gingham and a pair of nude heels, with a full face of cosmetics to complete the look: dark cat-eye makeup, pink blush, and candy-apple lips. The dress has been altered with a higher hemline, ensuring that in those shots where I have one foot perched atop a wooden crate, the retro-style garter belt and stockings underneath are on display.

And, unlike most photo shoots I've been a part of, there's not one stitch of camo pattern to be found anywhere. In fact, nothing about this piece for an Austin lifestyle magazine is what I'm used to.

To begin with, it doesn't really have anything to do with me—it has to do with my brother and his furniture company. When the magazine's creative team approached Trey and his business partner, Ryan, about featuring AustinMade in their annual fall design issue, good ol' Kukla and Ollie immediately offered my house—and me—as perfect fits for the vintage-industrial-meets-rough-tough-Texas concept they had in mind. But since my house is essentially a living showroom for Trey's work and I have experience hamming it up in front of a camera, I couldn't very well act as if the idea came out of left field.

Now, speaking of my publicity-and-camera-shy brother, it seems he's managed to make himself scarce yet again. I glance about the backyard where we've been shooting, looking for the messy blond hair covered by a backward Rangers ball cap that I know so well. Nothing but lighting equipment, assorted piles of gear, and a bunch of strangers scurrying about, so I head inside through the opened slider doors, striding past the setup for our next shot.

The Sunday supper scene, as the silver fox calls it, features the dining room table Trey gave me as a housewarming gift. The table is unforgivingly industrial and unapologetically big, large enough to seat twelve comfortably. The top is made out of reclaimed Greenheart boxcar planks, which sit atop a pair of antique French iron lathe bases. The centerpiece of today's tablescape is a very *fake* roasted suckling pig, with a very *cliché* red apple stuffed in its mouth. Another assistant busily works to polish a set of comically oversized carving tools, setting them near a vintage bumblebee-patterned apron that's draped over the back of a chair. I'm pretty sure that when I don that apron, grab those carving tools, and pretend to get after that fake pig, I'm going to look like a deranged trophy wife.

I give up a sigh and round the corner into my kitchen, where I finally find my brother. Mostly because I nearly stumble right over him. Trey's plopped himself on the floor like a little kid hiding out from the big, bad world, his long legs outstretched to span the width of my galley kitchen.

"For fuck's sake," I grumble. "Use a chair, you ruffian."

Trey glances up from his sketch pad, bends his knees to tuck them up toward his chest, and offers up his impossible-to-stay-mad-at grin. Lucinda's "Little Angel, Little Brother" kicks on over the speakers, just another reason for me to do nothing but jab him playfully in the shin with the pointy toe of my high heel.

He tosses a withering look at my shoes. "Those look dangerous."

"They're Jimmy Choos."

"Gesundheit," he deadpans, his eyes already back on the sketch pad.

My phone vibrates on the countertop. When I spy the preview window, a smile immediately breaks across my face.

A new text from Braden. With a picture. Even better.

I hop up on the countertop and try to keep my giddiness at bay, or at the very least, any sign of it off my face. I'm in Trey's sightline, and his disturbing ability to read people means he picks up even the faintest hint of shifting energies around him. So if I'm over here bubbling away like a shook-up can of RC, the kid will notice.

Unfortunately, it's almost impossible to keep my cool. Not when Braden and I are officially in a texting relationship. Up until our phone call last week, I couldn't have claimed our communication was much more than one-sided, but since then he's become positively chatty. From scouting reports in the area I plan to hunt, to pictures of his dog, the man is certainly holding up his side of the conversation. The only thing I haven't received is a picture of *him*, which I'd love to have—if only to confirm that my memory of his rugged form is as first-rate as what I picture in my mind on occasion. Like, for example, late at night, when my bed feels too big. Or early in the morning, when my bed feels too empty. Or in the middle of the day, when I'm bored and it's suddenly too damn hot in Texas, and I'm convinced Braden could inspire the same sort of heat, but for far more worthwhile reasons.

I swipe open the text, slightly disappointed to discover that the beasty creature in the pic isn't Braden, but a bull elk.

Not heavy, but he's even. 5x5. Mouthy, too. He's been busting around in the trees like he owns the place. Figured you might appreciate his style.

The bull elk pictured has five tines on each of his antlers. The tines are a little thin, but they're evenly spaced and symmetrical, just as Braden's described. The last of this season's velvet on the elk's antlers hangs from the tips, and he's tangled himself around some low-hanging branches on a tree, likely trying to rub those remaining bits of velvet off. His coat is a burnished copper color that's typical in late summer, smooth and glossy across his big body.

He's a good-looking bull, for sure. But I'm not sure if he's *enough*. I squint at the image to see if I can spot anything extraordinary, studying it for a few minutes until another text comes through.

You're being too quiet. I know he's not huge, but he's respectable. And a damn good bull for the unit you're hunting. So if your ego is sniping, remind her that not everything is about points.

I snort. From a few states away, he's managed to see right through me. Whether that's a good thing or not, I'm not sure.

I chose to hunt one of Braden's units for a few different reasons—and I'm not ashamed to admit that he was one of them. But even more so, I chose this unit because it would be a place where I would have to hunt hard, put all my skills to the test, and do so with little guarantee of success. Hunting in general offers no guarantees, but there, I knew I would be faced with long odds, which is exactly what I want. Because if I lose my show after taking this rugged path, then at least I'll know I have done my best to get back to my roots, to all of what my uncle Cal had taught me. I tap out a reply.

SHE doesn't need any reminders. And agrees that he's a damn good bull. Can't wait to see him on the hoof.

"Is that the yeti?" Trey asks, without lifting his gaze from where his pencil works over the page with quick strokes.

My head jerks up and I narrow my eyes on him.

"Were you snooping on my phone?"

He smirks at the page. "No. You've been floaty since you got back from Colorado. You've also mentioned the name *Braden*, casually, at least once a day since then, so he obviously left an impression. And you're currently smiling at your phone like a dope. Doesn't take a Sherlock to solve this mystery."

I look around for something safe to lob at him, hoping to redirect the conversation. All I find is a bag of store-brand sandwich bread, hefty enough to get my point across, but squishy enough to avoid injuring my only kin. The sack of bread careens off his sketch pad and lands on the floor.

"I have not been *floaty*," I mutter, then cock a brow. "What about you? Care to talk about the woman whose name you work so hard to *avoid* mentioning? How is Dayton, anyway?"

Dayton works for Trey. She is sweet and beautiful, far more

dedicated to AustinMade than any typical employee, and I've occasionally caught her watching Trey when he's all wrapped up in his head, contemplating him like he's her favorite riddle. Trey, for his part, does his own fair share of staring longingly in Dayton's direction but refuses to admit to anything other than a strictly professional appreciation. Essentially, his approach has been to play stupid or play dead when questioned on the topic.

Trey scowls at his pad. "You mean Dayton, my *employee*? My employee and nothing but? That Dayton?"

Ah. Seems he's gone with "play stupid" for today's round.

"Yup. That's the one."

"She's a competent and skilled accounting professional, as always," he replies flatly.

"Good to hear." I hop down off the counter and swipe the bag of bread off the tile floor. "You want a sandwich?"

Trey fights a small grin but loses. "Of course I do."

I shake my head. Make the kid a sandwich and you have a surefire peace offering. I slap together an almond butter and honey sandwich, taking a bite for myself before handing it his way. Trey reaches for it, sending me a quietly curious look.

"Does the yeti know about your soft-hearted, sandwich-making side?"

I reply with a self-conscious laugh, a warbling sound that reveals too much.

"There's my answer," Trey mutters, and then takes a sizable bite of the sandwich.

I sweep a few bread crumbs into the sink. Braden has seen my softer side, just a little, especially when I have enough cider rum punch on board. But nothing inside me believes that's a bad thing, or a risk not worth taking. He'd offered me his home, for God's sake. Trusted me to be there when he wasn't, and from every text he's sent recently, it seems he's thoroughly invested in the success of my hunt. Bickering aside, we genuinely like each other, I believe that. And we have chemistry, in fucking *spades*.

In the background, "I Just Wanted to See You So Bad" starts to play, Lucinda owning up to a craving she decides to see through, even if it takes her traveling. Even if it doesn't make a bit of sense, even if she can't explain why.

12

(Braden)

"In short, all good things are wild and free."
—HENRY DAVID THOREAU, "WALKING"

Finding a redneck on your doorstep at seven in the morning is a bit like discovering a door-to-door salesman there. The same persistence and determination, the same sensation they're about to shove their way inside with or without a proper invitation. The only difference here is that instead of hawking goods I won't buy, Garrett comes bearing a shopping bag full of junk food he knows I won't eat: Hostess Fruit Pies, Honey Buns, and those little powdered sugar–covered donuts that are the same size as the tumors they'll eventually find in your liver if you eat too many of them.

The junk-food offerings are symbolic, anyway. The guy equivalent of announcing that he needed to talk, and since it's too early for beer, he went with what he could find at the local gas station convenience store, where he consumes far too many of his meals. As Garrett knows, I'm an early riser, so he could count on finding me up and around after finishing my morning workout.

"This field is planted with milo, and this one with wheat. The rest of it's corn."

Garrett taps a finger on the plat map he spread out on my kitchen table almost immediately after announcing he'd brought breakfast and then worming his way into my house.

"There are two houses on the property. He'd keep the mineral rights, but one share of ditch water would come with the deal."

I nod, despite the way Garrett's position prevents him from seeing it. He's hunched over the table, his eyes still fixed on the map in front of him, speaking to it as much as he is to me. The map is of some Kansas farmland owned by an old farmer without heirs, who apparently isn't going to be able to work much longer and is looking for the right guy to sell it to. And Garrett is likely that guy. Despite having had to sell his dad's farm and finding himself working a dead-end job at the local co-op, Garrett remains a farmer at heart—he just happens to be a farmer without a farm.

The coffeepot on the counter hisses when it finishes percolating, and I push myself up from my chair to fill two mugs, setting one in front of Garrett.

He mutters a thank-you and grabs the mug, finally leaning back in his chair. His eyes are red, and the dark hollows beneath make him look twice his age this morning. But between being dumb enough to let Cara move back to Chicago without so much as putting up a fight and the marathon trip he's just made to Kansas and back, looking like shit is to be expected.

Garrett sighs, pushes up his ball cap to scratch his forehead before yanking it back down.

"It's too good to be true, right? A full section. For a fucking song, price-wise. And he's willing to take basically nil as a down payment and carry the rest."

He looks uneasy, more so than I've ever seen him in all the time we've known each other. I give a casual shrug.

"Either that or it's just the right deal at the right time. Maybe he knows guys like you don't come along every day. Not a lot of folks out there champing at the bit to farm, and even fewer who actually know what they're doing."

Garrett mumbles something in agreement, but it's obvious he's not convinced. Why? I have no clue. The kid has the brains and the heart for the life of a farmer, and not many people do these days. Not when farm profits are in a downturn, land costs more than it ever has, and most people would rather see a shopping mall where a cornfield should be. But Garrett's carrying around the knowledge of a fifty-year-old farmer in his head, on the back of a twenty-five-year-old—and this is his chance to put it all to use. So other than bullshit *fear*, I don't know what's stopping him.

"The soil is good, right?"

What I know about farming could fit in a beer can, but asking about the soil seems like an obvious place to start. Garrett gives a nod.

"Yeah, no worries there. I went to the FSA office while I was there, pulled all the soil reports. And I'd transition to no-till, which is easier on your dirt in the long run."

"No chance he's leveraged too deep with a bank or something? Grasping at a last chance to stay out of foreclosure?"

Garrett grinds his jaw and shakes his head. "I had my dad's old estate attorney check on that before I even went out there. It's free and clear."

I hit a sore spot—intentionally—but Garrett knows why I went there. After his dad died of a heart attack, he dropped out of college thinking he'd come home and take over the farm, only to find out the property was entirely upside down because his dad had too many loans out, leaving Garrett with no choice but to sell. The last thing Garrett needs is to find himself in another situation like that.

With that out of the way, it's time to poke at his other open wound. This one I'm a little more familiar with. I know how much your heart smarts when it's been stomped on. I also know that no matter how broken your heart might once have been, when there's an urge to put it out there again, all those old hurts can feel like ancient history.

I take another sip of my coffee before digging in, knowing that no matter how hard he flinches, this is for his own good.

"And are you thinking with your stupid, lonely dick? Because Cara might have made it clear she thinks this is what's best for you, but that doesn't fucking matter. Not really. She can't be the reason you do this." I jab a finger at the plat map. "You have to do this because it's what *you* want. You can't hang this deal on getting her back."

Garrett, surprisingly, doesn't flinch at all. "My dick has an opinion, but he's not running the show. This? Owning a farm for myself? It's my whole life's plan. I've just spent the last three years trying to pretend it wasn't."

"Good."

Garrett does his best to keep his expression neutral, but his eyes widen, when I don't say more.

"What?" I furrow my brow. "You want to know what I think?"

He groans. "Yes, asshole. That's why I'm here. Come on, you're the one guy I can count on to tell me exactly what he thinks. Don't fail me now."

I gather a long breath. Fuck, it's going to suck when Garrett leaves. But I'd be a shitty friend if I did anything other than tell him the truth, which means I set my coffee mug down and give him my full attention, crossing my arms over my chest as I lean back.

"I think you'd be an idiot not to see this through. Do your due diligence, research everything, then go back out there and get belly to belly with this guy to make sure you want to be on the hook for a loan payment to him for the next twenty years. If so, then do what you can to make it happen. I'll even help you move your shit out to Kansas."

My phone vibrates just before Garrett can launch out of the chair and try to hug me, which doesn't seem too far-fetched given the relief on his face. I shoot him a cautionary look as I extract my phone from my pocket.

> You are so dramatic. The Empire Ambassador is NOT a dump. I've stayed in places way worse than this.

My face wrinkles up and I let out a confused grunt. Don't tell me that shit-hole motel actually has a website. One that Amber might think she can use to determine its quality and condition. If so, you can be sure the photos she's looking at online are either fake, out of focus, or taken in the dark without a flash.

"You OK there, buddy? You're making some weird faces and even weirder noises." Garrett asks, around a mouthful of the Hostess Fruit Pie he's chowing down on now that he's not quite so stressed out.

"Fucking Amber," I mutter. "She's looking at some website for that motel out on Highway One Thirty-three, trying to convince me it's not as bad as I told her it was."

Garrett chokes a little on his sugar-laden death snack. "The Empire Ambassador? Is she nuts? That place is like every bad movie about serial killers and drug deals gone wrong."

"That's exactly what I told her. But she's determined to . . ."

My words trail off when another text comes through, along with a picture that's been snapped from over Amber's slim, golden-tanned shoulder. Half of her grinning face is in the shot, the rest showing a nasty motel room behind her. A bad painting on the wall, a gaudy table lamp with its shade askew, and two beds dressed with patterned bed coverings that would hide travesty all too well.

Look! Two QUEEN beds. Usually it's two doubles. Can you see the ancient clock radio? The disturbingly sticky ice bucket? The fine painting of possums above the bed?

I work to process the data I have at hand as quickly as I can. A picture and two texts, both of which imply she's not scrolling through a website, but that she's physically here. I close my eyes to think more clearly, then open them again; still trying to determine if the conclusion I just arrived at is the truth or just another one of my daydreams involving Amber.

"She's *here*," I announce, confirming it for myself even more than I'm proclaiming it to Garrett.

"What? Are you sure?"

I flip the phone around and point the photo in Garrett's direction. He leans forward and his face mirrors mine, screwing up into confusion. He steals the phone from my hand.

"Shit. Did you know she was coming?" His fingers start to flick across the phone face as I tell him this is all a surprise to me. His expression slackens a little. "Jesus Christ. You guys text all the time. What the—"

I grab the phone back. "Don't look at that."

An obnoxious smirk creeps across Garrett's mouth—one I'm probably going to want to knock off his face in about ten seconds.

"You fucking sly dog," he drawls. "You and she have a thing happening, don't you?"

"No."

My answer emerges firmly, absent of my own confusion on the topic. Is something happening between Amber and me? Maybe. But who knows if it's more than the two of us enjoying the way we rouse each other up? Odds are, it's not. Once she's finished up her elk hunt out here, she'll be off on some new adventure, and likely stirring up some other poor sap's hopes for more with her. My lip curls at the thought. My gut sinks at the same time because I can't help but pity that guy, whoever he is.

Garrett zeroes in on my changing expression in a way that means he's prepared to mock my every move if I back down from the rest of his nosy fucking interrogation.

"Hold up, is this for real? I mean, have you guys . . . ?"

I shoot him the hardest look I can muster as heat crawls up my neck and threatens to color my cheeks like I'm some pathetic kid again. I steel my voice because if it cracks, I'll never live this down. We'll be collecting our social security checks, stocking up on pudding cups, tottering around with our canes, and he'll *still* be giving me shit about it.

"No. We haven't."

Garrett's jaw drops open and a barking laugh emerges. "Holy shit. But *something's* happened. Maybe you haven't banged her—"

"Don't finish that sentence." I suck in a deep breath. "She's . . . hell, I don't know. I don't even know why she's here. Her hunt is scheduled weeks from now, and it was supposed to happen when I'm back home on my deer hunt. She knows that. I have no clue what she's up to by showing up here now."

Garrett doesn't reply; instead, he surveys my face for longer than I'm totally comfortable with, casually tapping his fingers on the tabletop.

"Want to know what I think?"

"Not really," I grumble.

He snorts. Another exasperating thrum of his fingers on the table, drawing out the moment. Unfortunately, now I *do* want to know what he thinks. Mostly because I'm at a fucking loss. Mercifully, Garrett doesn't make me ask, he just chuckles.

"Too bad. I'm going to tell you anyway. *I* think that the very fine Miss Amber Regan wanted to see you. I think she's here because for whatever crazy reason, she digs you and your porcupine personality. That's why she's been texting you constantly, and why she's shown up here with no warning. All the way from *Texas*."

Garrett slurps the last of his coffee, folds up his plat map, and then points it my way before heading for the front door.

"And *I* think you'd better get to the Empire Ambassador before she starts to think you don't give a shit."

13

(Amber)

"... as a rock-hopper, log-balancer, and rough-trail-scrambler,
you can also compete quite favorably with Mr. Average Man."
—*The Sierra Club Wilderness Handbook*,
"Women," c. 1971

After twenty minutes, I lurch up from my outstretched position
on one of the Empire Ambassador's properly saggy beds to sit up
straight. Peering into the dresser mirror across from me, I give
myself an admonishing headshake.

No response to my texts. Zero.

Stupid, silly, irrational human being that I am, I expected a
very different outcome this morning. An outcome that included
Braden beating feet to get to me and a surprised-but-thrilled look
on his face when I opened the door. Followed by the exchange of
one lingering look worthy of a subtitled NC-17 movie and then
a whole host of acts that would earn an upgrade on that rating.
Later, I planned to have him take me on a proper date. A date on

which I would wear the very tight, very hot blue dress I'd brought along, expressly to test out my previous theory about what look turns Braden's crank. If I was right, my plan also included that dress ending up on the floor somewhere in his house.

And yes, I know how crazy all that sounds. To start, Braden probably doesn't have a surprised-but-thrilled look in his arsenal of expressions. Furthermore, it's possible he has other things going on and, you know, wasn't simply waiting around for me to show up unannounced as I have. He could be working and out of cell range, busy nailing a poacher in the act of certain crimes against nature. Or maybe he and Garrett are off on some adventure, one that will end with them sharing some manly conversation over a breakfast of his sauerkraut and some sunny-side eggs. Or perhaps the Jolly Green Giant is sleeping in this morning, taking a break from his usual routine—one I know gets him out of bed by six a.m., because that is always when his replies to my nocturnal texts show up. *Always.* Although if this is a case of lazy snoozing, I hope it's not the result of a long night with some meek, mousy, agreeable woman. Because the mere idea of that sets my nerves on edge.

A heavy sigh leaves me. Stupid, silly, irrational . . . These are the misfortunes of those afflicted with a crush. Let your loins and your heart get muddled up in this sort of thing, and it's all bets off from there. Although reworking one's schedule to hop a flight to Colorado, without fair warning to the object of all your crushing, might be a new low in the realm of infatuation.

Another pointed look at my reflection in the mirror, followed by a glowering stare. Then I round things out with the ol' two-fingers *I got my eyes on you* hand gesture, which is enough to get me on my feet.

I kick off my sandals and set about pulling on a pair of wool socks and my hiking boots, tightening the laces with a good tug and a double knot. The July sunshine means my shorts and tank top make sense for the weather, but I've learned the hard way that hiking at altitude can lead to a wicked sunburn before you expect it, so I slather on plenty of sunscreen to be safe. My day pack contains some rain gear, a water bottle and snacks, a spotting scope and my range finder, plus the action camera I'll use to film some b-roll footage. In all, everything I need to do the extra scouting I'm here for, which *is* the reason for this little jaunt. At least that's the line I've offered to anyone who inquired why I was suddenly taking a whirlwind weekend trip to Colorado.

I tug on a ball cap, pull my ponytail through the back, and sling my pack over one shoulder. After grabbing my sunglasses and the keys for the rinky-dink rental car I picked up at the airport, I give my reflection one more scolding look, knowing that will be enough to remind me what demands my attention these days. And pining after a broody game warden is not it. Even if all that irrational pining is what drew me out here this weekend, my career has to remain my priority because if I lose that, I'll be on my own—with only a blech-worthy reality show to break my fall.

Opening the motel room door with a hard yank, I know the burst of sunshine on the other side of the door will redouble my efforts to focus on what matters: doing whatever it takes to save my show.

Minor problem, though.

A big body is blocking all those sunbeams.

I stop short with a gasp. Braden's hand is upraised as if he was ready to knock on the door, but he lets it drop heavily when our eyes meet, matching the move with a long exhale.

"Finally." His eyes scan my face for a moment then begin a slow descent. "The kid at the desk wouldn't give me your room number, like this is the goddam Four Seasons and he's the head of security. I didn't see your truck, so I was forced to start knocking on doors, which means I woke up more than one guy who smells like a half-empty beer bottle that's been used as an ashtray."

I raise my brows. "A more direct route might have been to text me back. Ask what room I was staying in."

"Still wasn't convinced you being here was real. That I wasn't dreaming this up."

"Dreaming it up? Sure it wasn't a nightmare?"

Braden's gaze has fixed on my bare legs, but his eyes now drift back up to mine. And say hello to the NC-17 look I was hoping for, because it's right there.

Right. *There.*

Our eyes lock, and everything about Braden tenses, fighting what looks like the sudden urge to barrel through the doorway and give me the rest of what I had previously imagined.

"Definitely not a nightmare. Not even close."

My lips part a fraction, in reaction and invitation, struck stupid by the reality of how much I want him—and how relieved I am to see the same on his face.

Braden's voice becomes a touch stern. "Now explain yourself. Tell me what you're doing here, why you didn't tell me you were coming"—he pauses and works over a labored swallow—"and how long I have you for."

All the sarcastic, mocking replies I've come to rely on with Braden go missing, just when I need them most. Instead, I take a moment to absorb the full picture of him, standing there in a pair of jogger pants and a graphic tee emblazoned with a logo for the clean supplement company I'd give anything to have an endorsement deal with. He has a ball cap on backward and his five-o'clock shadow is about twelve hours past.

I suspect he either was having a lazy snooze day or he was working out. And let me tell you, I'd love a chance to watch Braden work out. Even more so, I'd love to work out with Braden—

and I don't even mean it *that* way, I mean actually work out. Sweat it out together until we determine who can best who. I answer him almost robotically, while also imagining a very sweaty Braden trying to keep up with me.

"I'm here to get in one last scouting trip before season. I didn't tell you because I wanted to see you, but I wasn't sure what you'd say." Braden's jaw tenses, his hands flexing impatiently. "You have me for the next two nights."

"Good." Every inch of him relaxes slightly. "You headed for the trail right now? I have my day pack in my truck; we can go scout some of those game trails I sent you pictures of."

"Absolutely," I nod, giving him a smile, and eat up the way he very nearly smiles back. "Let's go play in the woods together."

Oh. My. God.

How did this happen? *How?*

How is this even possible? I ask silently, to every rock, tree, and bush in my path.

How did we not only manage to leave the motel but then drive to the trailhead and hit the dirt, all without greeting each other properly? And by "properly," I mean groping and kissing until we're nearly passed out.

That's the sort of *proper* I'm interested in.

To boot, we've now made it three of five miles into a laborious hike where I'm bringing up the rear. Behind his rear. Braden's very meaty but firm, sculpted, and mesmerizing rear. The one I'm currently too preoccupied with to feel entirely sure of my footing.

We come upon an especially steep section where a few large, jagged boulders interrupt the trail, unavoidable and inconvenient. When Braden clears them by taking long, max-incline StairMaster steps, then bounds over the last one with a nimble backside-becoming leap . . . I crack.

That's it. I'm *done*.

Unwilling and unable to take another step, I come to a halt in the middle of the trail.

"Wait," I blurt out.

Braden lurches to a stop and spins around. "What? You OK?"

I press a palm to my forehead. "No."

He curses under his breath and starts his way back down the trail toward me.

"Sit down, head between your knees, and take deep breaths. How much water have you had today? You can't mess around with this altitude, Amber. You have to take it easy and acclimatize yourself."

"That's not it." I sigh.

I spy a smaller, flat boulder just a few paces off trail. Stomping that direction, I step atop it to put myself reasonably eye to eye with the man who's now looking befuddled. I flick a hand toward my chest.

"Come here."

Braden approaches with caution, keeping his hands gripped tightly to the shoulder straps on his pack, stopping too far away for what my objective is. I flick my hand again, jerky motions to match my impatience. He steps in to close the distance, his toes nudging the boulder I'm standing on while eyeing me warily.

"Kiss me," I announce.

"What?"

I let out a frustrated rumble, trying to figure out where to begin, either in rationalizing my demand that he kiss me or my recent decisions in general. I set my hands on my hips.

"You have a great butt—you realize that, right? I mean, it's *great*. I feel like I should be paying for the privilege to watch you hump it up this trail, it's that good. And this is the second time I've been forced to walk behind you, trying not to stumble over my own feet. But at least last time you were wearing cargo pants and layered up for the weather. Today, though?" I wag a finger toward his jogger-clad lower half. "No relief."

Braden's lips part and he makes a garbled attempt to speak. I cut him off.

"We should've gotten this out of the way back at the motel, but we didn't. I don't really know why, but we didn't. Doesn't matter. The last time I saw you, your hand was up my shirt and we discussed sexing it up on your desk. Now I'm here again and I want to pick up where we left off. So don't play dumb. Just kiss me."

The hesitation written across his face a moment ago disappears. Even so, he doesn't do what I've commanded. Instead, his parted lips press together and he studies me for a moment, every second that passes sending a thrill down my spine.

"Say it again," he finally rumbles.

"Which *part*?" I counter.

Braden blinks once, slowly and deliberately, a wordless warning for me not to test his patience. A chaser of anticipation follows the earlier thrill that ran through me. I allow that sensation to fill my body until I'm equal parts emboldened and weak-kneed, like I'm suddenly the best kind of drunk—the sort that feels warm and good and worth whatever hangover comes later.

"Kiss. Me."

A smirk creeps across Braden's mouth, triumph mixed with unabashed want.

Based on that grin, I expect his mouth on mine instantly, in a rushed collision that's as blundering as it is hot and wild.

But what I get is nothing like that. Instead, it's the restrained advance of Braden leaning in slowly—in complete control—

allowing our mouths to meet in a tease, his lower lip brushing over both of mine so lightly it drives a whimper from my throat.

That sound is his undoing. Braden sets his large hands to my waist and yanks me forward, nearly setting me off balance until his body becomes an anchor, my hands landing on his chest to steady myself, keeping them there even after, my fingertips digging in despite the T-shirt in my way. Our mouths fuse together, teeth nipping and tongues teasing. Braden's grip slips down to my hips, then lower, then again. His hands settle where my thighs meet the hem of my admittedly *short* shorts. I tilt my hips back to encourage him, and his touch sneaks up underneath the cotton fabric, the rough pads on his fingertips gripping my ass like it belongs to him, and I *want* him to own it.

We break for air. For some relief. Braden's hands stay put, retreating enough to fix our eyes to the other's, searching. Braden's chest is heaving, and I can feel it working against mine.

"More," I whisper.

His eyes flare. "Here? As in, *more* more?"

I give him an overeager nod. Braden's jaw drops open, pausing as he tries to find whatever words it is he's looking for. He sucks in a long breath.

"I don't make a habit of carrying condoms in my pack. Do you?"

My eyes drop closed. Damn the practicalities of safe sex. You'd think that since something like this was on my agenda, I'd have come prepared. But—insert tortured sigh—I did not.

"No." I cut a look his way. "You don't have one in your wallet?"

He shakes his head. I stamp my foot like a disappointed child, letting out a huff. Braden chuckles and tips our foreheads together. "Sorry."

Another huff from me. " 'Sorry' won't cut it. I'm dying here."

We stay silent, breathing in each other's disappointment until

Braden's hands start to squeeze my backside, almost absentmind-edly. I give in to a soft moan and circle my hips, hoping he'll knead harder.

But he leans back instead, removes his hands from my behind, and casts a determined look to the area around us. I nearly stumble off the boulder when he grabs my hand in his, but my reflexes kick in as he drags us deep into the wooded area off trail, occasionally tossing a glance over his shoulder toward the main path. Twigs, leaves, and underbrush crunch beneath our feet as we edge down a small slope and into a stand of aspen trees. Sunlight dapples through the leaves, but the grove is still shaded, and when Braden comes to a stop a chill hits my skin. He shrugs off his pack and tosses it on the ground, then starts to help me out of mine before I have chance to catch up with what's happening and my arms get tangled up slightly. Once he has my limbs sorted out from my pack, he drops it next to his and eyes me from head to toe.

"Hat off. Hair down. I want to get my hands in it."

I balk only long enough to realize he's dragged me here for a reason—so we can greet each other *properly*—then immediately find my mettle. I shoot him a firm look while doing what he asked, slinging my hat to the ground and yanking the elastic from my ponytail before shaking my hair out.

"You, too." I wiggle a finger at his hat.

He tosses it off. His dark brown hair is longer than it was the last time I saw him, a few tendrils now sweat-dampened, curling his hair into a wild mop that matches the wild flare in his eyes. Braden reaches for me, slinking a finger around a belt loop on my shorts, tugging me forward while turning me so my back can rest against the trunk of an aspen tree.

No more talk after that. His hands are in my hair, tugging and tangling handfuls of it through his fingers as we start to kiss again, finding a rhythm, the pace we both want.

Braden's big hand leaves my hair and starts to work open the button on my shorts. When he yanks down on the zipper, I freeze, giving up a moan so he knows that I don't want him to stop; I'm preparing myself for what comes next. I want to be entirely present when he slides his hand over my belly, then lower, finally letting his middle finger slip to the place where I'm already so wet.

"Christ," I breathe, savoring the sensation of Braden's hand between my legs. I step my legs wider, allowing room for his one finger to become two, circling my clit softly. I curse again, bucking my hips enough to meet the heel of his hand.

He grunts and gives me a rough rub of his palm. "God, it's too much. You are too much. So wet, so fucking greedy. Love that."

I make a desperate sound, hoping he knows what I'm really trying to say. *Yes. Keep doing that. Keep saying those things. I am so fucking greedy, I must be.*

I start to fumble with his jogger pants, more thankful than I ever have been for a drawstring waist. If he couldn't decode that noise I just made, this should help. Drawstring loosened, I slip the waistband over his erection, sliding my hand down until the length of him is in my grip. Braden's busy hand stops and he sucks in a harsh breath. Even if the lust centers in my brain want his hand back on task, I understand why he's checked up, because a first touch like this demands it. I slide him through my gentle grip, up over the tip, where his precum coats my palm, and back down to the root. Braden drops his head, setting the hand he had in my hair to the tree trunk. Another heavy groan from him when I tighten my hand around his shaft.

"You . . . *fuck*." His words taper off into a moan. "You don't have to do that."

A soft laugh escapes me. "Yes. I do."

Braden sighs and starts to move his hand again, with renewed purpose, and I respond with the same, stroking him with an al-most rough grip he seems to like.

"Amber, I . . . God, don't fucking stop, OK? Please. Just like that. Don't stop."

My breath catches, soaking up the sound of him begging me and the feel of his hand working my body in all the right ways. My climax hits in a rush and his follows, spilling warm and wet into my palm and running over my fingers while Braden works hard to draw out mine, letting up on the pace of his fingers only slightly, all while trying to wring what he still can from his. Finally, we both slow our hands, nothing but fitful jerky movements between us and vain attempts to catch our breath.

Braden presses his mouth into my hair and sighs, holding my satisfied body up with his own. And it's a hell of a nice feeling. Sweet, safe, and indulgent.

Despite all my time outdoors, every excursion into the back-country and all those days spent afield, *this* is new territory for me. But I get it now.

No wonder Colin and Teagan find themselves off trail so often.

14

(Braden)

"... going to the mountains is going home ..."
—John Muir, *Our National Parks*

I'm not sure, but I think things should be awkward right now. Because human nature dictates that when two people who don't know each other that well end up in a grove of aspen trees doing what Amber and I just did, the next few hours could easily spell some uncomfortable moments.

But that's not the case. Instead, we've hiked in companionable silence, amicably debated the best spot for her to set up camp during elk season, and experienced a near mind meld when choosing this high vantage point to glass from today. We're above the tree line on a long, gently sloping hillside, with views to both a forest of dark timber and a large wallow, each of which will attract elk.

Amber has her spotting scope on a tripod, alternating between using it and her binoculars. I've succumbed to the need for a short nap, stretching out next to her using my pack as a pillow and my ball cap tipped low to shade the sun. My entire body feels weightless and drained, in a good way. Short of having had a condom on me a few hours ago, my day can't get much better. We're miles away from civilization, the weather is perfect, and the woman I've been crazed over for months just came for me. If someone were to hand me a beer, I'd probably laugh myself stupid at how good it all is.

Amber's hand lands on my chest, and I open one eye to squint her way. She's craned forward peering through her spotting scope while using one arm to grope blindly about until she lands on the two food wraps sitting on my torso. Both are from the stash of snacks I keep in my pack, one with dried apple chips in it and the other with venison jerky.

She gathers a small handful of the apple chips and starts to nosh on them, still hunched forward to scan a hillside in the distance. She breaks the silence from around a mouthful of chips.

"Where in the world did you get these fruit chips? Because I'm planning to buy a case to take home with me."

I grin from underneath my ball cap. "My kitchen. I buy fruit from the local orchards in the fall then preserve what I can. If I freeze the dried fruit chips, they last even longer. These ones have a chai spice mix on them."

Amber leans back from her spotting scope, sets her gaze on me, and sighs, but without the exasperation I'm used to hearing from her.

"I swear, you were born in the wrong century or something. You and this need to make things from scratch. You're like some hot, modern-day pioneer man."

She makes a play for the jerky, but I capture her hand in mine, bringing it close so I can set a quick kiss to her palm. A wary light flickers in her eyes, scattering when she realizes I'm not planning to keep ahold of her for any longer than the kiss requires, releasing her hand almost as quickly as I hooked it. Amber keeps her eyes on mine as she slowly draws her hand back. I tip up one brow, all but telling her with that expression to relax. *Calm down, I'm just being affectionate . . . and, trust me, it's as fucking weird for me as it is for you.*

Amber tips her own eyebrow as a reply, a reminder that, silently or not, I'm not to tell her what to do. She'll relax if and when she decides to. I snort to myself as she snags a piece of jerky.

"I made that, too," I say, smugly.

"Of course you did," Amber mutters. "Because it's awesome."

She finishes her bite, dusts off her hands, and downs a few gulps of water from her Nalgene. I decide to catch some more z's because we'll need to start down the trail soon but I'm still feeling properly wrecked. Just as my eyes drift closed, Amber clears her throat rather loudly, unzips her pack, and begins to rustle the contents around.

I keep my eyes closed, relishing how nice it feels to have laid down arms when it comes to Amber. We've moved beyond the way I was just a guy who hated hunting shows and she was just a woman with a hunting show, to two people who both love this way of life, under an open sky and in pursuit of a simple goal. That, I guess, might explain why getting each other off against an aspen tree felt anything but awkward.

"Hey, guys . . ."

My eyes flip open at the sound of Amber's *Record Racks* voice. A stage whisper that's all too common on hunting shows and does nothing but grate on my nerves, usually because most of the time whatever is being said, doesn't need to be. I cut my gaze Amber's way to find her with an arm outstretched and holding a small video camera in one hand, addressing her nonexistent audience conspiratorially. She's taken her hair down then put her hat back on, all her blonde locks artfully arranged to look casual even when they obviously aren't.

"It's late July and I'm back in Colorado, trying to get in one last scouting trip before season opens. The weather is great, but shooters are slim. I'm using my new Vortex spotting scope, so you know I can see everything. But I'm still looking for a bull that's *Record Racks*–worthy."

Then she winks at the camera, like she's sharing a secret she's not the least bit guilty about. I have to work hard to keep from snorting, scoffing, or rolling myself down the hill. So much for skirting past any awkwardness. One thirty-second recording of her being *the* Amber Regan—product placements, annoying stage whispers, contrived blathering and all—and we're right back where we started. No matter how much we have in common or how much we want each other, this career of hers is one thing we'll never see eye to eye on. All this preening and posturing? For people you don't know and will never meet? I don't fucking get it.

Amber turns off the camera and sets it in her lap, then draws her hair back up into a practical ponytail.

"How did that sound?"

I shrug one shoulder. My best chance of getting out of here alive is to keep my mouth shut. I might pass out from holding back every snide comment that comes to mind, but I'm going to at least try to avoid pissing her off.

"Is that a *you nailed it* shrug or a *try again, more cowbell* shrug?"

I swipe a hand down my face, tipping my head her direction. "It's an *ask someone else* shrug."

She makes a show of looking at the wide-open space around us, shielding her eyes with one hand as if she's looking for another biped who gives a shit. Once she's done with her performance, she shoots me an impatient look. I give up a grumble. I tried, anyway.

"It sounded like that shit always does. Stupid. No one actually says things like that when they're hunting. And the fucking whispering. That just makes whatever you say sound like complete bullshit." I rub my temple with two fingers. "But if that's what you're going for? Then yes, you fucking nailed it."

I try to tip my ball cap down as a means to communicate that I have nothing else to say on the topic, but Amber's hands shoot out and shove the snack wrappers off my chest and onto the ground. Then she flicks the bill of my hat to drive it up and she crawls over me with her legs astride my body so her knees can press tight to my hips. My hands latch on to her thighs, sliding up her bare toned skin until I can grip her hips roughly, immediately wishing she was naked and coming—instead of pissed off and fully clothed, as she is right now.

Her hands land on my chest and she gives my pecs a hard shove.

"I don't want to sound the way I always do. I'm trying to do something different here. I want it to come across that way." Her fingers curl in and her eyes leave mine. "I need it to."

I furrow up my brow, processing what she just said. Along with what she didn't say. How she managed to sound desperate, determined, and resigned all in a few sentences, I'm not sure, but she did. Combine that tone with the way this always-assured woman's shoulders have slumped and her lips are pressed into a thin line, and whatever plans I had to brush off this conversation are forgotten. I fix her with a matter-of-fact look.

"Then talk to the camera like you're talking to me."

Her shoulders sag once again. "I'm trying to. It's like I don't know how to be normal anymore, not when there's a camera around. I see that little red light and something in my brain switches on, then I'm doing what I've always done."

I tug on her ponytail playfully. "Maybe try not worrying about how you look so much. Keep your hair up like this." I grab the camera and start to fumble with it. "Just talk to me. Pretend we're on our own hunt, out here trying to fill the freezer. Like it's our own personal home video."

Amber snorts. "I'm guessing any home video you and I make might include the position we're currently in. Except we'd be sweatier. And wearing fewer clothes. Maybe something skimpy and lacy for me, but that's about it."

"I fucking hope so," I mutter, continuing to turn the camera around in my hands. Amber sighs and yanks it away, pressing a button on the side. She turns it so we can both see the viewfinder.

"It's powered up; just press this button to start recording. Press it again when you want to pause recording."

I gather it up from her hands and adjust the angle until Amber is center frame, then tell her we're good to go. Amber scans her own length.

"Wait, does it look like I'm straddling a Jolly Green Giant?"

I thrust my hips up once, roughly, when I assure her that no one will be able to tell. Amber's eyes fall closed and her head drops back on a moan, driving her core down to meet my body with a roll of her hips. Amber must feel the way I go heavy and hard, because she tips her head upright slowly, meets my eyes with a gleam in hers, and rolls her hips again. No matter how much I might want to play this game for a bit longer, I have to keep this train from going off the rails, otherwise this camera will capture some lively footage not meant for her viewers.

"OK," I tell her. "Do your thing."

Amber starts to fuss with her hair, tucking stray strands behind her ears and smoothing the length of her ponytail so it hangs over one shoulder. I use my free hand to give her fiddling one a swat.

"Knock that shit off. You look gorgeous. Like some guy recently slipped his hand between your legs." The blinking red light on my side of the camera scolds me. I whip the camera away from my face. "Shit. You can edit that out or whatever, right?"

She rolls her eyes. "Yes, Braden."

Good. She might be used to the idea of people knowing everything about her, but I'm not interested in playing that game, especially when it comes to us enjoying certain private privileges. Amber thumps two fingers on my forehead to remind me to stay on task. I bring the camera up, whirling my fingers through the air to prompt her, but Amber falters, everything about her shouting a need to fuss and fidget. She sighs and jiggles her shoulders about as if that might help shake off the discomfort.

Suddenly, no matter how much I couldn't give a shit less about a TV show, I just want to help her, so I find my inner director.

"Let's talk about why you're here. I know you came for this." I gesture to myself, sweeping a hand down my body, which earns a snorting laugh from her. "But I'm a sure thing when it comes to you. Not so much for these bulls. Tell me why you picked this unit, what it is about this hunt that's important to you. Tell *me*, though. Not the invisible 'them.'"

Amber takes a deep breath, holding back an exhale until she's buoyed herself.

"I picked this unit because it's where I shouldn't be. This unit isn't ripe with trophy bulls, or even big numbers. This is public land hunting at its best and worst. You have to do your homework, hunt hard, and be OK with going home empty-handed. All of that is exactly what people think I can't do." She gives me a sly smile. "And I hate it when people underestimate me."

"Sounds like you have something to prove," I prod.

She nods. "I have to prove my show is worth another season. This hunt hinges on that. Without it, I don't have anything. I'm as good as unemployed."

Amber locks her eyes on mine as if she wants to be sure I heard what she just said. Again, I couldn't give a shit less about a TV show, hers or anyone else's, but I'm smart enough understand that this is not only her income, but her identity. And if there is one thing I'd hate to see, it's this amazing woman not being one hundred percent of who she is. Even if that means there's not much room in her life for a guy who thinks her career choice is, at best, kind of ridiculous.

I add an edge to my voice, challenging her. "So what's it going to take to make sure that doesn't happen? How are you going to prove yourself and save your show?"

Amber takes the bait. Her gaze becomes steady and sure.

"I'm going to do the work. And I'm going to get it right. No matter the outcome."

I wait for her to say more, but she doesn't. I pause the recording and stretch my arm out to set the camera aside.

"Was that OK? Did it sound right?"

I blink once. Startled by the return of uncertainty to her voice, because now I don't know if what I just saw was real or for show.

"That depends. Was it bullshit?"

Her brow creases. "No. Did it sound like bullshit? Dammit, I'm trying to be real here, and it's not coming through. I don't know how—"

I grab her hips and give a rough yank to cut her off.

"You're doing exactly what you should. I only asked because you've spent years on camera and I don't know what your tells are. But I believed you."

"Good." Amber's posture relaxes and gives in to a little eye roll. "Because you're a tough sell."

Always a fucking smart ass, this one. Pulling her forward, I kiss her, soft and slow. I slide my hands up and down her thighs as we kiss, and Amber shoves my hat off so she can twist her fingers through my hair. A rumble sounds in the distance. Loud enough that both Amber and I freeze, waiting for the inevitable crack of lightning that will follow. It comes all too quickly. I mutter a curse word and give Amber's hips a swat to prompt her off of me.

Late summer means afternoon rainstorms in the high country. Rainstorms mean thunder. Thunder means lightning. And lightning storms at this altitude mean we could end up human barbeque. Silently, I tell myself off for screwing around and putting us both at risk.

Amber swiftly rolls off of me. "We need to go, huh?"

I nod, sitting up and working my pack on at the same time. "Now. And quick. I don't like how close that storm sounds."

She moves into gear, taking her spotting scope off the tripod so she can wrangle it into its case, then starts breaking down the tripod. I unzip her pack for her and open it up so she can quickly stow everything away.

Amber brushes off her legs as I start toward the trail, walking backward to be sure she's right behind me. She pulls on her pack but doesn't move. I call her way, asking if she's OK, struggling to keep my tone even when what I really what to do is tell her that now is not the time for plodding behind. She balls her hands into loose fists at her sides.

"What happens when we get back down to the truck?"

Another rumble of thunder. No time to play games.

"We get in my truck, I drive you back to that shitty-ass motel, and you pack up your stuff and check out. Then you follow me to my place in your rental car and stay with me until it's time for you to fly home. You said I have you for two nights. I want every minute I can get."

Relief crosses her face. Still, she's not moving.

"Permission to suggest an alternative?"

I look skyward, asking for patience, because the clouds have already turned darker. We need to get going. Now. Amber knows that, but looks determined for us to have this conversation before she'll even consider taking another step.

I flick my hand to encourage at least some sort of forward motion and answer her sharply. "Granted."

"You drive me back to the motel, but I don't check out." I send her a hard look that says *absolutely not*, but she ignores it. "Until later. I want you to take me on a date tonight. I'll get ready at the motel and you come pick me up. Like a real date."

I balk. "A date? In Hotchkiss? Where? You've already made it clear that True Grit doesn't meet your standards."

Her response comes in a rush. "There's a turkey foundation dinner at the Elks tonight; I saw a flyer posted at the gas station when I came into town. It starts at seven, and there are still tickets left—I checked. I want you to take me."

I know all about the dinner. I'm a member of both the Elks and this local conservation group that works to protect wild turkey habitats—but these dinners aren't my thing. I'm happy enough to send in my annual membership check, have them send me a bumper sticker, and leave it at that. No need to waste an evening listening to people spin yarns about some hunt they went on or wander around pretending that I want to bid on any of the junk they're hawking on the silent auction.

"I hate those things," I grumble.

Amber smiles. "Like how you hate hunting shows but just helped me try to make mine better? Like how you said you don't dance but caved when I asked? Because I brought a dress with me, one I think might change your mind about foundation dinners. An *all dressed up for a date with her man* dress. And *you* are my date."

I run my tongue over my now-dry lips, inspired by the mere mention of that sort of dress. Amber watches the gesture, looking smug. Shit. Nothing worse than knowing you're over a barrel—and the barrel knowing it, too.

"Those things go on forever. Do we have to stay through the whole thing?"

"Nope. Just so we stay long enough to feel like it's a date. After that we'll employ a code word. Either one of us says it and we're out of there." She humps her pack around to shift the weight and tightens the waist strap down. "I'm thinking 'sauerkraut.'"

"Sauerkraut." I tilt my head. "That's all I have to say when I'm ready to bail?"

"Yup. Sauerkraut."

Fine. If a bad buffet-style dinner and feigning interest in some crappy art is what it will take to get her out of that motel and into that dress she described, I'm game. She's here, and this may be the last time we ever see each other in person. There are too many miles between here and Texas, spelling the end of this, I'm sure—so I'm going to make the most of what we can.

I outstretch my hand in an agreement to her terms. Amber steps forward, takes my hand in hers, and we shake hands like bitter rivals, best friends, and bedmates all rolled into one.

Amber releases my hand and passes by me to take the lead on the trail. "I can't wait to meet Charley."

Aw, hell.

Some guys might claim the path to their heart is through their stomach. For me, it's my dog. Because if a woman falls for my dog, then she's golden in my book. And if she also meets Charley's canine approval? I'll give that woman whatever she wants.

Anything and everything—even if it's only for a little while.

15

(Braden)

"We need the possibility of escape as surely as we
need hope . . ."
—EDWARD ABBEY, *DESERT SOLITAIRE*

Let us take an inventory.

A roomful of guys telling hunting stories that sound too good
to be true? Check.

A buffet-style dinner with sad-looking lasagna and an even
sadder-looking iceberg lettuce salad? Check.

A silent auction overloaded with *once-in-a-lifetime* (overpriced)
guided hunting trips and *limited-edition* (ugly) framed prints of
game birds in a farmer's field? Check.

Every element I expect from a foundation dinner has been met
tonight. Only one thing is different: my date. A certain blonde
in a blue dress who is currently standing on the other side of
the room chatting up another local couple who can't seem to get

enough of all that sparkle Amber knows how to make use of. I'm proof enough of that—I'm *here*, after all.

I wander past the silent auction tables again, pausing once more at the blue lapis necklace-and-earrings set on display. As cheesy as it sounds, the stones are nearly the same shade as Amber's eyes. Enough that I've actually debated putting a bid in on them. The main thing stopping me has been that I have no idea how I would give them to her.

Would I present them ceremoniously, wrapped up in a gift box? Or would that be too much? Maybe I'd be better off to just casually toss them her way in a plastic bag.

Also, *when* would I give them to her? Before sex? After sex? Both assume that we're going to have sex, and even if that's the case, neither is a good option. Whether pre or post, both offer too much opportunity for misinterpretation—like I was putting a deposit on services to come, or a tip on services rendered. And I'm not interested in wading into *that* tsunami. The bigger issue is that gifts—jewelry, especially—are for girlfriends, fiancées, or wives. None of which I'm lucky enough to call Amber.

Still, I find myself fingering the small bid sheet on the table and darting a glance at the ballpoint pen laid aside it. Amber's laugh breaks my concentration, and my head jerks up, picking her out immediately in the crowd.

She's now talking to two old-timers, both of whom look like this is the best night they've experienced since some USO show back in the day. Amber gives the old guy on her left a playful swat on his forearm, then laughs when the one on her right obviously says something at his pal's expense. When they both return her laugh with their own, she offers up her signature Amber Regan smile, the one I now know is manufactured for the camera and conjured up for her admirers. Her private smile is something else entirely. Unguarded and honest in a way no camera could do justice to.

Fuck it. Right or wrong, girlfriend or not, I don't care. I grab the ballpoint pen, scribble down a bid that's sure to be enough, then toss it back on the table and walk away before I can change my mind. If the perfect moment to give them to her never arises, that's fine—I'll shove them in the back of a dresser drawer and try to forget they're even there. But if the moment does come and I don't take a chance on earning another private smile from her, I'll wish that I had.

I spot Garrett sitting at one of the folding tables near the bar, talking to Cooper Lowry as they each work on another beer. Cooper is a retired pro football player who recently relocated to the Grand Valley to play house with his hippie-dippy girlfriend Whitney and help run the organic orchard she owns in Hotchkiss. Their relationship works for reasons no one quite understands. Whitney also happens to be very, very pregnant. Perched on Cooper's lap, her belly acts as the perfect shelf for a paper plate holding a slice of chocolate sheet cake.

I make my way over to them and drag out a chair, dropping onto it so heavily the flimsy plastic creaks under the force of my weight. Garrett and Cooper both raise their brows, beer bottles poised near their lips.

"What?" I snap.

Garrett takes a swig of his beer then uses it to gesture toward the rest of the room. "Aren't you missing your new sidekick?"

I rub the back of my neck. "She's off being Amber Regan. Capital *A*, capital *R*."

"And you aren't allowed to be there when she is?" Cooper asks, frowning.

I shrug, slouching down in my chair. I don't know if I'm allowed to or not. I do know that I'm running out of steam on sharing her with this roomful of people, many of whom either want to fuck her or fawn over her. Selfish or not, I want her all to myself and away from prying eyes, even if I get why she's impossible to ignore. Amber dressed in a gunnysack would draw attention, but clad in a bold blue dress that traces every one of her many curves? A room goes silent when she walks in.

Whitney pipes in idly, managing to distill all of my frenetic thoughts into something that makes sense.

"He doesn't care about the capital *A*, Amber. It's easier to wait it out, even if it drives him nuts. His Amber will show back up eventually. That's the person he wants to go home with, anyway."

Whitney's eyes dart my way, a strange alliance between two no-bodies who found themselves falling for two somebodies. While the term "his Amber" is a reach, the rest is dead-on. My eyes flare just enough to silently tell Whitney thank you, grateful that she's put words to what I can't.

"Well, if it were me? I'd get my capital *A-S-S* over there before that guy tries to feel hers," Garrett says, his eyes trained on the other side of the room.

Hackles rising, I follow Garrett's gaze, knowing I'm not going to like whatever it is that's caught his attention.

Amber is easy to find again, a cobalt-blue fantasy in a room of beige and brown. She's standing near the far side of the room, flanked by a tall, skinny cowboy fuck who clearly has no sense of personal boundaries. Amber takes a few steps backward, her signature smile still in place, until the length of her back is pressed to the wall behind her. Cowboy Jones leans in, outstretching an arm to the wall just above Amber's head, and her body language changes the moment that he does. Shoulders back, chin up, spine straight. All to make herself seem taller or more imposing, while still keeping that smile on her face.

The chair creaks when I stand up to head her way, my entire body coiled tight like a python ready to strike. Amber is tough, I know that. She may not require my help, or need me to back her up, but if Cowboy Jones does anything that Amber doesn't want him to, I'm determined to be close enough that I can show him exactly what it feels like to have *his* space crowded.

I stop near enough to suit me, cross my arms over my chest—and wait. Amber sneaks a look my way and there's nothing particularly troubled in her expression but I notice that one of her lowered hands is twitching slightly. Maybe that's a covert signal—Amber encouraging me to go ahead and clothesline Cowboy Jones the way I want to. Either that or she's flexing her fingers so she can deck him herself. We can only hope, because that is a show I'd fucking pay to see.

I'm not sure, though, so I stay put . . . and wait.

Her smile fades when Cowboy Jones winds closer, boxing her in with his posture. Amber does not want to be boxed in—that much is clear, simply from the faint tick in her jaw and the caution now in her eyes. Five long strides put me a hairsbreadth away from Cowboy's neck, but I keep my hands to myself even when he cranes his face my way with a sneer and all I want to do is grab him by the neck and sling him across room.

"Sauerkraut," I growl, my eyes on Amber's.

Relief spreads across her features, and Amber ducks under Cowboy's arm. "Took you long enough."

I outstretch my hand. "Sauerkraut, sauerkraut, *sauerkraut.*"

Amber puts her hand in mine, letting out a little chuckle when she does. "Agreed. Let's get out of here."

16

(Amber)

"He had wished for a dog, and as though some good fairy
had waved a magic wand, there *was* a dog."
—JIM KJELGAARD, *STORMY*

Going home with Braden has one major drawback, one I hadn't
considered, even though I know enough about him that it probably shouldn't come as a surprise. The problem? His damn house
is too far away.

After he called sauerkraut on the banquet dinner, we made a
few hasty goodbyes, headed out to the parking lot, got distracted
for a bit by a private moment in which Braden made it clear that
he really likes my dress—then once my clothes were tugged back
down where they belong, we set off for his place, with Braden
leading the way in his truck while I followed in my rental car.

That was almost an hour ago. Braden's a prickly pear who
probably functions best with a buffer between himself and the rest

of the world, so it makes sense that he would live outside of town, for sure. I totally get that he's a curmudgeon of the mountain man sort, but come *on*. Jeremiah Johnson lived closer to civilization than this guy.

Keeping an eye on his taillights, I rummage around for my phone on the passenger seat, eventually snatching it out from underneath my hoodie. The display lights up the darkened car interior as I scroll through my contacts to find his number. It rings only once before he picks up.

"Five minutes," he declares.

My lips twitch. He shouldn't know me this well; it's unnerving. I mean, all the mystery is gone—already. And we haven't even had sex yet.

"Maybe I was going to ask about something else. Like the weather. Or the history of your rural homestead. The one that is evidently near the goddam New Mexico state line."

"Hang up and drive. We're turning left up here."

With that, he hangs up. I cast a halfhearted glare at my phone face then toss it back on the seat.

A single reflector mounted on a skinny T-post is the only marking at the dirt driveway we turn onto, which immediately ascends up a steep grade with multiple switchbacks. Eventually, the road flattens out and a clearing comes into view, along with a small cabin surrounded by pine trees, where two bright porch lamps near the front door light up the exterior of the house. The cabin's steep pitched roof slopes toward a covered front elevation that's framed with simple columns. Two log-hewn Adirondack chairs sit on the porch, but other than that, the place is plain and unadorned. Despite those spartan qualities, the house doesn't seem unwelcoming, merely . . . Braden-like.

Before I even have the car shut off, a toffee-colored Chessie barrels around from the far side of the house at a dead run, barking once, before hauling to a stop near the front door. A grin sweeps across on my face.

Hello, Charley.

She plops down into a sloppy sit, most of her considerable weight tipped onto one haunch, tongue hanging out of her mouth as she pants heavily. Her focus is fixed on Braden's truck, and even though she's nearly vibrating out of her fur with excitement, when he finally appears from around the side of his truck, she stays put and doesn't move from her perch. Her tail is the only thing that betrays her obedience, thumping wildly against the porch.

Well-trained *and* adoring. No wonder Braden finds me exhausting. The primary female in his life is submissive as hell.

Gathering my purse and phone, I pop the trunk release. When I step out, Braden has two of my three bags from the trunk already in hand. I nudge my chin Charley's way.

"How long did it take to train her like that?"

Braden's mouth lifts on one side. "The training never ends. We're both a work in progress, she's just making me look good at the moment."

I grab the remaining bag from the trunk. "Is she an outside dog? She came around from the side of the house pretty fast."

Braden lets out a snort. "No. She's a house baby. There's a doggy door around back so she can go in and out at her leisure, then I have an invisible fence just to be safe." He gestures toward the interior of the rental car. "Is that everything? Anything else you want to bring inside?"

I shake my head. Braden proceeds to stand there, staring at the empty trunk compartment as though he's not sure what comes next. I slam the trunk shut. Braden's gaze meets mine and he blinks once, allowing him to focus and take me in—just standing here waiting for an invitation. His eyes darken and my heartbeat begins to thump when the invitation comes wordlessly.

A tip of his head toward the house before he turns on his heel to head that way.

The moment his feet hit the patio, Charley springs forward, her body wiggling from crown to tail in greeting. Braden grins and, with my bags still in hand, bends over at the waist to plant a smooch on the top of Charley's waggling head. My knees nearly buckle when he all but coos his own greeting.

"I know. Yes, I'm home. Were you good today? Yes, yes. I know you were."

While some women might feel a need to fan themselves at the sight of a man holding a baby, this display is more my cat-nip. Burly Braden with his backside pointed my way, kissing and fussing over his dog. Charley immediately starts to whine and whimper, wanting more.

Join the club, girl.

It's possible some sort of appreciative noise has slipped from my mouth because Braden looks out the corners of his eyes, then whispers conspiratorially in Charley's ear. Charley bounces my way like she's just now figured out that Braden isn't alone. She drops onto her haunches at my feet and nudges my free hand with her muzzle, giving up a doggy groan when I scratch behind her ears. She sinks her full weight against my thighs, and I lock my knees just to be safe—she may be well behaved and beautiful, but she's also a big girl. Perfectly sized for Braden, but a bit outsized for me.

"Hello, Miss Charley. You're bigger than I expected." Leaning down, I work one hand under her muzzle and stroke the fur on her chest with an open hand, scratching lightly with my finger-tips. "And prettier. Yes. So pretty."

She starts to lick my face, and I sputter a laugh, squeezing my eyes shut until her weight suddenly disappears. I open my eyes and find her bouncing restlessly, nails clicking on the porch, one encouragement away from jumping up to put her paws on my chest. I brace myself for the impact and grin.

"Charley. Stay down," Braden warns. Her butt hits the deck on a dime. "Good girl. No getting your paws on that dress."

I wave off Braden's reprimand. "It's fine. I don't mind."

Braden sets one bag down so he can open the front door, letting it swing wide. Charley bounds through the open doorway and disappears.

"*I* mind. If anyone's going to wreck that dress by getting their paws on it, it's me."

He waves me forward. His big body leaves little room for mine when I pass by him in the doorway—not nearly enough room for our physical bodies *and* my rapid breaths *and* his potent energy *and* all this sexual tension.

When I step across the threshold, I can feel him behind me. His energy and his heat, near enough that I have force myself to continue forward instead of stopping in my tracks so his body will crash straight into the length of mine. I pair a deep breath with every footfall I take until I'm safely in his living room. I set my things on the floor and turn in a circle, surveying Braden's little warren, trying to determine if it's what I imagined.

A couple of table lamps brighten the room, throwing shadowy light across log timbers that frame the walls and line the floors. A stone fireplace covers nearly all of one wall, black soot darkening the stones below the mantle, evidence of its many years of use. The furniture is spare and casual—one armchair, one couch, one coffee table, and one console table—all made from brown leathers and dark woods. And everywhere one might expect to find knickknacks and novelties, Braden has books, all neatly arranged on sturdy shelves. Charley has flopped down on a dog bed near the fireplace, stuffed dog toys and rawhides surrounding her.

Braden strides past with my bags and disappears down a short hallway, returning empty-handed a moment later.

"I put your stuff in the bedroom. We can discuss sleeping arrangements later." He passes me without pausing, headed toward the small kitchen that's just off the living room. "You want a drink?"

I cast a quizzical look at the ceiling. *We can discuss sleeping arrangements later?*

He better mean a discussion about which side of the bed he favors. Or if he prefers to sleep with an extra blanket on the bed or the window cracked open to let in a soft breeze. Because he's insane if he thinks we're discussing anything that involves us *not* sleeping together for the next two nights—postcoital, sated, and satisfied.

I narrow my eyes on his retreating form. "Sure."

A freezer door opens, and ice clinks into glasses. "Is whiskey OK with you?"

Tipping my ear toward the kitchen, I listen harder for any nuance in his question, a hint of some sort. But there's nothing. No impatience, no nervousness. Just . . . Switzerland.

"Sure," I answer. Again.

Except this time, my voice cracks. Because I am not Switzerland. I'm, I don't know . . . a small, confused country in the middle of a heat wave. One that is best endured with fewer clothes on. A place like Vegas, mashed together with a tropical island, and crossed with something French—an all-inclusive resort that I really wanted to visit, but at the moment, I'm not sure intends to the provide turn-down service I expected.

Braden reappears with two highball glasses in hand and passes one my way. We tip our glasses together. I take a small sip of the amber liquid and study him, looking for anything that might explain why we both still have our clothes on. I find nothing. *Nothing.* A maddening amount of absolutely nothing.

I flick a finger between us. "What's happening here?"

Braden's eyebrows come together, enough that it's clear he doesn't get what I'm driving at. Maybe I'm on the wrong side of this equation. Maybe I'm crazy. Maybe I've tossed all men into a big bag of stereotypes with boners, and Braden doesn't belong in there. Maybe he doesn't want to have sex.

Huh.

My eyes dart upward as I try to process that theory. Frankly, it doesn't compute. The ice in Braden's glass clinks and my eyes drop to meet his. He draws the tip of his tongue across his lips, shifting his eyes to my mouth as he does, and the sight of his tongue teasing something other than *my* mouth, my skin, my breasts, or anywhere on my body shreds my remaining patience. I take a deep breath. Consent is everything, I remind myself—on both sides.

"Do you want to have sex tonight?" I blurt out.

Braden "Switzerland" Montgomery doesn't visibly react. He simply holds the moment silently. The highball glass in my hand begins to tremble, and I clamp my fingers down to make it stop.

His answer is unaffected. "Yes, I do."

I blow out a shaky exhale and take a gulp of my drink, swallowing quickly no matter the burn. "Well, I do, too. So what's the holdup? And what's with 'discussing sleeping arrangements'?"

I use my free hand to air-quote for effect, but there's a tremor in my voice that betrays the blunt indifference I was trying for. Braden calmly takes the highball glass from my hand and sets both on the console table behind him.

"I didn't want to assume." He steps close and tips his head to mine, near enough that his breath skates across the shell of my ear. "And I don't want to rush through this. I only have you for two nights, so I want to make this last."

The entire room falls away, along with every anxiety, every question, every confusing thought I had. All that's left behind is the two of us, intensely present and entirely vulnerable to whatever comes next between us. And I want Braden to decide what that might be, because I'm tired of taking the lead. I've made the first move more than once, and tonight, I don't want to ply him or convince him, or have it feel like he's simply succumbing to a craving he couldn't control. It's time for Braden to prove to me this isn't one-sided by taking the reins, just so long as I know I'll get them back at some point.

I caught a glimpse of the Braden I want earlier tonight, when the too-slick, too-skinny cowboy at the foundation dinner invaded a little too much of my space. Braden's protective yet patient gaze was on me, and I wanted to wrap myself in that sensation, sink into the experience of being watched over without being hovered over. Braden didn't storm over like a bull bent on drawing blood, or alpha his way in and deck the cowboy's lights out, even when I was ready for him to do exactly that. He acted like a man, not a hotheaded kid, and I wanted that man—the one in possession of all that control and composure—to want me.

Braden moves to stand behind me. He draws my hair away from the side of my neck, placing a kiss to the sensitive skin behind my ear, then traces his fingertips to that same spot, and my entire body comes alive. Another sweep of my hair to the side, exposing the zipper on my dress, the one he could so easily yank down. Instead his hands land on my shoulders, fingers splayed wide so he can gently knead the muscles there. My eyes drift closed.

"I haven't done this in a while," he says.

Eyes still closed, my brow knits. This impromptu neck massage is diverting, but not so much that I don't find what he just said a little surprising. Sure, Braden isn't exactly a poster child for sociability, but he *is* hot. His looks alone could open a few bedroom doors, and anyone who bothers to peek under his surly

Superman cape would find a man who never neglects to answer a text and sometimes checks his best friend's forehead for sign of a fever. Add in that big, masculine body of his and the guy could easily get some if he wanted to, so there must be a reason why he's been on hiatus.

Braden's thumbs begin to work over deep knots near my shoulder blades that I didn't know were there.

"Why has it been a while?"

He continues to knead until he feels my shoulders wilt in relief.

"I got burnt by an ex a few years back. I hadn't met anyone worth the trouble since then. Until now."

My curiosity doubles down on those last two words. "Why me?"

I'm not sure what it is I want him to say, so long as they aren't trite words about how I look. From another man, that sort of desire might be enough, but with Braden I need something else. What, I'm not exactly sure. I just know I need more than the superficial.

Braden's hands drop to my hips and he grips them firmly, pressing his groin to my backside.

"Because you make me feel like a goddam live wire. You're in the room and I feel you. I don't have to see you, even. Because you're fucking everywhere. It puts my teeth on edge and sets my skin on fire. And I can't get enough."

He'd heard my thoughts. He had to—that's the only explanation for his being able to say exactly what I needed to hear, yet couldn't name for myself. I calm the urge to all but shout, *Take me, sailor!*—like some swoony matinee star from back in the day.

Slowly, I turn in his grip and meet his heavy-lidded gaze, intent on kissing him or dropping to my knees, whatever feels right. But Braden slinks one arm tight around my waist, trapping me in his grip so he can run his fingers across my mouth, his eyes fixed there so intensely my face heats under the lovely scrutiny. My lips part a fraction, ready to speak or kiss or moan, I'm not sure which.

Braden continues to stare at my mouth. "Because it's been a while for me, I need you to let me set the pace this time. Can you do that?"

My chest begins to rise and fall raggedly. "Can we take turns after that?"

Braden's face immediately cracks into a broad grin. One that's wry and exasperated, but above all, charmed . . . charmed by *me*.

A slow shake of his head. "You couldn't just say *yes*, could you?"

"You know you would have been disappointed if I had. I just want to be sure I get my turn. I want to drive you crazy, but in a *good* way."

His grin fades, his eyes darken, and I find myself tossed over his shoulder before I can even act like I might object.

"Fucking live wire," he mutters, striding down the hallway and ducking when we make it to the doorway, flipping on a light switch at the same time. Braden sets me back on my feet near a single nightstand next to an enormous bed.

The room itself isn't huge, so the bed takes up most of it. The frame is gray-stained pine trimmed with black wrought iron, and if I didn't know better, I'd think it was one of Trey's designs because it's industrial-looking and impossible to ignore. The nightstand holds a tower of books and an alarm clock, and there's a grocery-store bag tossed there, partially open to reveal its contents.

Condoms.

Good man, Braden.

I waste no time after that, reaching for him with a tug while trying to work his belt open and yank his shirt off all at the same time. Braden's hands swoop in and latch on to mine, letting out a low rumble as he spins me to face the other direction, still somehow able to keep my wrists in his loose but commanding grip.

His lips meet the crown of my head, whispering, "My pace. We agreed."

Being denied means I end up whimpering. He's apparently unmoved, because he uses one hand to begin unzipping my dress while continuing to hold my wrists in his other hand. My dress starts to slip from my shoulders on its own, and I have to fight the impulse to wrestle free of his grip so I can shimmy the dress to the floor as quickly as possible.

Fortunately, I don't have to struggle for long, because as soon as the zipper is down, Braden gives in and uses both of his hands to push the dress off completely. The material hits the floor in a soft pile, and I'm left standing there in heels and my favorite matching set of underthings. While both pieces are skimpy enough to leave almost nothing to the imagination, the white floral lace is unlined and delicate, so I always feel both pretty and sexy.

Behind me, Braden gives up a curse but doesn't touch me. His breath is labored, as if he's working hard to hold off. I tip my hips back so our bodies brush against each other, and that's all it takes. His hands come to my breasts, cupping them fully with a gentle squeeze before teasing my nipples with the tips of his fingers. When I let out a long moan and grind my body to the front of his pants, Braden spins me around, kisses me once, and then tosses me on the bed, where I bounce once. I lean back on my forearms and watch as he draws his hands down my calves and pulls off my heels, tossing them on the floor behind him. His eyes skim my body as he starts to undress.

"Here's the thing: this first go-around, I'm bound to be a little quicker on the trigger than I want to be, so I need you to tell me what you like. I promise it won't always be that way, but like I said, it's been a while—and you drive me completely out of my fucking mind. Help me out, OK? Help me make sure this first time is good for you. Tell me what gets you there."

Braden continues to eat me up with his eyes as he loosens his belt and tosses it on the floor, then does the same with his shirt, using one hand to yank it off. My eyes go wide at the sight of his bare chest. He's not built like a model with washboard abs that go on for days, or some smooth waxed torso that mimics a Ken doll—he's built like a *man*. Defined pecs and biceps, strong abs, and a dusting of dark hair on his chest that tapers to a trail disappearing under the waist of the pants he's now unbuttoning. My mouth falls slightly agape, and I start to feel a little dizzy. And when he starts in on a lewd quiz, that only makes the wooziness worse.

"Do you like being on top so you can ride it? From behind so I can play with your pussy while I get deep? Under me and your legs spread so you can rub your clit? Is there something else you like?"

My mouth goes dry and my voice disappears along with it. Not only because it's hard to decide between all those filthy and fabulous options, but because he's naked now, standing there asking me how I best get off while he strokes himself. With every twist of his fist over the head, his abs contract and the muscles in his forearm flex—and I can't think, let alone speak.

"Amber," he rasps. "Answer me."

I close my eyes. At this point, I think any of what he's mentioned will work for me, but I take a moment to imagine each one in my mind as a flickering, full-color fantasy. Braden starts to press again, but I hold up my hand to quiet him.

"One second, please. I'm picturing all my options. Just finished riding you; now I'm bent over the mattress with you behind me." I bite the tip of my tongue between my teeth gently, still considering.

A long groaning curse from Braden. His hand starts to trace up the inside of my leg, eventually meeting the edge of my panties, sliding his thumb across the bit of lace that covers my pussy.

A few passes over the material, then he sneaks beneath it, cursing again when he feels how ready I am. That touch and my last image are enough to make a decision. My eyes flip open.

"Like this. My legs spread and you above me."

Braden doesn't delay. He grabs my legs behind the knees, tugging me a few inches closer, and reaches over to grab a condom. Watching him, the quake in his hands but the surety in his actions, is a sight on its own.

Seconds later he's over me, his mouth on my neck and his cock pressed to my core, grinding in long passes over the lace still covering me. I work my hands down between us and stroke him once, then tug my panties over, thinking I might actually cry if we stop and try to take them off properly. Braden seats himself where we both want him, pushing forward slowly. Too slowly. I dig my nails into his backside.

"Braden. Don't tease. I can't—"

He drives deep in one thrust and my words become nothing. Braden pushes upright so he can spread my legs wide, his hands gripping my knees for leverage. I arch my back and instantly feel one of his hands on my bra, yanking down each cup roughly, my breasts falling into his demanding grip. I dip one hand low over my belly, then lower, until my fingers meet the slick space just above where our bodies meet. Braden's eyes jump to track my movements and his jaw flexes tight as he watches my fingertips work in frantic, tiny circles.

"Fuck yes," he groans, "Rub that clit. God, that's the way you like it, isn't it? Fast little circles. Show me more so I know for next time. Next time, I'll do everything, I promise. All you'll have to do is take it, let me fuck you and make you come."

I respond with a moan. *Next time.* I love the sound of that, the idea of that—even if it seems he's already forgotten that we agreed to take turns.

Braden gives up his hold on my breasts so he can press my legs wider, opening them so much it's almost painful, but the fullness of him and the steady thrum of my fingertips mean I feel nothing but pleasure.

"Tell me you're close," he urges. "Or tell me what you need. Come on, baby."

I nod frantically, a nonanswer that he somehow unravels and figures out what to do with. Braden's thrusts become rough and short, exactly what I need—and everything behind my eyes goes blazing white as my body turns to shrapnel. And when Braden follows, I nearly come again because he keeps going and going, refusing to let it end until he's damn good and ready.

Finally, his body nearly collapses on mine. I scratch my nails down his back, soaking up the weight of him for as long as I can, knowing eventually I won't be able to breathe. But putting aside that basic need, I could get used to this: Braden impossibly close, the heady buzz of pleasure swimming through my body, and the way every problem in my life feels a million miles away.

"My live wire," Braden whispers, dropping a soft kiss to my neck. "You were so worth waiting for."

17

(Braden)

"Getting up too early is a vice habitual in horned owls, stars,
geese, and freight trains. Some hunters acquire it from
geese, and some coffee pots from hunters."
—ALDO LEOPOLD, *A SAND COUNTY ALMANAC*

The warm body I wake up next to is not the one I'm expecting—
it is, however, the one I typically share my bed with.

Charley's snout is resting on my chest, her perpetual doggy
morning breath wafting toward my face. She opens her eyes lazily
a moment after I do and looks pleased as always to see me. Greatest dog ever. Even so, her furry muzzle is not the face I wanted to
wake up to this morning.

I lift my head and peer about the room. Amber is nowhere to
be seen, but all of her bags are where I left them last night, which
is a good sign that she's here somewhere and didn't decide to bail
on me in the middle of the night.

Although why she isn't lying here next to me remains to be

seen. If she were, that would make it a hell of a lot easier to commence with what I had mind when I woke up. Now I have to get out of bed, drag her back in here while listening to her gripe about it being her turn to set the pace, then see how many licks it takes to quiet her complaints. My head flops back to the pillow on a groan. I don't care how many licks it takes, I have a taste for every last one.

Before tossing back the covers, I apologize to my morning wood. A quick glance at the clock reveals that I not only forgot to set my alarm, I also overslept long enough that once I'm done giving Amber a sweet tongue-lashing, there won't be time to enjoy more before I'm due in town for work.

Despite the multiple rounds we went at last night, it would still be pretty rude to saunter out there dick-first, so I tug on the pants and shirt I tossed on the floor last night, then run a hand through my hair. Charley bounds off the bed and pads out ahead of me, breaking into a scamper when she registers that someone is in the kitchen. I nearly do the same when I spot Amber standing with her back to me, hands on her hips as she stares at the kitchen table. She's wearing a pink silk robe with a short hem that barely meets her thighs, and when Charley bounds over, Amber immediately starts to fuss over her.

"Good morning, pretty girl." Charley burrows in for some affection, and Amber's intent on indulging her, so she starts to break at the waist, and when she does—whether my pants are on or not—I may not be able avoid going into this conversation the wrong way if she bends over too far.

Whatever you do, mountain sprite, don't bend over. Please. Don't bend over, don't bend over, don't bend—

She bends over.

Evidently, she's capable of refusing anything I ask of her—even if it's all in my head, because Charley gets a thorough nuzzling on the head and I get a perfect peek of what kept me up too late last night.

I remind myself to keep my greeting simple, ensuring that I don't say something she may not find charming at this hour. She seemed to like every blunt, dirty thing I said last night, but it might not go over the same way if those are my first words at sunrise. I just need her to stand up straight as quickly as possible. There are too many soft, pretty, and pink areas in my view right now, all of which my gutter-dwelling mind is far too focused on.

Gravel-voiced, I offer up my only PG-rated thought.

"Morning."

Amber cranes her head my way but takes her sweet time rising upright. When she does, she quickly starts to tuck a few locks of hair behind her ears, escapees from the loose knot atop her head.

"Morning." She casts a hand behind her, gesturing toward the table with a fitful flick of her wrist. "I woke up a few hours ago and couldn't get back to sleep, so I made breakfast. Well, not *made* breakfast. Technically, all I did was dish up breakfast. I wanted to make eggs, but you don't have any."

I glance at the table. Two bowls filled with granola, another bowl with sliced fruit, and a gallon of almond milk. I return my gaze to Amber, who's now awkwardly smoothing the front of her robe.

"I don't like eggs."

She turns away and drags one of the kitchen chairs out. "That's too bad. I make a mean veggie frittata." She points to the seat. "Here, sit."

Woodenly, I take a seat where she's indicated, casting a wary look at both the table and Amber—because between her fidgeting and this vaguely domestic scene she's tried to set, I'm not sure what's happening here. I may have found Amber's bold, brash confidence a little hard to take when we first met, but now that is one of the traits I like best about her. She doesn't hedge her personality for anyone—certainly not me—which makes her self-consciousness this morning even harder to understand.

Amber doesn't take a seat herself. She starts to fiddle with the bowl of fruit, giving it a half turn and then moving the serving spoon she set in it, from one side over to the other. When she reaches for the almond milk, I intercept the move, grabbing her hand before she does God knows what else. I twist our fingers together and stroke my thumb against the back of her hand.

Amber lets out a sigh. "I'm not good at this part."

My forehead creases. "What part?"

"This," she announces, rather loudly, flailing her hand over the table. "The domestic-goddess, wow-him-with-your-ability-to-serve-up-a-morning-after-breakfast-in-bed crap."

She sighs again, still assessing the tabletop as if that's actually the problem here. Which it isn't. The problem is that she's trying to be someone other than who she already is, and for no good reason. I've already wasted too much time attempting to confine Amber to a variety of neat little boxes in my mind, thinking that if I reduced her to a stereotype—gorgeous but lazy, beautiful but difficult, amazing but intent on driving me insane, etcetera—it would be easier to ignore the way I felt about her. But no matter the box or the label, she's shattered each one, every time.

And this box? The one she's confined herself to as a less-than domestic goddess? I'm not interested. A domestic goddess probably cares more about keeping me from dragging dirt into the house, rather than coming along for the ride to where all that dirt originated. But Amber not only wants to ride along, she wants to beat me up the trail, and see who comes home with the most dirt packed in their boot treads.

To hell with domestic goddesses. I just want Amber, dirt and all.

"Of all the things I thought about this morning"—I run my

eyes up and down her form—"I promise you that 'Gee, I hope she makes breakfast' wasn't one of them."

Amber covers her face and laughs, her entire body relaxing when she does, and I take the opportunity to reach out and tease the bare skin on her legs, tickling the inside of her thighs just below the hem of her robe. She turns and rests lazily against the edge of the tabletop.

When she drops her hands from her face, the woman I've come to know is back. One side of her mouth tilts up.

"If breakfast wasn't one of your thoughts, what did you come up with?"

I start to move my hand that's teasing the inside of her thigh upward.

"Waking up with your head on my chest. Waking up with your mouth on me. My mouth on you." My fingers meet the crease between her legs, and Amber's eyes drop closed.

A soft whimper leaves her mouth. "Pretty sure it's supposed to be my turn to set the pace. You got two turns last night."

"Then you should have put your time to better advantage when you woke up. I was lying right next to you. You chose to come out here and fuck around with breakfast."

I give the flimsy tie on her robe a tug. The silk falls open only slightly, so I reach up and part the fabric, exposing and framing her. And just like last night, my mouth goes dry at the sight of her smooth, golden skin, her flat torso, and the feminine taper near her hip bones that highlights how insanely fit she is.

"Christ," I whisper. "Look at you."

Last night, I shied away from words that might make her feel like she was just a body to me, because she isn't. I love the physicality of her, yes, but I don't want that to be our story. I want there to be more between us. But this morning, it's harder to keep those words at bay.

I slide one hand down the center of her body, my fingers

spread to skim the inside curve of her breasts along the way. Once I meet her belly button, I circle a finger there lazily before reaching around her so I can rearrange the breakfast buffet she's set out, clearing some room on the table.

I rap the tabletop with my knuckles. "Up."

Amber does what I ask, but not without commentary. She babbles about my being bossy and claims the only reason I'm getting away with it is because I give great orgasms. I stand up, crowding her space so that she's forced to make room for me between her legs. When I slip the robe completely off her shoulders, I urge her body back to the table at the same time—and she's still talking. I drop my hands to either side of her, listening while I look my fill.

"You are the worst smexy-times business partner," she huffs. "Fifty–fifty, we agreed. But last night you wouldn't let me have a turn, and I get the feeling it's going to be the same story this morning."

I latch my hands to her ass and give her body a quick yank so she's at the very edge of the table, which quiets her for a beat. Long enough that her eyes meet mine just before I drop to my knees. I could draw this out to toy with her, but I don't want to. I press my hands to her inner thighs to part her legs wider, then trace my thumbs up and down her smooth pussy. Amber draws in a stuttered breath that momentarily interrupts her continued jabbering.

"Do you not remember that part of our discussion last night, Braden? The taking-turns agreement? I told you I want to drive you crazy but in a good way, and now—" She sucks in another hard breath. "Oh my *God* . . ."

The rest of her words dissolve into gibberish when I sink my mouth onto her, all but devouring the sweet taste, drawing a long moan out of Amber. I take another pass, slower this time, lingering over her clit with the tip of my tongue. She goes silent, nothing but the rush of her breath to be heard.

Mystery solved.

Two, that's my answer.

When I woke up this morning, I wanted to see how many licks it would take to quiet her complaints, and now I know. It's two—two wet, worshipful, sweet licks.

I make another pass, relishing the way her taste and scent grow headier with each one. But when her hips buck up to meet the press of my tongue, I give her clit some more attention, suckling gently until she lets out a whimper and grinds her pussy to my face. I soak up her impatience and consider how much better this could be if I weren't due at work so soon. I'd let her do that all day if I could. Since I can't, I bring one hand up and tickle two fingers to her opening, parting her with the just tip of my middle finger.

"Fuck *yes*," Amber hisses.

I debate using my free hand to jerk myself off, but decide against it because I want her orgasm more than I want my own. I curl my hand around her thigh to encourage her leg to my shoulder. Amber takes the cue and does the same with her other leg, giving her leverage to press closer to my face and me the room to slip two fingers inside her. I give her both at once because she's wet enough to have already coated my mouth and my scruff, but she still groans at the fullness. I work my fingers in and out, long slow strokes to start, until the cadence of her breath turns ragged.

My tongue flattens to her clit, working in persistent circles, and I give her my fingers in shorter strokes, faster and harder, until she gasps wildly. When she comes, I nearly laugh, pleased as fuck with this moment, this morning, this amazing woman. I plant a few kisses to her clit as I slow my fingers entirely, drawing them out gently.

Amber lets out a satisfied sigh and pats my forehead with her hand, like I'm her adorable lapdog—something I could try to deny, but given that I'm currently on my knees in front of her and panting a little, there's not much point.

"Fifty–fifty is overrated. No need for me to set the pace; I like this arrangement just fine."

I rise up and look Amber over—her robe open, her lush body on display, and her cheeks flushed. A soft smile on her lips, her glassy and glittering eyes on mine.

That beats any social media pic she's ever posted, in my opinion. Even better, I get to claim some part in what made her look this way. Pardon me while I pat myself on the back and enjoy the beautiful, sated evidence of what I just helped make happen.

Unfortunately, duty calls so I can't enjoy the view for long. I glance at the kitchen clock. Amber checks the clock for herself, casts a look at my fly, and notes the grimace now on my face.

"I have no idea if you have to work today. Do you?"

I nod, jaw tensing. "Public hours at my office. I have to get going, otherwise I'm going to be late."

She draws her hand down and grips me through my pants.

"OK. So I need to be quick then." She starts to work open my zipper. "Condom? Or I could give you what you just gave me. I like the sound of both, so you pick. Tell me what you need."

Closing my eyes, I make a futile attempt to block out the image of either. It doesn't work. With a groan, I lay my hands over hers. "I can't."

"What?"

I open my eyes and sigh. "Right now I could probably come in a hot minute. But even that won't be fast enough."

"Seriously? You're going to leave?" She points accusingly at my fly. "Like that?"

I nod and Amber sticks her lower lip out in a cute pout, and I'd do the same thing if it wouldn't look totally stupid on me. All I can do is hang my head in surrender.

"Trying to be a responsible adult right now."

Amber laughs softly. "Ah, *adulting*. I know it well." She swats my ass. "Good luck trying to walk with that boner."

I give myself a painful adjustment, changing the subject in hopes that might offer a little relief. "What are you going to do today? Scout some more? You can take my truck if you want to. I'm driving my work truck into town."

I point to the hooks near the back door, where the keys to my personal truck are. Amber smiles, rests a hand to the center of her chest.

"You know the way to my heart, Braden. A real truck to drive. Thank you, because that rental car is a joke." She hops off the table and closes her robe up. "Breakfast was a bust, but what about dinner? I saw an elk backstrap in your freezer when I was snooping around this morning. Will you be back in time? I could throw that tenderloin on the grill and cook up something to go with it."

Amber then goes still, seemingly caught off guard by what just came out of her own mouth, and begins to backpedal.

"I mean, whatever. Just—if you want, but if you don't . . ."

I smirk. "Is this domestic goddess part two? Are you fumbling over asking me when I'll be home so you can have dinner ready?"

Amber averts her eyes. "No." She grins. "Yes."

I remember how often my ex used to ask this same thing of me—trying to pin me down on a time for dinner, then resenting it when I wouldn't play along. But with Amber, I don't feel the way I once did: pressured to make plans I couldn't care less about and frustrated by the fact that it seemed to be the one thing my ex *did* care about. Today, all I want is to make this small commitment to Amber, and see it through.

"I'll be home by six. If you can handle dinner, I'll bring wine and dessert back with me."

Amber sticks her hand out. "Deal."

18

(Amber)

"Love flowers best in openness and freedom."
—EDWARD ABBEY, *DESERT SOLITAIRE*

"**M**ore?" Braden asks.

"Never enough," I reply, encouraging him with a wave of my hand over the pot of polenta simmering on the stove top.

Braden dumps in another heap of freshly grated Parmesan. I stir it in, taking a taste once it's all incorporated. Needs salt, maybe. I gather another spoonful and hold it up for Braden to try.

He narrows his eyes after tasting it. "S&P. Needs both."

After a dash of each, I turn the heat down another notch. Braden drops the box grater into the kitchen sink and returns to his work at the small butcher-block island in the center of the kitchen. We decided that a quick puttanesca-style sauce would go well with the rest of our dinner, so Braden is chopping up tomatoes, green olives, capers, and garlic. The elk backstrap is ready for the grill, slathered with more garlic and some rosemary. We'll wait until the last minute to throw it on to cook because backstrap is a coveted cut, equivalent to the best chateaubriand of beef, but with big game medium rare is the only option. Anything beyond that and you'll end up with a hunk of shoe leather on your plate.

Braden works quietly, either because he's spent or because he's hungry—or both. He showed up right on time at six o'clock, but he did not arrive calmly. He basically stomped into the house while slamming the front door shut behind him, strode right past me in the kitchen, and disappeared into the bedroom. Only to storm back out and lurch to a stop a few feet away from me, clasping a condom in his upraised hand. He looked as if he'd barely made it home without cracking, and I'd barely made it through the day myself, so I switched off the burner and crooked a finger his way. Neither of us said anything until I had the counter edge in my hands, Braden behind me, one breath away from him sliding inside me.

"Longest day of my fucking life. All I wanted was to get back to you."

I swear, I nearly came right then. Instead, that happened only a few minutes later for both of us. The shower we took together afterward was ten times longer than the act itself, but almost as satisfying because when Braden decides to wash your hair for you, he doesn't half-ass the task—he massages and lathers, and kneads everything along the way. It's like going to the salon, but one where you can feel free to moan as loud as you want while someone deep-tissues your scalp.

As a result of all that, dinner is later than planned.

I take a sip of the wine that Braden brought home and watch him for a moment, sure-handed with the knife as he works it through a small pile of olives. His back is turned, so I'm safe to stare without him questioning me. If he did, I'd probably mutter something cheeky or call him a Jolly Green Giant—anything other than disclose the truth, which is that I'm trying to figure out how it is that he's still single.

He's hot, smart, and actively employed. He's awesome in bed. He's a great dog dad, a good friend, and a dedicated employee. Basically, he should be someone's husband by now. But he's not, and I'm curious why.

"Tell me about the ex."

Braden doesn't flinch or falter, and continues chopping without slowing the knife.

"What do you want to know?"

I shrug even though his back is still to me, hoping the casual gesture comes through in my tone.

"What's her name? How long were you together? You said she burnt you, but what is she like? Is she a health nut? Is she the reason you do all this cooking and sauerkraut-making?"

Braden snorts. "My mom's the reason I cook and browbeat people about food. She had breast cancer about seven years ago, and when she got sick I wanted to know *why*. Both of my parents are professors, so I did what we egghead types do best: I buried myself in research. I came out of all that reading scared shitless about every FDA-approved additive that's out there." He notes my *oh, shit* expression. "Relax. She's fine. It took radiation, chemo, and a double mastectomy, but she's in remission now."

I let out a long exhale. Braden sets the knife down and returns to the stove, setting a skillet on a free burner and lighting the flame. He adds some olive oil before turning back to grab the cutting board he's been chopping on.

"As for the ex, her name's Laurel. She's healthy, but not a health nut. She's a preschool teacher, she's a democrat, she likes jam bands, and she's a perfectly nice person. If I'm being honest, she's probably too nice. We were together for three years." He pauses. "We were engaged."

Engaged? Braden was engaged? Apparently I was spot-on about the notion he should be someone's husband by now, because he'd been well on his way to exactly that.

"So what happened?"

Braden tips the contents of his cutting board into the pan, and everything sizzles at once. He sets the board aside, grabs a spoon, and stirs the sauce until it quiets.

"When we were together, I was still working as a hotshot, which Laurel hated. Her family wasn't exactly a Hallmark special; her dad bailed when she was a kid, and her mom couldn't keep a steady job, so she got bounced around for years among relatives. Growing up that way meant stability was huge for her, and here I was, doing this job that wasn't safe and took me away for weeks at a time. Finally, she asked me to quit. I loved her, so I did it. I gave up my spot on the hotshot crew and got a job as a park ranger."

I watch as the puttanesca simmers away and decide that even without hearing the rest of this story, I already dislike Laurel. She likes jam bands, for Christ's sake—that's reason enough, but I'm pretty sure that isn't the worst if it. I suspect by the time he's finished I'm going to hate her. Braden reaches over and turns the burner down.

"A month later, I come home one day and she's sitting on the stoop outside our place, some guy next to her with his arm around her, and all her shit is packed up and loaded into the back of a pickup truck. She was bawling. Said she was sorry, but she figured out that she fell in love with him long before she asked me to quit my job, hoping that might make her fall *back* into love with me."

My jaw drops open. I pause my spoon midstir, letting it droop to the side of the pot.

"Are you fucking kidding me?"

Braden shakes his head, and I blow out a measured exhale so I can calmly summarize this bullshit that's worthy of a daytime talk show, just to be sure I have it all correct.

"Let me get this straight. She was all 'wah-wah, I want you to quit your job,' then gave it a big thirty days to see if that would do the trick and make *her* feel better. When things didn't miraculously improve after a *month*, she took off with another guy. One she must have cheated on you with, long before she gave you this selfish-ass ultimatum."

He nods. I clench my hands into loose fists. I was right. End of story, and I hate Laurel.

"I cannot believe you can stand there and say she's a perfectly nice person. She's rotten—to the core. Rotten, manipulative, and awful."

"No. She's not." Braden faces me, his mouth pressed into a thin line. "She's just not like *you*. She's not able to say exactly what she's thinking, when she thinks it. This is a woman who would rather risk food poisoning than send back a plate of chicken that's raw in the middle—that's how much she hates anything remotely confrontational. And I knew that about her, but I never bothered to put in any real effort to get her to talk to me. By the time she finally worked up the nerve to tell me what she needed, it was too late."

It's my turn to shake my head, mostly to keep from grabbing Braden by the shoulders and shaking *him* until we can declare in tandem that Laurel sucks. After that, we'll dig up an old picture of her, mount it on a 3-D target out back, and commence to demonstrate our archery skills on it. I cross my arms over my chest.

"I'm going to hate her. And you can't stop me."

Braden leans in and takes my face in his hands so he can place a single kiss to my forehead. "Go ahead. God knows that's how

I felt when it happened, and why I thought I needed to move four states away from her. But she wasn't the only one to blame. Either way, this shit happened three years ago, so it's old news at this point."

"How very mature of you," I mutter. Braden snorts. I lower my voice. "I still hate her."

"Thank you," he whispers.

Out on the back porch, Braden runs a stiff-bristled brush over the hot grates of his barbeque before using a pair of tongs to take the backstrap off the plate I'm holding and place it on the grill. I trot back inside to dump the plate in the sink and return with a clean plate and our wineglasses. Braden takes the plate and his wineglass, takes a sip, then sets both off to the side.

"Since you asked about my ex, does that mean I get to ask you about something, too?"

I flop down in one of the rickety folding chairs he has set up on his flagstone patio and cross my legs, gazing out at the garden Braden has planted behind his house. He's enclosed the small plot with tall panels of chicken wire to fend off the deer, but continues to fight the rabbits who want to sample his harvest. Even so, he has a thriving patch of cucumbers, peppers, squash, and carrots growing—not to mention the cherry tomatoes and herbs that made their way into our dinner tonight.

"Go for it. But I'll save you the trouble, because I don't really have an ex. At least not one worth mentioning. And I definitely don't have anyone like Laurel. Also known as the founder, the mayor, and the mascot of the town of *Rottenville*."

Braden gives the grill an absent smile before turning the meat over. "That's not what I want to ask about."

"Oh. Well, ask away, then."

"I'm curious about what's going on with your show. On the mountain, you said something about being unemployed if this hunt doesn't go the way you need it to. Tell me what you meant by that."

My breezy attitude breezes away. For nearly one full day, I hadn't given much thought to my show, at least not in a dire way. I'd been enjoying myself too much to dwell on the fact we still hadn't heard anything significant from the programming heads over at Afield or that one of my biggest sponsors had just announced they'll be cutting their marketing budget in half next year and I currently have no idea which side of the fifty percent I'm going to fall on. But Braden's curiosity means every anxiety comes rushing back. I haul in a long breath, hold it for a few seconds, and then exhale audibly. Braden continues to give the grill all of his attention, so I train mine on my wineglass.

"What I meant by that is exactly what I said. If this hunt doesn't go well, I'm probably going to lose my show. My ratings are in a downtick, and in this business, a downtick means you're as good as dead. Because TV? She is a fickle, fickle dame. Everything hinges on ratings, loyal sponsors, and fresh content. Without the trifecta, you may be the darling of your channel today, but tomorrow, nobody will return your calls. That's where I'm at right now. The place where the head of programming at Afield won't return my manager's calls. Or mine."

I smooth my hair down and take a sip of wine—for fortitude and all. "My brand needs a reboot and this hunt is all about trying to do that. People are tired of seeing me hunting high-fence ranches, and I'm tired of filming them. I want to get back to what my uncle Cal taught me, the skills I learned from him in the field—"

"Before you had boobs," Braden interjects.

I chuckle, grateful for some levity, no matter how small.

"Exactly. The boobs are part of the problem at this point. So filming a solo hunt, DIY, on public lands, is the best chance I have to save my show. If it doesn't work—meaning either I screw up or it doesn't impress the programming head at Afield"—I pause and tip my eyes skyward—"then I'm getting paid to go topless."

Braden jerks his head my way, frowning. "Ending up on a stripper pole sounds like an extreme outcome to losing your show. Try putting in an application at Cabela's first. Pretty sure they'd hire you."

"I'd be hella good at the gun counter," I return drily. "But I didn't mean stripping. It's this reality show that's been calling my manager for a few months. They're filming a show down in Mexico and want me to join the cast as a sportfishing guide. The topless part was a joke because some girl's bikini top always goes missing on those shows. But if another season of *Record Racks* doesn't get picked up, then that's my next best option."

The grill top slams shut with a loud clang. Braden leans over to shut off the propane, and despite his craning down, I still see his jaw flexing tight.

"I highly doubt some crappy reality show is your next best option. Like I said, try Cabela's. Bass Pro Shops. Shit, any no-name sporting goods store from here to Austin would be happy to give you a name tag."

Braden then points the tongs directly at me. I raise my brows at the gesture. He clicks the tongs together a few times, leveling them on me in a challenge.

"But it isn't going to matter anyway. Because if anyone can make this hunt a success, it's you. You're smart, you bust your ass, and you know what you're doing. Even if you don't kill an elk, just show them what you show me when you think I might be underestimating you. Do that and you'll still have a show. A show that *I'd* watch."

Braden draws his tongs down and lowers his voice.

"Even if how I feel about you isn't at all what it was when we met, my feelings on hunting shows haven't changed. If these pricks at the Afield Channel don't get why you're worth the airtime, then fuck them. You hear me? Fuck. Them."

I nod my head jerkily, overwhelmed by the conviction in Braden's voice. I didn't realize how badly I needed that pep talk—from *him*. The same words from Trey or Teagan, Colin or Jaxon, wouldn't have had the same effect.

"Yeah? Fuck them?" he goads.

I nod again, more certain now. "Fuck them."

"Good. Now, let's eat. I'm hungry." He stomps off. The back door thwacks shut when he saunters inside, leaving me alone on the patio.

I take a deep breath and stare at the now-closed door. Braden seems to truly want this success for me, even when there was confusion in his eyes just now that made it clear he doesn't understand why anyone would want it in the first place.

Braden may love the outdoors the way I do, and after last night, I'm confident that he certainly *likes* me, but there's no question that this part of my life will never make sense to him. If tomorrow we try to say goodbye, then look at each other and realize that goodbye just won't do, my job might always be something Braden accepts but never embraces—the same way his wretched ex tried to do with his work as a hotshot. We all know how *that* turned out.

Even so, I'm still grateful for the pep talk, despite his rude departure. In truth, though, I like Braden's brand of rude, I think. It's the sort that keeps me on my toes and makes it so I feel well within my rights to keep him on *his* toes.

Braden—tough-love pep talks and rude exits included—whether he knows it or not, just gave me exactly what I need to get through the next few months.

~⁓

In the morning, I get my turn to set the pace. Finally.

And it is *so* worth the wait.

Unfortunately, morning also brings along with it a few too many grown-up realities. Things like long drives to the airport, plane tickets back to Austin, and the unspoken possibility that this may the last time Braden and I see each other. We manage to ignore those realities until Braden is loading my bags into the trunk of the rental car and jabbering on about the particulars of me crashing here while he's gone.

"I'll leave the hide-a-key out back, under that cinder block by the grill. Don't worry about putting it back when you go, just lock the door and leave it inside on the table. Charley will be with me, but you might see my neighbor from down the road around with her dogs. She's going to bring my mail up and water the garden for me unless we get a cold snap and everything freezes before I leave."

I nod almost robotically, watching him rearrange the bags in the trunk, lining them up neatly side by side—for no reason whatsoever, other than to keep from shutting the trunk lid, which will bring us one step closer to me leaving.

"Don't worry about buying any groceries, just eat whatever you want from here. Plenty of meat in the freezer, and if the garden's still kicking, harvest what looks good." He finally slams the trunk shut, then immediately shoves his hands in his pockets. "I'll make a batch of those millet energy bars before I leave and put them in the freezer for you. Did you like the figs? If not, I can make them with something else, maybe cranberries or cherries. Just promise me you'll eat them. Take a selfie with one of those shitty bars for your Instagram if you have to, but don't *eat* it, OK?"

My answer is an eye roll, partly out of instinct and partly because my eyeballs feel weird. Weird in a watery, emotional way because he's going to make special energy bars for me and I want to kiss him all over and stay here instead of going home.

"And promise me you'll stay safe. Hunt hard but drink plenty of water, watch your footing, and make good decisions. Be sure you don't set your pack down and walk away; you'll lose track of it in the—"

"Oh my God, *stop*," I blurt out.

He's just fucking talking—about everything and nothing, at the same time—to avoid the inevitable. I pinch the bridge of my nose with two fingers and take a long breath. Exhaling, I open my eyes to find a slightly startled Braden studying my face.

"I do not need a lecture on the basics of outdoor safety. I'm a very competent woman and a very capable hunter."

Braden fumbles over a protest, claiming he knows exactly how capable I am, but I carry on right over him. I *know* he knows that—I just needed him to knock it off with the pointless chatter.

"I hate that you won't be here when I come back, Braden. Hate it. If I didn't understand what it's like to spend multiple seasons chasing one specific buck, I'd try to convince you to change your plans. But I do understand, so I'm just going to wish you good luck. Now please kiss me goodbye."

Braden's jaw drops open a fraction, then he sets his teeth to his bottom lip and leans in, slipping his hands into my hair, and the demanding way he pulls me to him turns my insides into a muddled-up mess of disappointment and need. Braden skates his lips over mine until I'm teetering on the edge of a whimper, then offers up a goodbye kiss that makes leaving feel nearly impossible.

I break the kiss before he does, not because I want to—because I have to. Braden keeps his hands in my hair and tips his forehead to mine with a sigh.

Finally, he leans back and shoves his hands into his pants pockets, then pulls them out and holds them open for me. A pair of blue lapis earrings are in one hand, and a matching necklace is in the other.

"I bid on these at the silent auction. They're for you."

I volley my eyes between his face and his palms. He looks nervous, which is making *me* nervous. I want to say the right thing, not only because they're beautiful and just my style, but because I want him to know how much these few days with him have meant to me.

"Braden," I sigh. "Thank you."

I wrap my hands over his and he releases a held breath.

"Not sure what I'm going to do if this is the end of the road for us, Amber. Tell me this doesn't have to be all there is. I know there are a hundred different reasons this probably can't work, but I don't really give a shit. We don't have to make any promises—just say this isn't it."

My body replies with a sharp swell of relief that works its way up from my belly, through my heart, and meets my lips with a grin. Last night after his rousing pep talk, I imagined this moment. I wished for it, really—and this morning, nothing has changed. Here I was, about to drive away from the best sex I've ever had, with a great guy who is better than most I've ever known, potentially leaving behind what could have been the beginning of something more. Now I don't have to.

"No promises? I'm not sure I like that." I say slowly, tilting my head and locking my eyes on Braden's. He doesn't nod or flinch; he simply takes my gaze and meets it with his own. I lean in a fraction.

"Let's make one promise, OK? Just one. That we ignore all the reasons this can't work . . . and see if we can figure out a good reason it *will* work."

Braden nods, a short and sharp gesture that would be more appropriate between two warring military generals than two people who just decided they want more than a few nights together. A shadow of relief follows, creeping across his face until he's nearly smiling.

"One reason, then," Braden says. "Easy enough, right?"

19

(Braden)

"And after all, there lies the soul of the sport. The fragrance of
the earth, the deep purple valleys, the wooded mountain
slopes, the clean sweet wind, the mysterious murmur
of the tree tops, all call the hunter forth."
—Saxton Pope, *Hunting with the Bow and Arrow*

Every year near the end of August, I can be found here, on the
two hundred acres in Central Oregon that my parents have owned
since they were first married in the '70s. The forested land and its
accompanying fairy-tale-worthy cabin was their one-year anniversary gift to each other, knowing it would be the perfect place for
two academics to spend their summers, noses buried in whatever
research project occupied their thoughts.

Continuing to spend every summer here after I was born
meant that once I was old enough, a weird little kid like me could
easily lose himself in the woods for hours at a time. Add in parents
who believed in free-range parenting before it was an actual thing,
and this land is where I came to understand risk by crossing rush-

ing streams and climbing trees, and learned patience by lying in wait for rabbits to emerge from their burrows.

When I wasn't busy doing that, I was reading. Jim Kjelgaard books were my gateway drug to adventure, and I devoured every story he wrote about boys and their dogs, game wardens, and hunters and trappers—every word felt like it had been written for me and about me. I begged for a .22 rifle when I was eleven years old and my liberal-but-libertarian parents indulged me, with the caveat that they needed some assurance I would be safe. After a few lessons in firearm safety at a local gun range, I was all in. Learning to hunt came with an endless number of challenges, ones I didn't always overcome, but when I did, every success made the next challenge all the more tempting—which is what, to this day, always brings me back to these woods.

After a two-day drive, I spent yesterday scouting the spots where I already have tree stands, trying to determine which would be the best one to set up in today, based on what fresh sign of deer I could find in the area. I woke up this morning with what I'm convinced is a foolproof plan, and with that, everything is just as it should be.

I'm perched in my favorite tree stand, a gentle wind is in my favor, and here in this infinitesimally small part of the universe, the world is nearly silent. Back at the cabin, there's a batch of antelope chili in the slow cooker, a case of Coors in the fridge, and my dog is waiting for me.

Everything is *exactly* as it should be.

So I shouldn't wish I were anywhere other than right here, right now. I definitely shouldn't wish I were back home in Hotchkiss where Amber is. I shouldn't be worrying or wondering about her, or stewing over the possibility she might need something. But no matter how hard I try, my body is the only thing that's here. My heart and my mind are elsewhere.

A heavy sigh escapes me, loud enough to spoil the invisibility offered by my camo, my face paint, and my position high above the ground. A fact confirmed by the buck that just wandered into the opening below, who immediately tilts his head at the sound, locking his eyes on the lovesick idiot sitting in a tree. As if being spotted isn't bad enough, when the buck lifts his head to study me, I spy a set of distinctive markings on his chest.

Christ. That's *my* buck. The one I've been chasing in these woods for three seasons.

The same one who is now off to live another day, bounding through the brush to clear a downed tree with one graceful leap. He disappears into a cluster of pines, and it suddenly feels like this season is over almost before it starts.

~⁀~

When the sun dips low enough on the horizon to signal that dusk isn't far off, I crawl out of my tree stand and start the trek back to the cabin. The end of my day followed the same script as the start, with my mind wandering and all the deer in the area acting as if I was nothing but a pitiable distraction to their safe, pastoral lives.

By the time I step out from a thick bank of trees and onto the rough two-track we use to access our land, I'm exhausted—even when there's no good reason for it. All I've done today is sit on my ass in a tree stand, and other than fussing about a woman who is hundreds of miles away, nothing else raised my heart rate beyond that of a sedentary sloth. While some archery hunts are physical enough to rival a Spartan race, this was not one of those days. Even so, when I spot the cabin's chimney peeking over the tops of the trees surrounding it, my feet become impossibly heavy. The dirt road curves lazily toward the front of the house, but when I round the last bend, I draw up short because the front porch light is on, as are most of the lights inside the house—none of which is how I left it this morning. Either the Grimms' fairy-tale qualities of the cabin drew in a Goldilocks, or one of my parents is here.

The answer is parked next to my truck. A twenty-year-old Subaru wagon that probably hasn't been vacuumed out or properly washed since I left home, more than likely has potting soil and fern fronds littering the floorboards, and definitely needs the last remnants of the *Ralph Nader for President '96* sticker scraped off the liftgate glass.

I pause on the porch to take off my boots, picking up the faint sound of a James Taylor song playing inside, off of an album I heard so many times as a kid that when I was eight, I went through a short-lived phase in which I wanted to be a folk singer. Then I discovered BB guns. I'm sure the music world still considers my change of heart a huge loss.

Opening the door as quietly as possible, I greet Charley with only a low murmur and a scruff behind the ears. My mom showing up here unexpectedly means she needs the unique solitude this place provides, signaling that she's either trying to finish a scientific paper or wading her way through the initial draft of one. Either way, other than James's crooning, she requires peace and quiet to get through it.

The timer on the oven buzzes loudly the second I finish saying hello to my dog, and I curse the sound on Mom's behalf as I start toward the kitchen.

"Corn bread," Mom announces from the far side of the living room.

She's sequestered behind her writing desk, everything but the graying blonde hair on top of her head obscured by towering stacks of books and two large ferns in black plastic pots that sit on either corner of the limited workspace. Her research work at the university in Corvallis is on plant phylogenetics, specifically those with polyploid lineages. Translation: she knows *a lot* about ferns. Oddly enough, with the exception of her ferns, she's no green thumb. My dad and I basically had to eighty-six her from getting within five feet of the family garden, because things seemed to wilt in her mere presence. I suspect the tomatoes and cucumbers didn't like being stared at in the way my mom tends to scrutinize plants.

After shutting off the timer, I grab a pot holder and pull out the cast-iron skillet of golden-brown corn bread, setting it down on a burner so I can pierce the center with a knife tip, turning the oven off after determining everything is cooked through. The chili in the slow cooker is more than ready since it's been on low for eight hours, so I clear off the small table in the kitchen and set out dinnerware for two.

Charley gets a dish of her kibble, and then I serve myself some chili, along with a big slice of the corn bread on the side. I twist open the band on the mason jar of honey Mom carts along everywhere with her, dipping a spoon into the dark, slightly cloudy amber nectar that's straight from my Dad's hives, then drizzle a dollop over my corn bread. I dig into my dinner, knowing Mom will join me when she's ready. The only dining rule in the Montgomery family is that there are no rules. People eat when they're hungry, make conversation when they want to, or read at the table if it suits them—and no one gets their nose out of joint about any of it.

Just as I'm finishing my dinner, she strides into the kitchen and pours herself a glass of wine from the bottle I opened for her, fully expecting that she would want some with dinner. She dishes up and sits down at the table across from me, takes a few bites before exhaling slowly. A sip of her wine. Finally, she looks directly at me, tucks a few wayward curls of her short hair behind her ears, and removes her reading glasses to set them aside on the table.

"Hi."

I grin and return her perfunctory greeting. Mom is notoriously compartmentalized, shifting gears between her roles as academic, wife, and parent so intentionally it's like watching someone close then open a garage door. The upside is that when she's with you, she's truly with you, and her attention never strays until it's time to change roles again.

Mom proceeds to slop two spoonfuls of honey on her corn bread. I cast a glare at the action.

"Don't start," she warns. "It's honey, not plutonium."

"It's still sugar. Cancer likes sugar, thrives on it. And with the way you dump that stuff into your tea all day and then—"

My rant comes to a halt when she dips into the pint jar again, scoops up *another* spoonful, and proceeds to shove the whole thing in her mouth.

I curl up my lip. "That's gross."

She ensures the spoon is clean before pointing it at me. "I love you. Please shut up about the honey." She drops the spoon to the table with a clang. "Did you have any luck today?"

Answering her with a grunt, I shrug a shoulder and stare at my beer bottle. Silence follows, and I start to reconsider my half-assed answer. She won't press, so if I want to talk this out, it will fall to me to pick up the conversation again.

"You know how I feel about luck," I mutter. "But luck or not, it wouldn't have mattered. My head wasn't in the game today."

"Why was that?"

"I just . . ." I peer up to find her gaze has turned assessing, and I start to understand how those tomatoes in our garden must have felt. She tilts her head slightly and softens her expression, Mom-style, and I wilt a little more inside.

"Is it because you're here when Amber's in Colorado?"

Well, shit. That made things easy. My having written about

Amber in my letters meant I didn't have to figure out how to mutter my way through saying exactly what Mom just did. I labor through a dramatic exhale, blowing it out from one side of my mouth.

"I can't keep my mind on track. I keep worrying about her, which is stupid because, like I've mentioned, she's about as expert as they come in the field. She doesn't need me, so it's annoying that I can't focus on anything else."

Mom takes a few more bites of her chili, still studying me as she does. Finally, she sets her spoon down and leans forward a few inches, intently enough to send me slouching down in my chair by the same measure. I may have gotten my bulk from Dad's side of the family, but Mom more than makes up for her slight frame with her eyes: dark brown and downright dogged when they're fixed on you.

"Have you considered that her needing you—or not—isn't what this is about?"

I narrow my eyes and answer flatly. "No, Professor Montgomery. But I'm not sure I want to hear your theory on what it *is* about."

Mom offers a patient smile, in the way parents do when they're about to offer an adult child some uncomfortable life lesson they probably thought they'd outgrown hearing.

"You're selfish, Braden."

Yup, here it comes. I could claim that her declaring I'm selfish stings, but it doesn't. I'm perfectly aware that I can be an autonomous, selfish asshole sometimes.

"That being said, I'm selfish, too. So is your father. Human beings in general trend toward selfishness. We all have to work at selflessness."

She takes a sip of her wine then pauses, and I find myself squirming in my chair. There are certain types of honesty that inevitably inspire a desire to take cover, and right now that means I vaguely want to crawl under the fucking table.

"Laurel never challenged you. Up until the end, she rarely asked anything of you—or at least nothing of significance. But Amber is different. She challenges you at every turn, and you've found yourself considering her in ways you're not used to. For the first time in your life, you want to be there for someone else. Not because she *needs* you to, but because you can't imagine otherwise."

I furrow my brow and think on what she's just proposed. It doesn't take long to figure out that what she's said makes sense. It also doesn't take long to find myself counting the days between now and the end of elk season back home—or to realize that if I hit the road and make good time, I might be able to help Amber finish out the last half of her hunt.

Mom finishes her chili while I continue to think. When she's done, she stacks our empty dishes together, patting my hand with hers before rising to head for the sink.

"Don't leave tonight. She'll be OK. Go to bed and then head home in the morning."

20

(Amber)

"A deep chesty bawl echoes from rimrock to rimrock, rolls
down the mountain, and fades into the far blackness of
the night. It is an outburst of wild defiant sorrow, and
of contempt for all the adversities of the world."
—ALDO LEOPOLD, *A SAND COUNTY ALMANAC*

Decision time.

I glance at the midafternoon sky and try to calculate how
many remaining hours of good light I can hope for today. About
four, I'm guessing. More than enough time to put a stalk on the
bull elk that's appeared in the draw below me. All I need to do is
pack up my spotting scope, grab my bow, and work my way down
from the high ridgeline I've been perched on for the last four
hours. Once I climb the next draw, I can then drop down into
position near the watering hole I know this bull must be headed
to. I've watched two young raghorn bulls plus a few still-single
ladies make their way over there already today. This big guy and
his harem of cows are bound to take the same trail, I'm sure of it.

So long as I keep my steps steady but quick—and that elk continues to take his sweet time meandering around and bugling like a moronic frat boy catcalling on spring break—I'll make it to the watering hole long before he finally arrives.

Elk are in the rut this time of year, so bulls are consumed by the need to breed, single-mindedly doing whatever it takes to attract all the cows they can and show dominance over any other bull in the vicinity. This guy already has a decent-sized harem, but that doesn't stop him from giving up a loud, squealing grunt every ten steps and rubbing his body across each pine tree he passes by to leave his scent, all so he can add yet *another* cow to the group.

Bull elk. They're controlling, mouthy, narcissistic, belligerent, and totally unfaithful. What a catch, right? It's a good thing they have biology working in their favor.

The bull comes to a stop, draws his head down and arches his back, then lets out another ear piercing bugle. The sound is beautiful and obnoxious, wild and ancient—and it also sounds like he's taunting me.

That's it. I'm going after him. This will work, I know it. Just so long as everything works in my favor.

Unfortunately, that right there is the problem. Not much of *anything* has gone my way so far. I spent the first two days of my hunt trying not to puke or pass out from an unexpected bout with altitude sickness, and the following two days on what felt like a never-ending nature hike for the sheer lack of elk. I finally picked up and moved my camp on day five. A good decision it seemed, because that afternoon I heard what sounded like a nice mature bull bugling in a thatch of dark timber below my tent. I hustled my way through a deep draw nearby and proceeded to spend the next forty-five minutes luring him my way using a reed-based cow call, only to have him suddenly go silent and then seemingly disappear entirely.

After that, I decided it was time for a reboot—and a shower—so I spent the night at Braden's. Lying in his bed last night, I could practically hear him giving me a stern, well-timed pep talk, and I woke up this morning ready to tackle the mountain again.

After stowing away my spotting scope and cinching down my pack, I use my binoculars to make one last pass over the area, sweeping them over the bull and his harem, who are now up and on the move. As the crow flies, there are probably a good two miles between where I am now and where I need to be, but with the wide berth I'll need to maintain so the elk don't scent me along the way and terrain that doesn't offer a straight shot to my destination, I have one hell of a climb ahead of me. And standing here thinking about that doesn't get me any closer. Bow in hand, I settle on a route and start to hustle in that direction.

Here goes nothing.

An hour and a half later, I finally reach the water hole, finding the area surrounding it a little more exposed than I expected, so my options are limited when it comes to cover. But after ducking under a low tree limb, I spot a small boulder that will work. The rock is big enough to provide cover but low enough that when I'm ready, I can rise up on my knees and have a clean shot into the clearing that lies twenty yards beyond. Doing my best to keep from snapping too many of the dry twigs scattered on the ground, I hunker down behind it and remove my pack then adjust the action cam mounted to my hat, cursing the damn thing for all its awkwardness.

When I see Colin again, I'm going to throw myself into his arms and smooch his cheeks until he blushes tomato red. I will never take his expert cameraman skills or his human packhorse qualities for granted ever again. And as for all those luxury ranch hunts I thought I was so tired of? After this trip, some overpriced pampering and a little five-star cuisine sounds pretty damn good.

Solo hunt. DIY. Public lands. In arid, high-altitude Colorado. Stupid, stupid idea. Muttering under my breath, I swear to myself I am never doing this again—and even if I know I'm lying, it's a soothing thought in the moment.

I drop down and sit back on my heels, bow in hand so I can nock an arrow in preparation. Based on the growing sound of his bugles, the bull and his harem aren't far off. I can hear my breath and it's too wild, so I tell myself to calm down and forget everything but staying invisible. But my skin is slicked with sweat from the near-trail-run pace I kept in order to get here and after just a few minutes in this position, I think my right foot is starting to fall asleep. No time to adjust my perch or strip off a layer of clothing, though, because a series of bugles pierces the air, followed by tree limbs falling and bark coming loose in the wake of my elk's approach. I hold my breath for a moment, waiting to see or hear him. I know he's close; I can *smell* him. Earthy and ripe, the presence of elk in the rut has its own distinctive scent, one that in large doses is pungent enough to make your eyes water.

When he steps into my sight line, I freeze. All I can see is the tip of his snout, but that's enough to turn my breath wild and rushed again. Adrenaline takes over, drowning out everything but the rush of blood I can hear pounding in my ears. He steps forward again and stops, raising his head to rotate his ears, listening as best he can. A few beats pass, and he relaxes his posture.

Come on, come on, come on. Five more yards. That's all it will take.

He raises one hoof, gingerly taking one new step. Slowly, I rise up on my knees and raise my bow, watching his movements as I question whether to draw the bow now or wait a few more seconds. Once I'm at full draw, I want to spend as little time as possible holding that position before triggering the release and sending my arrow, staving off the fatigue that will eventually cause my arm to shake. If I'm there too long and my form starts to break down, I may have to abandon the shot altogether.

The bull prepares to take another slow step, and I know this is my chance. I draw back and center my sights, curling the tip of my index finger around the release so that when it's time, only a small squeeze will set it off. All I need now is for the bull to take that final step.

But suddenly, his head lifts. His ears prick up as his nostrils begin to flare.

And then I feel it. A tiny breeze working in from behind me, skating past my ear, and downwind from there. Straight into the snout of the seven-hundred-pound beast with the epic olfactory senses, who immediately takes two steps backward. His head swivels from side to side, seeking out what he scents as unfamiliar, predatory, and out of place.

When he pauses and fixes his gaze in my direction, I see the glossy shine of his coal-colored eyes, and it feels like he's staring directly at me, but I can't say that's the truth. It doesn't matter, anyway. Because he's already gone, disappearing back the way he came, bumped into action by one squirrelly moment of shifting wind.

I let down my bow and sink back onto my heels, all my earlier adrenaline waning into something sticky and suffocating. Something that goes beyond frustration. Beyond disappointment. Beyond defeat.

Failure.

~

By the time I make it back to my camp, it's dark. The moon is only a sliver in the sky, but the stars cut a bright swath above.

With darkness came the cold and now the sweat on my skin feels like shaved ice melting under my clothes.

As soon as my headlamp illuminates camp just ahead of me, I quicken my steps and immediately off-load my pack inside the tent. I know I should take a few minutes to make a short video diary entry about the failed stalk from this afternoon, so the experience of it all remains fresh, but it's *too* fresh, and I don't have it in me to hear my own voice as I retell it for an audience.

Headlamp still on, I zip up the tent and trudge the seventy yards to get to the tree where I've slung a rope over a high limb and tied a bear-proof bag to it. While this isn't major bear country, it's always better to take a few precautions when it comes to keeping Yogi and Boo Boo out of your camp. Untying the end of the rope from the trunk, I give it some slack so the bag slips down from where it was hanging about twenty feet in the air.

Once it's down, I survey my choices for dinner: freeze-dried chili mac, freeze-dried beef stroganoff, freeze-dried lasagna, or freeze-dried beef stew. So many sodium-laced, gummy, depressing delicacies to choose from. Unfortunately, they all pretty much taste like the same bad lunch-line slop I remember from my elementary school days, so I grab the bag that's on top and let fate decide for me.

Stroganoff it is.

The bear bag goes back up into the air and I head back to camp, knowing that I shouldn't cook near or eat in my tent just in case a Yogi Bear does decide to wander by, but I'm willing to take the risk tonight. I set up my backpacking stove—essentially a miniature fuel canister set on a tiny tripod with a small cooking pot attached to the top—and, using what's left in my water bottle, fill the pot and then light the burner.

It takes only a few minutes for a pot of water to reach full boil, but when you're beat down, hungry, and tired, time doesn't pass the way it should. To keep from letting those too-long minutes eat away at what sanity I have left, I use the time to snap a picture so I can post an update on social media, using my headlamp to light a shot of just my boots and the camp stove on the ground.

Dinner. After this, sleep. More miles to put on tomorrow.
#hunting #longday #neverquit #coloradoelk #worththeclimb #grateful #stayingstrong

Decent signal strength means I don't have to go wandering around with my arm stretched above my head to post the pic, saving me from questioning whether I believe half of what I just hashtagged. After today, I can't say if I have a clue what I'm doing out here. Maybe the skills I thought I had were nothing but a delusion created to convince myself I could do this.

The water comes to a boil, so I shut off the burner and tear off the top of the freeze-dried meal's pouch and prop it open on the ground to carefully pour the water in. With my dinner in hand, I head inside the tent and set the pouch off to one side so it can steep in the hot water as directed. *Add water. Wait nine to ten minutes. Stir. Enjoy!*

Sure. Enjoy. That's not a reach at all.

Quickly, I take my boots, my coat, and my brush pants off, then crawl into my sleeping bag in my base layer gear and wool socks, sitting cross-legged so I can set my dinner in my lap. I take a deep breath and relish in the relief that a little warmth can bring about.

But after only a moment, I realize that a strange hissing sound is competing with my deep breathing. I dart my gaze around the small tent. Not the hiss of an animal or a snake. Not the sound of my dinner "cooking." And since the wind has already been sucked out of my emotional sails, I can't blame this noise on that.

I peer down at my lap, now noting how my body seems to be . . . *sinking*.

Oh, come *on*. No. This can't be happening. The universe cannot be this cruel; it isn't possible.

But it is, apparently. Because my sleeping pad—the one-inch cloud of comfort I dragged up here in my backpack, then spent a good fifteen minutes blowing up puff by puff when I set up camp, and is the only thing between me and the rock-hard ground when I sleep—apparently has a fucking *hole* in it.

I'm sure there's a rock somewhere that's to blame, but who knows. All I know is that now, I have the distinct pleasure of feeling every rock beneath me as each one digs into my back tonight.

Now, to those who've never slept in the backcountry, this might seem like a minor setback. Not worthy of the jaw-clenching, guttural groan I just let out or the dizzy sensation of uncontrollable anger that's clouding my vision a little. But for those of us who have spent multiple nights afield, we understand that there are small luxuries you come to rely on when regular-world comforts are miles away—and without them, you can easily start to lose perspective on *everything*.

If this weren't a solo hunt, and if I weren't slowly working over my very last nerve, this would be one of those moments that Teagan and Colin and I would laugh ourselves stupid over. Teagan would have heard the hissing first, widened her eyes, and waited until Colin heard it, too. Colin would make a predictably male joke about musical fruits or toxic gases, or *something*, until fatigue and stupidity would have us all in tears from laughing so hard.

But without them the humor is hard to find. Suddenly, I feel impossibly, utterly, entirely alone. More than merely lonely. More than solitary. Alone.

When the last of the air seeps out from my precious sleeping pad, all I want is someone here, with me, because I miss everyone in my life so deeply it feels like my heart is about to crack open. Trey and Jaxon, Teagan and Colin. My parents. My uncle Cal. I miss them all.

And Braden? I miss him, too.

Because Braden understands this life better than anyone. He would remind me that this isn't bad luck, because luck is for suckers. Out here, hard work is all I have—and the only thing I can control.

Wild, unruly frustration begins to rush though me, tension coiling in my chest so tightly that the tent becomes too small to breathe in. I haul myself out of my sleeping bag, yank on the tent zipper, and crawl out so I can stand under the near moonless sky. The cold beneath my feet feels damp, and even through my socks, that sensation roots my body to the dirt.

I ball my hands into fists, tip my head back, and stare at the blanket of stars above me, my breath curling into the cold air as nothing but silence surrounds me.

Alone means no one will hear me.

One long breath in through my nose. I hold it, then close my eyes.

Then I scream my weary little heart out.

21

(Braden)

"What business have I in the woods, if I am thinking of
something out of the woods?"
—Henry David Thoreau, "Walking"

After almost two days on the road, last night I finally made it
home, completely exhausted from the long drive. When I walked
inside, evidence of Amber having crashed here was scattered about,
from her thank-you note on the kitchen table to the empty peach
Snapple bottle she left sitting beside it, likely giggling to herself
when she did. In my bedroom, I found one of my T-shirts neatly
folded at the foot of my bed and—since I've apparently become a
total fucking nut job—I actually *sniffed* it. Strawberries, of course.

Once I skulked through the house like I was on an Amber-
themed scavenger hunt, I dropped into bed and crashed for a
good ten hours. All my restlessness, and the disquiet I couldn't
shake when I was in Oregon, feels long gone when I wake up.

Maybe using the Amber-scented T-shirt she left on my bed as my own personal pillow sachet helped. If so, then *Mr. Creeper, party of one? Your table is ready.*

It was too late to text her when I got in last night, but it's all I can think about the moment my eyes open this morning. I drag my phone off the nightstand and shoot her a message.

I'm back in town. Need help?

Her reply takes a bit, but just as I start to drift off into another strawberry-induced slumber, my phone beeps.

What? You're back? You filled your tag already? You are SUCH a
show-off. I want to punch you . . . or maybe do other things to you.
I'm not sure. DO NOT GLOAT. I'm too tired to deal with that.

A sleepy grin slinks across my face. Feisty *and* frustrated. A combustible combination that would make for a good time if she were in my bed instead of on a mountain. I tap out a reply.

No gloating. Decided to come home early. Send me your coordinates.
I'll come help you.

I start to worry when five minutes pass. Then ten minutes. Eventually, twenty minutes, then just as it nears thirty, she replies.

I want your help . . . I do. And if you'd texted me yesterday, I would
have taken you up on the offer. But I can't. I have to finish this out on
my own.

A string of sad-faced, teardrop-soaked emojis follow the last sentence. Everything in my chest sinks and what feels like rejection stings. Deeply enough that the selfish jerk inside me wants to fire off a rant about *my* hunt, the one I sacrificed, all to come home to *her*. Followed by a guilt trip about the vacation days I save up every year for, which I'm now going to spend stuck in my house, crawling the walls.

But I count to ten and take a deep breath, all to keep from doing anything stupid. Reason wins out when I finally start to type.

> If you change your mind, text me. I'll keep my phone on. And keep me updated. I want to know you're safe.

Her reply?

More fucking emojis.

⌒

Well, there it is. A new low.

Charley is pissed at me.

Not that I can blame her, really. Too many days spent around the house, fussing like a cranky toddler while trying to keep busy but available just in case Amber reaches out, means I've become the worst version of my already-prickly self. Poor Charley normally acts as a salve to my disposition, but even her furry charms can't salvage my current mood. She's kept to her bed for most of the day while giving me some seriously ticked-off side-eyes. So much for unconditional love. New low. Seriously.

Launching up from the chair, I toss the book I'm reading onto the side table and set off for the kitchen to check on the wild turkey carnitas I have braising in the oven.

I spent all day yesterday trying to decide what to make for dinner today, because it's the last day of season and Amber will be off the mountain no matter what. Based on the updates she's sent me, she's had a tough time finding elk, and when she finally did find a decent bull, a change in the wind blew her chances. But she's determined to hunt straight through until the last minute, and short of a scenario in which she shoots an elk late in the day, she'll still be here for dinner, and I want to be sure she has comfort food waiting for her. Something other than the freeze-dried meals she's been subsiding on, because after a long hunt you're too tired to cook but all you want is real food. Knowing that, I went into town earlier and picked up some corn tortillas, avocado, red onion, and sour cream at the store so we can use the tender shredded meat to make tacos, then grabbed a six-pack of a Mexican beer to go with it.

After taking a look at the carnitas, I set the lid back on the cast-iron pot and shut the oven door, then grab a few dog biscuits from the pantry in hopes I can buy back Charley's affection by plying her with snacks. The rattle of the box is enough to get her attention and she skitters into the kitchen, tail wagging and all her grievances long forgotten. If only biscuits worked this sort of magic with people.

My phone beeps just as Charley nudges her snout to my hand and I slip her the biscuit while digging my phone out of my pocket with my free hand. I swipe open the text, knowing it's Amber and hoping she has good news.

> Packing up camp and heading out. I had a good bull at 30 yards. I missed.

"Shit," I wince.

That is not good news. She missed. At *thirty* yards.

For an archery hunter, yardage is everything. Without the luxury of the firepower that comes with rifle hunting, hunting with a compound bow demands a closer range. Experienced hunters will sometimes take a shot on an elk at fifty yards if everything is perfect, but most of us feel far more comfortable at half that range. Thirty yards, though, is a sweet spot—close enough to help ensure shot consistency but far enough to stay undetected. You can't ask for much more when it comes to the spot-and-stalk scenarios of elk hunting.

That being said, we all miss. It doesn't matter how much you practice, how much you commit, how well you normally shoot. We all miss. Sometimes we miss for reasons we can explain—poor form with your bow or shitty follow-through when you take your shot—but sometimes we miss even when everything seems to have gone the way it should. *Those* are the worst. You'll replay the moment a million times over, trying to figure what went wrong and why, blaming the wind, your bad luck—or yourself. It will drive you out of your mind if you let it.

Which is why I'm already in my truck, headed for the trailhead. I want to be there when Amber arrives, even if all I can offer as comfort is me.

~

Amber emerges three hours later, burdened by her pack and what looks like the weight of the world given the sag of her shoulders. She sways a little as she takes the last few steps down trail, lurching to an unsteady stop when her feet meet the asphalt of the trailhead parking lot. When she sees me, I have to fight the urge to barrel over there, wrestle the pack from her body, and then carry her back to my truck.

Once she gathers what may be the last lump of resolve she can muster, she strides my way, stopping ten feet away from me, all of her features rigid and tethered. The message is clear: now is not the time for coddling. I attempt to look casual, even when I'm anything but, leaning against the side of my truck with my forearm resting on the top of the bedside, hoping she doesn't notice the way my hand is balled into a fist.

"Hey."

"Hi," Amber returns flatly.

The game warden in me asks the one question I need to. "Was it a clean miss?"

"Clean miss. It landed in the dirt about ten inches away from his front hooves. He probably thought it was a skinny tree limb that broke off in front of him." She raises a weary fist pump. "Yay for that, I guess."

No response in the world would be right, so I keep my mouth shut. Amber's arm wilts down and swings at her side.

"I've had seven miles to think. I don't want to think anymore, Braden. I want you to take me home, feed me, fuck me, put me in a warm bath, and make it all go away for a bit. Can you do that?"

I lift a brow. "In that order? Because I'm thinking warm bath first, food second, and then the fucking. You've been without running water for days, and even if I can't smell you from here, you have to reek. Probably best to address that first. But I am open to switching up the order of the food and fucking."

I'm rewarded with a tired smile. Amber's shoulders sag again, but in relief this time.

"I can't tell you how much I love that you get it. All of this. You are the only face I wanted to see right now. Because you *get it.*"

I try to hide the way her words hit me square in the gut, how much I want to take all her troubles away. Instead, I approach her slowly, unbuckle the waist strap on her pack, loosen the shoulder straps, and gently work the pack from her shoulders. She lets me, without putting up a fight or a protest. I set her pack in the bed of my truck. Taking her face in my hands, I put a kiss to her forehead, and Amber slips her hands around my waist with a sigh.

"Now let's get you home and into that bath, mountain sprite. I was right. You *reek*."

～～

"I liked your house before, but now? I love it. I love this couch, especially." Amber uses one hand to tug up the wool blanket I draped over her earlier so it's bunched up under her chin. "And this blanket is the best blanket ever made. I'm also a fan of this T-shirt of yours that I'm wearing. And this pillow. And these socks you lent me."

One of her feet sneaks out from under the blanket and she wiggles it onto my lap. She's stretched out on her back, slumped against the arm while I sit in the center. I take her foot in my hands and rub gently, careful to keep my touch away from her ankle because I saw the blisters there when she stripped down to sink into the bath I drew for her.

I chuckle. "What about the three beers you drank? Are you a fan of those?"

"*Yes*," she drawls. She's not drunk, but she's limbered up, for sure. A hot bath helped her onto that path, and the comfort food and the beer only hastened her travels. Before I can offer up one other surefire suggestion for further relaxation, Amber is casting off the blanket and slithering onto my lap. Guess my suggestion would have been beside the point. Amber draws her hands up over my chest, across my shoulders, and links them behind my neck.

"Confession time," she says. I widen my eyes a fraction. She leans in and mock-whispers. "I already wore this shirt. When I was here before."

She's wearing the shirt I found folded up on my bed when I got home. It's cute on her, but equally enormous, so she's swimming in the fabric that hangs down nearly to her knees.

I lean in and whisper the same way she did. "I know."

Amber grins goofily and suddenly my entire world becomes nothing but the space between us, so I pull her closer and slide my hands up the back of the shirt. She's bare beneath—no bra, no panties—because when she stepped out of the bath, she wanted nothing but to dry off and eat, and so my shirt was as far as we got with clothing. Nothing but her warm, soft skin under my palms. Amber purrs a little, encouraging my hands to continue exploring, up her rib cage and lingering just below the swell of her tits. She tips our foreheads together and lines our lips up so she can speak against my mouth.

"Confession time again. But this one's on you." Amber's body presses closer to mine, her core meeting squarely with my dick, which responds by thickening beneath her. "Tell me something. Did you come home early just so you could help me?"

My breath catches. I hoped the second round of confession time would follow the format of the first, maybe something along the lines of Amber whispering all the wickedly hot things she did to herself while wearing my shirt and lying in my bed. Instead, she's calling me out on truths I'm not entirely comfortable owning—at least not out loud. My heart is beating wildly and heat is crawling up my neck, but when Amber whispers my name softly and rubs her pussy across the ridge of my cock, I give in.

"Yeah."

She purrs again, and this time it sounds like a thank-you. Especially when she follows up by sneaking her hands down to my waist and toying with my belt.

"And were you mad when I didn't take your help?"

I feel my belt slip loose, the button on my pants flick open, as Amber's fingers begin teasing over the zipper. Was I mad? Kind of. But if this is her way of making up for that, she's already forgiven.

"A little," I admit. "But not mad *at* you. Not really. I couldn't stop thinking about you and I wanted to help, make sure you were OK. It was frustrating that you wouldn't let me."

"I wanted to, so much. But I couldn't." She sighs. "I'm sorry that you missed out on *your* hunt, baby."

In the time she uttered those words, she's managed to unzip my pants and work my boxers down enough to take me in her hands. My head drops back to the couch when she twists her fist over the head with just the right amount of pressure.

"Nothing to be sorry about. I was where I wanted to be. Here—just in case."

When Amber lifts her body up, I know she's about to sink down on me at any second, and before she does, I have to use my non-beer-addled brain to make sure we're safe, so I take advantage of our position and slink my hand into my back pocket to extract my wallet. Grabbing the condom I stowed inside, I toss the wallet onto the couch. Amber snorts.

"I thought you didn't carry condoms in your wallet? That's what you said that day we ended up off trail."

The wrapper tears under my teeth and I send it to the ground before working the latex over my length.

"I didn't. And I don't, except when you're in town. I wasn't sure if you'd come down off the trail wanting a go, so I made sure to show up prepared."

Amber curves away to give me some room, watching as I stroke my hand down to the base a few times. Then she bats my hand away and doesn't delay, taking me deep in a slow push that forces my eyes shut, letting out a grunt from behind my teeth.

Once she's taken all of me, she leans back but doesn't move. I open my eyes, taking in the way she looks languid and already sated.

"I'm glad you came prepared. Too bad I could barely stand up, let alone have a go." She rolls her hips, slowly and just once. "But there is one thing I want from you that I decided while I was on the trail."

I wait for her to tell me what she wants. Every second that passes making it harder to keep from grabbing her hips and getting her to move the way I want her to, or just do the work myself and fuck straight up into her, hard and fast. She must see the frustration on my face because she tilts her head and starts to ride me in a slow rhythm.

"I want you to come visit me in Austin. Drive down, bring Charley, stay with me for a few days."

Whatever I thought she was going to say, that wasn't it. My body reacts by lighting up from the inside out, and it's a sensation I haven't felt in so long I can't be sure what's happening—if I'm simply falling for Amber in some new way or if this is merely a cardiac situation brought on by wanting to fuck her so hard she screams. Hell, maybe it's both.

"Will there be barbeque?" I ask. "The sort that proves your Texas superiority complex about brisket isn't just some statewide delusion?"

Amber tosses her head back on a laugh.

"Damn straight. One bite and you'll want to burn True Grit to the *ground*."

Her tits are moving gently under the T-shirt, and even if I might normally want to strip it off her so I can see, touch, and taste without anything in my way, in this moment, I want her just like this. She isn't trying to put on a show and neither am I; we're just two people caught up in the sweet intimacy of fucking someone you know and love, still half-dressed but not holding back. No bells or whistles, no lingerie or luxuries. Just her pussy taking my cock deep like she owns it and me not giving one fuck that she does.

I grab her hips to halt her. Amber whimpers.

I kiss her once. "Then count me in."

22

(Amber)

"I saw your face so clear and bright, I must have been crazy
but it sure felt right, I just wanted to see you so bad."
—LUCINDA WILLIAMS, "I JUST WANTED TO SEE YOU SO BAD"

If someone were to ask what my strengths are, a few things come
to mind.

Dependability. Persistence. Self-reliance.

One trait that doesn't make the list? Patience. Only when I'm in
the field doing whatever it takes to stay put and keep quiet does patience become me. In every other area of my life, I hate waiting—
especially for things I want. And right now, I want Braden.

He's due here at any moment, but after spending the last few
weeks apart, with only phone calls and texts to keep us connected,
I'm jonesing. Not to mention that I just turned in the final cut
of my elk hunt in all its unsuccessful glory to the programming
heads at the Afield Channel, and I desperately need a distraction

while we wait to hear back. The distraction I want is six five with sage-green eyes and an occasionally bad attitude I love figuring out how to make disappear.

I spent the morning cleaning up my house. Once that was in order, I set about prettying up my person—curling irons, razors, loofahs, and tweezers were involved—only to end up plopped on my couch in front of the television for the last hour. I'd hoped a little daytime TV might provide some mindless amusement, but instead I've found myself caught up in this soap opera, confused and full of questions.

First off, were soap operas always this poorly acted? Pretty sure I was a teenager the last time I sat through one of these, but I don't remember it being this bad. The story lines haven't changed much, though. Which begs the question: Why are people always stealing someone's baby? Taking care of a baby is hard work. How come they never steal their dog? Or their car? Their ATM PIN? Or all three? Put the dog in the car and drive to the ATM. Boom. You're golden until they shut off the account.

My imaginary crime spree comes to a halt when the sound I've been waiting for hits my front door. The unmistakable knock of a big, similarly impatient, man. I leap up from the couch and give my favorite halter sundress a quick smooth-out with my hands and then shove my feet into the cute heels that go perfectly with this dress. The heels are high and my hemline is, too. If I do say so myself, for reasons both fashion *and* carnal, I'm good to go.

When I open the door, my favorite fix is standing there with a duffel bag cast over one shoulder and his dog sitting obediently at his feet. Braden's eyes glide over me with a mix of awe and frustration. I return his inspection with my own, fascinated at the way seeing Braden again inspires the exact same sort of woozy appreciation it did the first time I saw him. He's glowering as he did that first day, but I now know what comes with that look. I also know the exact breadth and power of his body in ways I didn't before. Which means if I were to topple onto him today, it sure as hell wouldn't be an accident, just my hormones getting two steps ahead of me.

"An hour ago, when I was sitting in traffic outside Fort Worth, I was questioning my sanity. Trying to figure out what in the fuck I was thinking by asking my boss for time off with basically no notice, then loading up my dog and driving sixteen hours across three states." He shakes his head slowly. "One look at you and I have my answer."

I give him a sly smile. "Feeling a little live-wired?"

"You have no idea."

"Oh, I think I do." I swing the door open wider and encourage Charley inside, then bend over to give her a good nuzzling.

Behind me, Braden groans loudly—my high hemline and all—as his bag thumps to the floor and the door shuts with a heavy thud. Still leaning down, I peek over my shoulder. Braden's gaze is glued to my backside, his eyes hazy and unfocused.

"Charley could use some time outside," he states. An obvious addendum that Braden could use some time *inside* goes unsaid.

I whistle to encourage Charley to follow me over to the slider door at the rear of the house and she bolts straight outside, diving on a plush dog toy that's in the middle of the yard, which keeps Trey's dog occupied when he's here. Charley circles the perimeter, takes a drink from the water bowl I set out for her, and goes about frolicking on her back in the grass.

"Water, a new yard, and a toy," Braden says, his arms slipping around my waist. "She'll be happy for hours."

I hum softly. Braden wastes no time after that, his hands drift down until he can slide them under my dress, lingering on the backs of my thighs. His face presses into my neck, kissing and nipping the sensitive skin there. Between kisses, he grips my thighs harder, digging his fingers in with a bite that promises more. His mouth finds the shell of my ear.

"So glad we talked before I came. I love that we don't have to stop, even for a second."

I, in my infinite wisdom, broached the all-important *let's go without* conversation the night before he started his drive here. We talked about birth control and clean bills of health, and admitted to not seeing anyone other than each other—and more important, not wanting to see anyone else. Which means we get to have all the fun, without delay, the entire time he's here.

Braden starts to work my panties down my legs and when I step from them, I spin on my heel to face him putting an open hand to his chest so I can urge him farther into the house. I don't live in a penthouse in the sky, I live in an old-town suburb with low fence lines and oodles of neighbors who work from home. And as much as I'd like to have Braden press me up against the cool glass, I'm not interested in putting on a show for the entire 'hood.

His back hits a wall in the living room. Braden eyes me intently and waits for my next move, his breath turning harsh as I undo his belt and work his pants open, pausing before tugging down his boxers and taking him in hand. One stroke and he snaps, reversing our positions. His hands come to cup my ass, grinding the length of our bodies together before giving mine a lurch upward with the power of his, taking me off my feet for a split second. When my feet find the ground again, one of his hands moves between my legs, sliding two fingers across my slippery opening. Once, twice, three times.

"I need you, Amber. And I want this pussy. Now."

I lean up and take his earlobe between my teeth gently, then flick that spot with my tongue. "Then take it."

Braden lifts me up, my feet off the floor in one smooth move, using the wall behind to keep me in place. I twist my hips impatiently. Braden leans back a fraction so he can guide my body to his, and then he's deep. We both lose our breath for a moment at the delicious sensation of nothing between us.

Braden kisses me, soft and slow. Mid kiss, he starts to move in long, deep strokes that quickly grow rough and punishing. Gripping his shoulders means I can press my body to the wall, and the way my hips pitch means he lands right where I need him to. A few thrusts are all it takes. My body goes taut but Braden keeps on, wrenching every bit of pleasure out of my body—and his—that he can.

When we both start to catch our breath, I work my hands through his hair.

"I have plans for us, Braden. I'm going to make this trip so worth it." I give his hair a little tug and he lets out a satisfied hiss. "We're going to pop your Texas culinary cherry by getting brisket at Franklin Barbecue, go paddleboarding at Quarry Lake, and Trey told me about a vintage store I think you're going to love. Lots of dusty books and old LPs. Oh, and there's a distillery on Rainey Street that has the best whiskey in—"

"Stop," Braden cuts in, letting out a low chuckle, one I can feel radiate from his chest to mine. "No need to try so hard, baby. You make the trip worth it. Already. Just you."

23

(Braden)

"May your trails be crooked, winding, lonesome, dangerous,
leading to the most amazing view."
—EDWARD ABBEY, *DESERT SOLITAIRE*

Playing host to Amber's hostess during a backyard barbeque
comes with the obvious expectation that we'll both do what we
can to ensure every guest has a good time and relaxes. In my mind,
that means my primary job is to keep the beer cooler well stocked
and properly iced. It does *not* mean I should act as a human lawn
chair . . . for Jaxon.

In my defense, I don't want Teagan to sit on my lap, either.
Or Colin. Or anyone else milling about Amber's backyard at the
moment. Only one person belongs in my lap, and she's already
there, acting as the shield I need.

"But he has *two* thighs. And there aren't any other chairs left,"
Jaxon tipsily announces, sweeping his hand to gesture at the yard.

Amber draws her legs up to drape them over my other leg as a safeguard. "Stop. You're making the Jolly Green Giant blush. And I'm stingy when it comes to him. Go see if Teagan's friend with the Zac Efron eyes will play along."

Jaxon's own eyes brighten and he turns on one of his Top-Sidered heels to amble away.

"Swifty's for brunch tomorrow, doll." He thrusts one finger up in the air. "And I'm drunk enough to declare *now* that I'm ordering the banana brûlée French toast. And bacon!"

Amber laughs, her head tossed back, exposing the slopes of her neck. When her laugh subsides, she curves closer to me and I wrap my arms around her waist to encourage her head to my chest. A sweet blush has pinked her cheeks, likely brought on by the sangria that both she and Jaxon have been sipping on all afternoon.

Amber ticks her eyes up to meet mine. "Thank you for hosting this with me."

"You're welcome."

She ticks her fingers under the collar of my T-shirt and tickles there. "Have you had fun?"

I drop a quick kiss to her forehead. "Yes."

When Amber said she wanted me to meet some of her friends, I expected an awkward outing to some dive bar where I'd be forced to drink overpriced PBR and try not say anything too sarcastic, only to find out that a shindig in her backyard is what she had in mind. And while she claims she's no domestic goddess, the woman absolutely knows how to throw a party—with good music and great food—so it's not a lie to say that I've had fun.

Colin provided a wild hog for us to roast, one he shot on his family's ranch just yesterday. After we got it prepped and onto the smoker, we spent the rest of the morning setting up tables and stringing lights from the trees. I put together a batch of purple cabbage slaw to go with the roasted pork, and Amber made some of the ice cream she's apparently known for, one a simple Dutch chocolate and the other a honey bourbon peach—and both are concoctions I'd happily consider drowning in, despite all the sugar. When her friends started to arrive, it was clear I was on trial for the first hour or so, but by the time we pulled the fully-roasted hog off and started to shred the meat, I'd survived the worst of their interrogations. I'm sure the vast amount of beer and sangria that's flowing also played a part in warming everyone's previously cool attitudes.

The jury's still out on her brother Trey, though. He's been relatively quiet most of the day, but I suspect that's his norm. Even so, it's obvious that no matter how little he says, the kid is *definitely* listening. He's one of those people who can go unnoticed enough that people probably say more than they should, simply because they forgot he was in the room.

Amber, however, is not one of those people. Trey might duck or hide from her view occasionally, but he never gets too far, which means that Amber sits up straight when she spies him across the yard, tugging on his zip-up hoodie as if he's about to take off.

She cups her hands over her mouth and calls out over the music that's playing.

"Trey Regan! Don't you dare leave without saying goodbye to me or I won't do your laundry tomorrow!"

Trey halts in place and makes a show of slinking our way with his hands up, kowtowing to a woman who is half his size.

"Never joke about my delicates, laundry whisperer." He tips his chin to me. "Is six too early for you in the morning? The drive to the lake takes almost an hour, and the bass are jumping early these days."

"Fine with me. I've been waking up before dawn since I got here. My brain hasn't caught up with the time change."

Trey casually asked if I'd like to go fishing with him in the morning and since I like to fish and already knew that Amber had plans to brunch it up with Jaxon, my decision was easy. Plus, Trey's invitation was code, anyway. What he really wants to do is determine if I'm an asshole or not, and I respect that, so if that means we need to go somewhere he can cross-examine me and threaten my life in some roundabout way, fine. And adrift in a small boat is an ideal location for him to dispose of my body if he decides I *am* an asshole.

"I'll see you at six, then. I have the boat and the tackle; you're in charge of the refreshments." Trey sticks his hand out for a parting handshake, then waggles a finger at Amber. "*You* are in charge of ensuring my T-shirts smell like lilacs by the time we return."

"Lilacs? Does Dayton like that? Because it's a little girly. Maybe that's the problem."

Trey lifts a wry eyebrow and shoots Amber a hard look, then rounds the yard and calls out to his dog, Saint, who is Charley's new best friend. Trey and Saint then disappear out the side gate, leaving Charley to look longingly at the gate. She barks once then saunters our way and flops down underneath my chair.

"Who's Dayton?" I ask, once I'm sure Trey is gone.

Amber snorts. "His unrequited love. Well, more like the love he won't requite . . . or something. She's his employee, they want each other, but neither of them has the cojones to do anything about it." Her eyes brighten mischievously. She pokes me in the chest. "*You* should ask him about her tomorrow. It will irk the shit out of him."

I shake my head. "No. Guys who just met don't go asking each other about their unrequited *anything*. And why would I want to irk him? He's your brother. I want to be on his good side."

Amber's mischief eyes fade, and she tilts her head thoughtfully. "You *do*, don't you? Be on his good side."

I nod. Her eyes remain on mine, asking for more without saying a word. Asking why I care what her brother thinks of me, wanting to know if that says something about us.

Maybe later I'll answer her. Maybe in some quiet moment that feels right, I'll tell her all the reasons why.

~

Two hours later, we have the house to ourselves again and we're finishing up the last of the cleanup that we can't put off until tomorrow. Amber is putting lids on plastic containers filled with leftovers while I finish hand-washing the things that wouldn't fit in the dishwasher. After giving a large stoneware bowl one more rinse, I grab a dish towel and start to dry the bowl off, my eyes landing on Amber as I work, taking in everything about her.

She's wearing a little outfit that's essentially a one-piece combo of shorts with a top in a silky yellow fabric, and paired with heeled sandals that show off her lean, tan legs. The top is strapless, held up by her full tits and a laughable strip of elastic. I've spent most of the day trying not to leer at her in front of her friends and doing my best to keep from going hard when she planted herself in my lap. Both became more difficult as the evening wore on and once I was a few beers in, the image of her on her knees in front of me with the top part of her outfit rolled down popped into my mind one too many times.

Amber catches my stare when she puts the containers in the fridge, her mouth lilting up on one side. "What's up there, Braden?"

"Just thinking."

She shuts fridge door with a bump of her hip, then turns to face me. "Yeah? Thinking about what? Is it dirty?"

I set the dish on the counter and toss the dish towel next to it, waving my hand toward her outfit. "I like what you're wearing. The shorts-and-top-sewn-together thing."

She laughs, tosses her head back a little when she does. "You are such a man. It's called a *romper*. But I'm glad you like it."

Romper. I don't think that's supposed to sound dirty, but it does. And now I kind of want to tell her to *romper* her ass over here so I can feel her up and then let those tits spill out into my hands.

I won't, but I want to. I do try to keep my filthiest thoughts to myself, just to be sure I don't accidentally say something that might make me sound like one of her creepier fans. In general, my rule is, if something I'm thinking might earn a "like" from some prick that trolls her Instagram, I won't share it with her or ask it of her. I'm thinking that "Come over here in that romper, get on your knees, and suck me dry" definitely qualifies.

Amber's eyes turn wicked as if she can read my every thought anyway. "What do you like about it?"

I latch my hands to the countertop on either side of my body. "That you're in it."

She takes a step toward me. "Yeah?"

I nod as she continues to prowl forward. Her kitchen is tiny, so it only takes a few steps for her to land right in front of me, looking up at me with her blue eyes full of heat. I grip the countertop harder. Amber leans up and draws her soft lips across mine, not in a kiss, but a tease.

"Tell me," she murmurs.

"Tell you what?"

"Whatever naughty thing is going on in that head of yours. Tell me."

Her hands drift onto my waist, flicking and fingering near the button on my jeans. I shake my head as my entire body tenses. "I can't."

"Why?"

"Because," I grit out.

Amber must feel the rush of tension in my body and hear the same in my voice, because she tips her head back to scan my face.

"Hey. What's with being made of stone all of a sudden? Why is your heart beating like a jackhammer? And why won't you tell me what you're thinking about?"

I'm screwed now, because she's called me out and that means I can either fess up to my thoughts and risk looking like a perverted jerk, or I can refuse to say more and look like a withdrawn jerk who won't communicate. I debate my two shitty options with a long exhale, answering when I decide there's only one grown-up way to deal with this.

"Because what I'm thinking right now involves saying things that might make me sound like one of those assholes who write screwed-up sex comments on posts where you happen to be on your knees or your top is tugged down or your lips look all plumped up and swollen." I suck in a quick breath. "And I never, ever want you to think I'm like them. Or think that I think of you the way they do. I don't. You're more than a fucking picture to me, OK?"

Amber's jaw drops open, likely because I've raised my voice more than necessary and I'm having a hard time looking her in the eye for more than a second at a time. She slowly draws her jaw closed then flops it open again, clearly reconsidering whatever it was she planned to say. Finally, she lets out a breathy chuckle.

"Have you been worrying about this? Do you actually think

I'd confuse whatever dirty thoughts you share with me, with what happens behind a computer screen? Seriously?"

My eyes dart up and I start to study the ceiling. When she says it like that, it doesn't sound the same as it does in my head. In my head it's a big deal and not to be taken lightly, but when she says it, it sounds melodramatic and stupid.

Mumbling, I drop my gaze and give her a scowl. "I guess."

Her face relaxes into a patient grin.

"Well, *don't*. You get all of me, Braden. Parts of me that those people will never see, or touch, or understand."

She takes my hands and sets them low on her hips. Her hands return to my fly, grazing a lazy pattern there.

"I want you to tell me whatever you're thinking. You just have to trust that I'll tell you if it's too much or it makes me uncomfortable. Have I given you any reason to think I would hold back my thoughts?"

I shake my head. God knows she doesn't hold back—ever.

Amber slips from my hold and slowly steps backward until she's back where she was when this conversation started.

"Then let's give this another try, OK?" She lifts her arms up to mime as a director might, clapping her hands together. "Take. Two."

We lock eyes for what feels like minutes, until Amber's expression becomes that of a goddam temptress. "Tell me."

Every hesitation melts away when I recognize how alone we are. It's just the two of us here. All those nameless and faceless people, they aren't here. They never will be. What happens in this room, in this moment, is for Amber and me alone.

"Come here." I crook a finger lazily. Amber approaches the same way, in a slow amble that drives every thought I've had today right up to the surface. "Hurry the fuck up."

She smiles—and doesn't do a thing to quicken her pace. When she finally arrives in front of me, I dig my fingers to her hips and give them a rough jerk.

"You want to know what I'm thinking? What I want from you?"

Amber lets out a breathy moan when I yank on her hips again. She nods, closes her eyes. *"Yes."*

I slide one hand down to palm her ass with a light touch, then rear back and swat her so hard that we both moan. Her eyes flip open in surprise, then hood and go hazy.

"All fucking day I've watched you. Watched you laugh and smile and be amazing, dressed in this whatever-you-call-it, with your tanned legs teasing me and just this little piece here"—I draw a finger over the upper edge of her top—"to keep my hands off your beautiful tits. And it's been *killing* me."

Amber arches her back, pushing herself into the grip of my hands.

"I want you on your knees, that top tugged down so I can touch you while my cock is in your pretty mouth, fucking it while you suck me." I give the silky fabric a teasing tug at her breasts and grab another handful of fabric with the hand I still have on her ass. "That's what I want. Now tell me what *you* want."

She licks her lips and nods. "I want all of that. Just promise me you won't make me stop. Not until you're there, all the way. I want to *taste* it."

My answer is a curse, one I keep repeating as she starts to lower her body, trailing her hands over my chest, my abs, my thighs, until she's exactly where I want her.

Amber's blue eyes peek up to mine and I can't mistake the desire there. I grit my teeth to pace myself, but Amber clearly wants none of that because she parts her lips just enough to peek her tongue out. My words come in a rush—spoken before I can figure a way to tame them, either with some endearment or a simple "please."

"You're making my cock hurt. Fix it. Take me out and give me the rest of what I want."

Amber doesn't hesitate, setting me free in a few smooth moves and straight into her warm, wet mouth. The first full stroke of her lips across my shaft is enough to force my hands into her hair, keeping her still because the last thing I want is to come too quickly. She fights my hold by whimpering but the sound only prompts me to knot her hair through my fingers, just to hear her do it again.

Once I'm in control, I ease my grip and Amber starts to slip her mouth over my cock, slow at first. When she adds in a hand with the perfect rhythm, I sink into the feeling, loving every second until her mouth suddenly disappears. My eyes flip open. I peer down to find her giving me an impish smile.

"Oops. I almost forgot."

She uses her free hand to pull down her top, and her breasts tumble out with a little bounce that drives a groan from my throat. I reach down immediately and grasp her flesh in my hand. Hard. Her nipple feels like a diamond in my palm, and Amber moans before setting her mouth on me again. After that, I can't keep from saying every single thing that leaps to mind— begging her to not stop, telling her how good it is, how much I love her hot little mouth. When Amber draws back and lets her tongue work circles across the sensitive underside, I can't take anything else, coming harsh and hard and for what feels like forever.

Amber continues until I let out a hiss of discomfort. My cock is still in her tender hold, but she sits back on her heels and turns her face up to mine. Her eyes are shining and soft all at once—and suddenly the only thing I want is her *not* on her knees. I wrestle my weak hands under her arms and haul her up, pressing our bodies together until it feels like nothing exists beyond the two of us, right here and right now.

24

(Braden)

"And you can bury me beneath the deep blue skies of Texas."
—AARON WATSON, "TEXAS LULLABY"

When my line jerks again, signaling that I have yet *another* bass hooked, I actually laugh out loud. This morning's fishing trip with Trey has been borderline absurd. We arrived at the lake at seven, had Trey's little Ranger boat in the water by seven thirty, and had our first hits ten minutes after that. By nine we both had our limit, but kept at it catch-and-release. I'd never tell her this, but if Amber weren't already worth the drive down here, the bass fishing would be. I'll just add it to the list of things I could get used to about Texas—like the barbeque, which is every bit as good as they claim, the water that is still warm enough for paddleboarding even into the fall, the used bookstores you can get lost in for hours, and the beautiful blonde who gave me a sleepy smile when I kissed her goodbye this morning.

God bless Texas, y'all.

I reel in my latest catch, unhook him, and return him to the water quickly. The midday heat means we're finally seeing a break in the action, so I set my pole aside and dig around in the cooler sitting by my feet to grab a beer. Trey reels in and follows my lead, rustling through the ice and extracting his own beer. He inspects the other cooler contents before letting out a snort.

"I think I have you to thank for our lunch options today. Normally, when Amber and I come out here together, all she does is slap together a few PB&Js. These fancy-looking subs must be her attempt to impress you by taking a stab at sandwich artistry." He takes another peek in the cooler. "And there are cookies . . . which look suspiciously homemade."

I tip my ball cap down to better shade my face from the sun and take a sip of my beer.

"I'm the sandwich artist. The cookies I made a few days ago because your sister was threatening to buy a bag of Chips Ahoy!, and I couldn't let that happen. She was in charge of packing the cooler, that's it. Claims she has a patent-worthy system for layering the ice, and I decided not to challenge her on that."

Trey chuckles. "Jesus. How in the hell did you two *happen*?"

The question is clearly rhetorical given that he's staring at the shimmering water while shaking his head, so I offer nothing in return. Not that I could explain how Amber and I happened, anyway. Something about us might make sense on paper, but it took us a while to find the proper translation in person, and now that we have, I'm working hard to avoid overthinking it. Trey takes a long slug off of his beer, swallows, then turns his attention to me.

"I have no smooth segue here, so let's just get it out there, yeah?"

I nod, rest my arms on my knees and lean forward, my beer still clasped in one hand. Trey mirrors my posture.

"She's not as tough as she seems," he announces.

I resist telling him that I've already suspected as much. He knows her better than I do, though, which means if he's offering a few insights, I'd be stupid not to listen. Trey looks over my shoulder to the water.

"When our parents died, our uncle Cal was the only relative around who would take us in, but he wasn't exactly the kind of guy you'd look at and think of as a reliable guardian. I mean, he *was*, he just didn't fit the part. Think Archie Bunker meets Jeremiah Johnson meets John Wayne, but with a backwoods Texas accent and missing one of his front teeth—that was Cal."

My eyes go wide. Trey grins.

"Exactly. So he had to go to court to keep us out of foster care. But it was my sister who really saved us. She took the stand at ten years old, sitting on a stack of phone books so she could look the judge right in the eye. She sat there, with her hair in these cute pigtails and wearing a totally girly pink dress, and told this old geezer judge that she knew what was best for me, for her, and for us. Then she told him if they split us up and put us into the system, she would do whatever it takes to *fix that*." Trey laughs softly. "Basically, she looked like a menacing Strawberry Shortcake with a vengeful side. I think he was scared stiff because he didn't even ask what she meant by 'fix that.' "

I conjure up an image of Amber then and it brings a half smile to my face. The same hair, the same sparkle, and the same blue eyes that can melt you or skewer you as she sees fit. But the smile fades when I consider how much pressure she was shouldering then, trying to ensure she and Trey had the best future they could given their shitty circumstances. And despite knowing even at that age Amber could shoulder whatever came her way, the fact that she had to is hard to accept.

Trey continues with a sigh. "That was Amber hustling, round one. Not much has changed since then. Scrambling and busting ass is what she does. She hustled to keep us together, did the same to get out of the town we grew up in, and the same to get her show."

He shoots me a knowing look. "Hustling" would never be the word I use, but I've seen her in action, so I get what he means. I give him a nod.

"But she also thinks that's a good way to protect herself. That she can just hustle her way out of anything, unscathed." Trey takes the final draw on his beer, crushes the can, and tosses it on the floor of the boat. "But losing her show? If she can't scrabble her way out of this, it will hit her hard. The last thing she needs in her life right now is something or someone else that she can't count on."

The "someone" remark sounds like an opening, so I take it. "Look, Trey—"

"She's soft inside," he cuts in and presses on. "She's got this loving heart, you know? The woman still does my laundry, and I let her, even though I can obviously do it myself. But she's been taking care of me since I was seven, and that's a hard habit for someone with a big heart to let go of. I just want to know if you understand that."

He pauses—finally. I think he just said more in the last five minutes than he did this morning and all day yesterday, combined. I answer him quickly, before he decides to start in again.

"Yes, I know that."

"Good. Because this isn't her norm with guys. By this point she's usually given them a speech about why her show makes it hard to have a long-term relationship, while blinding them with her smile and sending them on their way. But instead she's parading you around for her friends to meet, like she's invested in this going somewhere. So tell me you feel the same way, that you aren't jerking her around."

I'm definitely not jerking her around, but giving Trey anything more than that as an answer is tough. On the drive here, I questioned what we're doing and where we are going, but I squashed the thoughts as quickly as they came. Too much, too soon. If I started to consider real life with all of its sticky practicalities—living states apart, her career, and my shitty history at keeping a woman happy—then this trip might seem like a worthless waste of vacation days I don't even have.

I let out a sigh. "I don't know."

"You don't *know*?" His face goes slack. "I tell you to say that you aren't jerking my sister around, and your answer is *I don't know*?"

"Don't drown me in the lake just yet." I raise my hands up. "I'm definitely not jerking her around. But beyond that? I can't say. She and I haven't had that conversation."

Trey doesn't look as if my answer suits him, so I try again, steadying my eyes on his.

"Look, when she came down off the trail after missing that elk, I saw her hurting. And it tore me up. So, I can tell you this: I'm not interested in doing anything to cause her hurt. Ever."

Trey considers my answer silently, squinting my way. Then he digs into the cooler for two more beers.

"Fair enough." He hands me a beer and cracks the tab on his.

Fair enough.

Easy for him to say.

He's not the one who just realized he's got a big-ass question mark in his life—and he doesn't like it.

25

(Amber)

"If we forget that life itself is a cruel contest, especially in the wilds, then we are shocked and pained by the hunters' story."
—Saxton Pope

After the hostess seats us, she hands Jaxon and I menus the size of postcards, then inquires about our drink order, rattling off all the usual brunch libations. Bellinis, Bloody Marys, micheladas, and the like, but Jaxon politely interrupts before the word "mimosa" comes out of her mouth. He removes his amber-lensed horn-rimmed sunglasses and holds up two fingers listlessly.

"Turmeric tonics for both of us, please."

When the hostess disappears, I wrinkle my nose for Jaxon's benefit.

"I'm nowhere near hungover enough to require anything being billed as a *tonic*."

Jaxon tosses his sunglasses on top of the leather messenger bag sitting next to him, then peruses the succinct menu.

"Trust me. A tonic will do you good today."

Anxiety wriggles its way up my spine, slowly, until I can feel it needling across my neck. If I was a little less perceptive, or Jaxon were a little less blunt, I might indeed blame this sensation on a hangover. Instead, I label it for what it is.

Dread.

We spend far too long pretending to read the menu, especially given that we've been here before and the fact that there are only seven things on the menu. Three of those items are omelets with weird fillings that don't appeal to me, and of the other four, two are vegan and one is oatmeal. The former doesn't enter my lexicon, and the latter I eat every damn morning at home, which leaves us with what we always have. French toast that is stuffed with sweetened cream cheese and drenched in brûléed bananas. It's the best sort of comfort food—nothing but fatty, sugar-drenched carbs—and something tells me I'm going to need all the comfort I can get.

Jaxon sets his menu aside, prompting me to do the same as he leans forward, arms resting on the tabletop, fingers clasped together. Reflexively, I lean back, lengthening my spine to the back of the chair while mentally willing the crown of my head to meet the ceiling.

"Bud Smeltzer emailed me last night. I saw it after I got home from your place."

A mustachioed man with too much pomade in his hair appears tableside, sets our tonics on the table along with drinking straws, and sidles away without a word. Jaxon taps his straw from the paper liner, and I do the same, forcing my mind to stay on track. There's a fault line under my career, and it's about to crack right open, I just know it.

"They're not renewing *Record Racks* for next season."

I tap my straw to the tabletop again, too hard, and it buckles. I toss it aside and grab the glass, going bottoms up on the orange-colored concoction, swallowing before the taste can truly hit my tongue. Even so, my face squishes up, so I chase it with a drink of water before speaking.

"Because *why*? I'm interested in hearing what half-assed excuse they used."

"They feel, quote, 'The future of the Afield Channel does not lie with *Record Racks* or align with Ms. Regan's brand.'" Jaxon's expression turns droll, and his eyes then roll up to the ceiling. "And yes, Smeltzer referred to you as *Ms.* Regan. Like he hasn't made twelve thousand thinly veiled comments in the last five years that imply he'd like to roll over next to you in the morning."

"Well, *Ms.* Regan is curious where their brand does lie. *Ms.* Regan wants to know if they even watched the tape of her Colorado elk hunt. Because *Ms.* Regan feels like they might have strung her along, even though they had already decided to ax her like a gangrened appendage."

"Tell Ms. Regan to stop talking about herself in the third person. It's obnoxious." Jaxon sighs. "Supposedly, yes, they did watch the tape."

"And?"

"They claim the production quality was not what they anticipated. Then some tagline crap about "world class-production with engaging storytelling and dynamic film sequences." I don't speak television technical mumbo-jumbo, but there was some mention about certain filming specifics. I have no idea what any of it meant, and I'm guessing Smeltzer doesn't, either."

I grit my teeth to avoid unleashing a curse-laden tirade. Production quality, my ass. Unlike big-budget shows on major networks, I don't have a studio backing me. What I do have is a team of brilliant freelancers behind my show, including production guys who have more talent in their beards that Smeltzer has in his entire body. But we're a shoestring operation, and my neck has been the one on the line this entire time, financially and otherwise. From monopolizing Colin and hiring Teagan, to sourcing the right company to edit and package the final cut, I've done all of that from day one. Even after I scored my last three—far more lucrative—contracts with Afield, not much changed except that I had more money to invest. The result of that investment was Smeltzer once proclaiming that *Record Racks* had redefined what outdoor programming should look like.

Now they want me to believe it's not up to par? Bullshit.

I make a valiant attempt to loosen my jaw and breathe like a normal person, instead of a bull in the chute. Jaxon takes a sip of his tonic, and try as he might, his own face squishes up a little.

"Just so we're clear, is it worth my time to show up at Smeltzer's office? Is there room to talk this out with them? Or is this a full-stop rejection?"

He shakes his head. "Full stop. No room to talk, nothing between the lines. He values your previous partnership with Afield and wishes you the best in all your future endeavors, blah, blah, blah. I'd say the door is closed."

"So I'm done. I need a new gig."

Jaxon doesn't answer. He gets that I already know the answer, but my saying it aloud will help it to sink in. My leg begins hopping under the table like the needle on a sewing machine, the result of an impulse to bolt from the table, go home and get to work on what's next. A new project, a new gig, a new way to make my living—and I want to get to work *now*. But Jaxon knows me too well. Without a word, he raises a hand to settle me down, then extracts a glossy folder out of his messenger bag, tossing it on the tabletop in front of me.

"That is the latest from Bona Fide. A full media kit and links to the sizzle reel. Investors are on board now, so they're anxious to lock down talent. They want you for this Los Cabos thing, doll. Badly."

Emblazoned on the cover is a color photo of a white-sand beach with a predictably gaudy but luxurious mansion hovering in the background. Taking a closer look, I try to find evidence of a hellmouth lurking under the sand, or a two-headed creature of some sort that suggests this is a breeding ground for unnatural things but find nothing. It all looks harmless, really—like a warm, relaxing place where I could lick my wounds, earn a paycheck, and buy some time to figure out my next move.

A server appears, a small notepad in one hand and a pen in the other.

"Are you two ready to order?"

French toast as usual, but I want a side of bacon, too. And a piece of their strawberry cream pie to-go. After today, it's nothing but lean proteins and colorful veggies—no beer, no Braden cookies, no white flour, no potatoes.

The topless bikini diet.

～

An hour later, Jaxon drops me off at home, full of French toast and caffeine, courtesy of the two cortado coffees I drank after finishing my tonic. The caffeine combined with the anxiety means my body needs a release. Braden, unfortunately, isn't home yet, so any hope for his playing a part in that release isn't an option, leaving me to go about it another way—with a good, hard, sweaty workout. Punishing my body has always been the best way to quiet my mind, so here's hoping it will work today.

Forty-five minutes later, I'm in the backyard working through another set of box jump burpees, with a very specific X Ambassadors song blasting in my ears on repeat. The urge to puke or pass out dissipated early on, leaving only angry energy, the kind that makes it easy to focus on hitting my marks, even when Braden emerges from the house. He pauses at the edge of the patio, his stance wide and Charley acting as his dutiful shadow. Even without giving him my entire focus, I can feel his gaze from here.

I push through the rest of the set, then lean down and grab my water bottle, taking a long slug before walking his way slowly. When I take my earbuds out and lift my sunglasses up, Braden scans the length of me, lingering on the flat of my torso between the sports bra and workout shorts I'm wearing.

"Do you have any idea how fucking hot it is to watch you work out that hard?"

I level my eyes on him, but his remain on my body. "I imagine it's almost as hot as it would be to watch *you* work out hard."

"Yeah?"

I nod. Braden shoves his hands in his pockets, so forcefully the gesture reads as a calculated precaution to keep him from reaching for me. He lifts his gaze to mine, and I expect something heated when he does, only to have it disappear in a flash.

The corners of his eyes crinkle. His forehead does the same. "What's wrong?"

My heart lurches in my rib cage, halts for a beat, then thuds unsteadily. I have zero time for—or interest in—a confessional, so I avert my eyes and pretend to brush grass off my legs.

"Nothing."

"Nice try," Braden says. "But your eyes are red and your makeup is all smudged. Have you been crying?"

Stupid tear ducts, stupid eyeballs—giving away my secret, nearly an hour after I gave in to a crying jag that lasted all of ten whole minutes. After that, I put on my workout gear and decided to leave self-pity in a pile of sweat on the grass. I tip my sunglasses down.

"I'm fine."

Braden tries again, stepping close so he can clasp one of my hands in his.

"What happened at brunch? Did Jaxon—"

I step back, jerking my hand away, cutting him off before he starts to sound like the therapist I did not make an appointment with. My only getaway is the house, so I set off that direction.

"Afield isn't renewing my show. They looked at the tape of my elk hunt and didn't bite. It's over."

Behind me, Braden hisses his way through a few curse words. A large tub of black raspberry–flavored hydration supplement is on the kitchen counter, and by the time Braden slinks in, I've added a scoop of it to my water, screwed the lid back on my bottle, and started to shake it up leisurely.

"Fuck. I'm so sorry about this, Amber."

"Not your fault."

Braden stiff-arms the countertop, his palms flat to the granite surface as he takes in my stone-faced expression.

"Do you want to talk about it?"

"Nothing to talk about." I inspect the pink concoction in my water bottle, looking for any undissolved crystals, hoping I can shake them into submission if there are.

"Really?" Braden scoffs. "You're losing your show, the thing you've committed the last five years of your life to, and that doesn't bring up anything? Because those red eyes that you're trying to hide behind your sunglasses—inside the fucking *house*, by the way—tell a different story. I'm here, Amber. Talk it out. I'll listen."

I realize then how stupid I must look standing in my kitchen wearing a pair of aviators, studying my water bottle like it's the answer to everything and trying to pretend this doesn't hurt. The way Braden has grown to understand me makes it hard to hide no matter what, so I don't stand a chance at stumping him when I'm this raw. But I don't want to talk. I want to move on from this without some deep dive into my thoughts and feelings, when that shit won't change a thing. My best defense is to distract him—and sex is a distraction Braden and I do well. I yank my sunglasses off and tuck them into the center of my sports bra.

"I don't need to talk it out because I'm fine. That reality show I told you about, the one where I'm a fishing guide in the tropics? It's a go. So I have things to do to get ready for that. Do you want to be on that list, Braden? Of things I *do*?"

Braden's expression doesn't particularly change, but the temperature in the room drops a good twenty degrees. Slowly, he pushes up from the counter and shakes his head.

"No. I don't want to be on your list of things to *do*."

I shrug, leaving him where he stands as I stride back out into the sunshine, extracting my phone from the band around my arm. Taking a seat on the wooden box I used for my workout, I hold the phone up, adjusting until I have the right light and a pose that shows the perfect amount of skin. With my sunglasses back on to hide all evidence of my shitty day, after a few clicks I'm out in the world as I should be, filtered and absolutely fine.

Braden is back on the patio, stationed there like an angry sentinel. One I should ignore—but can't.

"Something you want to say?"

He crosses his arms over his chest. "You don't see the irony, do you?" I send daggers and a silent message his way. *I don't want to play. Spit it out.* Braden sighs.

"Life as you know it is ending and all you can think to do is take a fucking selfie. Fucking shallow as a wading pool."

The sting smarts only long enough to get me on my feet and put us toe-to-toe.

"I'm shallow? That's the best you can do? I've heard it before, and I'll hear it again. You saying it means nothing to me. Because when you leave tomorrow, Braden? Nothing in my life changes. *Nothing.*"

～◡

An hour later, I emerge from the long shower I escaped to and discover that Braden and Charley are nowhere to be found. After looking outside, I breathe a sigh of relief because his truck is still here, which means wherever they've disappeared to, it's on foot. But if Braden had packed up his things and left for home today instead of waiting until tomorrow as planned, I couldn't blame him.

The hot water and steam did a number on my body, easing my limbs until I was so unsteady on my feet I needed to press a palm to the shower wall for support. My mind followed, leaving too much room for every uncomfortable, restless thought I tried to push away. Now, on top of everything to do with my career, I've managed to screw up the first real relationship of significance I've had in years, all because he'd had the balls to ask me how I *feel*.

After curling up on the couch, I draw back the curtains to keep an eye out for Braden and Charley, then dig out the media kit Jaxon gave me at brunch from my bag. The last few hours have cast a pallor over the white-sand beach on the cover, along with the images of beautiful people who grace the interior. Maybe it's the darkening sunset light outside, but the whole thing looks far less harmless than it did earlier. I grab my tablet and type in the Web address for the sizzle reel, clicking on the video player when the page loads.

A terrible samba-reggae track blares loudly from my speakers, and I grimace, turning down the sound as far as I can without muting it entirely. The camera pans over a shot of the beach, then zooms up a stone walkway leading to an enormous patio, and crosses over a shimmering infinity pool. A quick cut takes us to the house, through opened slider doors that run floor to ceiling, revealing a Spanish-style living room with high ceilings supported by teakwood beams and covered in decorative tile.

Nice digs, no question about that.

The opening track fades out, replaced by a hip-hop ode that somehow manages to outsuck the first song by a stretch. Non-sensical lyrics including "Patron pahr-tay," "jiggle-wiggles," and "saltshakers" are to blame, along with a rapper who sounds like a cigar-smoking Elmo. On the screen, a bedroom door swings open, where—naturally—we find three gals jumping on a bed, grabbing at one another to keep from falling over, clad in only skimpy boy shorts and cropped tank tops. Giggling ensues until they all flop to the bed in a tangle of tanned limbs. Then, because there is only one way for this to go, one of them grabs . . . a pillow.

Feel free to smother me with a pillow, because a pillow fight commences. Complete with the feathers swirling about in the air and plenty of slow-mo close-ups of bouncing cleavage.

I force myself to finish watching despite the sudden migraine-like pain brewing behind my right eye. Mercifully, the masterminds behind this nightmare know to cut straight from the cleavage to the pitch, with appealing data designed to lure in advertisers. The reggae track from hell sounds again just as my front door opens and I slap the cover on my tablet shut, like I've just been caught streaming a particularly dirty Tumblr video.

Braden unhooks Charley's leash, walks through the living room without looking at me, holding a carryout bag from a ramen noodle joint that's a few blocks away from my house. He fell in love with the bowl he ordered when we went there on his first night in town, one that features a spicy, lemony-garlic broth teeming with fat noodles, diced pork, and wood ear mushrooms.

He raises the bag in the air. "Dinner."

We eat in silence except for the slurping. When we finish eating, I start to clean up, brushing off Braden's attempts to help. He doesn't protest, disappearing down the hall toward the bedroom. I waste as much time as I can wiping down the countertops even when no actual cooking has occurred today, washing the two forks and two glasses we used during dinner by hand. I let Charley out to do her thing in the backyard for a bit and stand there drinking a beer in the dark.

After that, unless I want to start vacuuming or scrubbing the grout in the bathroom, there's nothing to do but go in the bedroom and see what I find. Clasping the media kit and tablet to my chest tightly, I linger at the threshold to gather the humility I couldn't summon up this afternoon. Deep breath. There will be more to lose if I don't try to fix this.

Braden is sprawled out on my bed in just his boxer briefs, an arm crooked behind his head, and reading a book clasped in his other hand. Charley is snoozing at the foot of the bed with the top of her head nudged up against Braden's leg.

I stop short when Braden lowers the book an inch or so to peer my way because it feels like the first time in *days* he's looked at me, even if I know our fight started only hours ago. Not to mention that the sight of a nearly naked Braden in my bed with his brown hair a little messy, just lounging there for the taking while reading, is apparently a masturbatory fantasy come to life for me. And one I didn't even know I had—because my entire body believes this can be fixed with one good, long round between those sheets.

"I'm sorry," I croak.

Braden lowers the book completely, laying it on his chest still opened. His now-free hand rests on his abs, low enough that his fingers tick just under the top edge of his boxers and I catalog the sight for later use.

"I didn't mean what I said earlier. You leaving tomorrow isn't easy for me. Especially now."

His face slackens. "*I'm* sorry. The shit about you being shallow? I don't think that. That was just my fucking ego taking a cheap shot."

I make my way to the bed and crawl up on it, resting on my heels and casting the tablet onto the duvet cover. Braden lifts his head to one side.

"When I came home today, Amber, all I wanted was to talk to you. About . . . *us*, I guess. Then I saw you out back—the sweatiest, sexiest, most kick-ass woman I've even seen—and my plan changed. I wanted to let you finish your workout, fuck you until you saw stars, then talk. Instead, we ended up here. Pissed off and hurt, the both of us." Braden clears his throat lightly. "But I'm still here if you want to talk. About your show, about us, about what's going on in your head. About anything."

This was the moment I flinched earlier, when I thought it would be better if I pushed him away. Since that definitely didn't work out, I have to stay put, no matter how hard this is. I shift my position so I'm sitting cross-legged, cutting a glance toward the tablet.

"This Cabo thing? I'm not a hundred percent sure about it. Honestly, it's not what I want to do, it's what I *have* to do." I grab the media kit and tablet, replacing the book on his chest with them. He gives it all a cursory glare. "That's the media kit. And there's a promo video cued up on my tablet. Look at it, tell me what you think."

Braden shakes his head. "You don't want that."

"I do."

"No, you don't. Because you already know what I think."

"You said you would talk to me about anything. I want to talk about this." I scoot a little closer to him. "Humor me."

He shimmies up to sit with his back against the pillow and the folder and tablet tumble off his chest and onto the bed.

"You should know by now that I'm truly shit when it comes to humoring people," he grumbles, snatching up the folder and opening it.

I snort, waiting as he reads through the folder, then set the tablet in his reluctant hands once he's finished. The opening track begins to play, and I blush when Braden's head rears back a few inches at the horrific sound of bongos and maracas being played by what sounds like a passel of angry monkeys. As the video plays, Braden's expression remains in check, betrayed only by the tiny flare of his nostrils when the sorority sisters start to thump one another with pillows. Although I can't tell if it's because his libido is flaring at the bouncing breasts or his dander is rising at the icky spectacle of it all.

The video ends and he hands the tablet back without a word.

"Well? Tell me."

"I think if you do this, it will be a mistake."

"OK. But *why?*"

He scrubs a hand down his face. "Because you are nothing to them. If you pass on this, they'll just find another hot blonde willing to do what they want you to do. But if you do take it, you will *become* just another hot blonde. They will reduce you to tits and ass."

"I *am* just another hot blonde," I state. "I have tits and ass worth camera time. And they want to pay me a lot of money."

Braden's eyes harden. "Do not say you are just another hot blonde. You aren't. No one is *just* anything. I get that showing the results of all your hard work on your body is part of your brand and it's why these companies pay you to endorse their products, I do. But that's just a fraction of what you're capable of and you shouldn't take a gig that doesn't allow you to be one hundred percent of who you are. Don't fucking *settle*, Amber."

"I wouldn't be settling forever. Just this show, then I'll be able to go back to the drawing board and find something better."

Braden grinds his jaw tight, then loosens it as if he's about to say something else, only to clamp it shut again.

"What?"

"I can't watch you settle. Even if it's for a little while. And . . ." Braden grabs the media folder and flips to a FAQ page, holding it up in front of me. He points to a header printed in red, bold-face letters.

"I also can't know that you're down there being someone else's love interest. I'm sorry, I know this isn't about me, but I can't sit here and talk about this without saying that. I can't."

My eyes drop to the bold-face header and the details below.

Interested in falling in love while in Los Cabos? We sure hope so! Cast members won't be at a loss for opportunity to find love, not if we have anything to say about it—and when you do meet someone, you'll have six sun-soaked weeks to get to know them! Viewers love a good "will they or won't they?" so we cast with potential love interests in mind. Think of us as your very own matchmakers . . . with the sexiest, most spontaneous, fun-lovin' matches in mind JUST FOR YOU!

I want to roll my eyes the way I did the first time I read it, but I stifle the reaction just in case Braden then thinks I'm mocking him, instead of this FAQ that sounds like it was inspired by a website for some high-end girlfriend experience. I grab the folder and toss it onto the floor.

"I'm not interested in being anyone's love interest but yours.

Even if they use editing magic to make it look like I was interested in someone, it wouldn't be real."

"From my side of the screen, it would feel real. And if you think I'm evolved enough to not have that gut me, you're wrong. I'm not. I couldn't do it."

His expression, paired with that last sentence, sounds a lot like Braden drawing a line in the sand. Tears threaten to pool in my eyes, but I will them away by letting my pride do the work. He may have said he knows this isn't about him, but he went ahead and made it about him anyway.

"So you're pulling a Laurel. You're blackmailing me with your feelings and asking me not to take this show."

Braden's face turns stony. "Low blow, mountain sprite. I took my own earlier, so I'd be a fucking hypocrite if I called you out on it, but I'll just state the obvious. No, I'm not asking you to do anything based on my feelings. I'm just telling you where I'm at. It's called *communicating*."

I start to scoot away so the physical distance between us matches the growing divide that's come every time we open our mouths today, but he latches a hand on to one of my ankles.

"Don't. If either of us holes up or backs away, we're fucked. The only chance we have is to keep talking."

I dip my head and fix my eyes on the gentle grasp of his hand to my ankle, his thumb now skimming up the back of my calf in a slow, winding pattern. Despite the size of him and the power I know he has, there's nothing aggressive in the gesture, and I don't feel trapped in the way I might have expected—because no one has seen me the way Braden does. Truly and righteously *seen* me, every facet and from all sides. And he never acted as if he wanted a little more of this or a little less of that, he simply took note and moved on to the next thing. I draw my fingers up and down his forearm through the dark hair there, watching as gooseflesh rises under my touch.

"What am I supposed to do, then?" I ask, voice lowered. "Get a job at Cabela's? I thought we were joking around when we talked about that."

"Lots of people have regular jobs, Amber. They have someone who loves them, things they like to go do, places they love to visit. They're happy. They have ordinary lives that they wouldn't trade for anything."

My heart sinks like a stone. What Braden just proposed—an ordinary life—was noble and simple. But I don't want that. I'm greedy because I want everything. I want him, and what I had, and the guarantee there will be even more to come.

When I don't reply, Braden's hand goes still and he slowly lifts his fingers one by one. He draws his hand away and slinks down so he's lying on his side, staring up at me. His eyes are sad. Defeated. Worst of all, accepting. Because once again, he's seen me. He could see that the ordinary life he'd presented, the one he could so easily give me, wasn't enough. He was making note . . . and moving on.

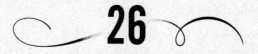

26

(Braden)

"This is how you talk to her when no one else is listening,
And this is how you help her when the muse goes missing,
You vanish so she can go drowning in a dream again."
—Jason Isbell, "24 Frames"

I wake up to Amber. Her beautiful face studying mine as I blink away the last of what was a restless night's sleep. Once I'm fully awake, her tired eyes seem to say that she's been at this for a while. Watching me sleep, taking in these last moments quietly so she could file them away in some special part of her memory.

Amber sneaks one hand out from under the covers and gives me an impossibly sweet, childlike wave, her fingertips curling only a little. Then she presses her fingertips gently to her mouth and skates the pads across her lips thoughtfully. A faint smile curves across her mouth.

"My heart hurts," she whispers.

I take a rough breath. "Mine, too."

She smiles again, somehow grateful as much as it is sad. Her hand slips back under the covers, coming to rest over my chest. She keeps it there, her open palm pressed to the place where she can feel my heartbeat, a slow and heavy thump that backs up the claim that my heart hurts, too.

Her hand starts to move, a slow descent across my chest and down my abs, until I'm in her warm grasp. Amber starts to stroke gently, still over the fabric of my boxer briefs, yet that barrier isn't near enough to keep my cock from stirring to life completely. My poor dick has equally poor judgment, so he doesn't understand the circumstances here. He thinks this is one hell of a way to start the day. But my head and my heart know what a mess Amber and I have found ourselves in, and even if I'm hard and hurting, that still doesn't make this a good idea.

"Amber," I croak, "we shouldn't do this."

She wiggles closer, near enough to kiss the base of my throat and up across my neck, so that the scent of her honey-muddled strawberry hair tickles just under my nose. Her bare thighs are touching mine, and her breasts are pressed to my chest.

"Why?"

"Because . . ." My words falter when her fingertips steal under the waist of my boxers. I suck in a harsh breath and hold it, closing my eyes as I wait for her hand to find my length. When she does, I sink into the sensation with a slow exhale, knowing that nothing in my life will ever be better than this—better than waking up next to Amber, her sweet smile for me, her body pressed to mine, and her hands on me.

"Because? Because why, Braden? Tell me why we shouldn't enjoy this and love each other this morning."

That's because why, I want to say. Because we love each other. She may be saying it another way—as some flowery euphemism for sex—but the words alone, without any redefinition, spoke the truth. *Because we love each other.* But last night that love wasn't enough. I couldn't see past the choices she was about to make, and she couldn't fathom going another way. In the end, we chose ourselves.

I open my eyes, peering down to Amber's face tipped to mine as I try to figure out how to give her an answer—without bringing love into the mix. But her bright blue eyes are wide and wanting, nothing but openness in her gaze. My mouth finds hers before I can give her a reason why, or give myself a good reason why not.

Amber starts to work her hand over my length as we kiss, using the touch she knows I love. An easy roll of her hand, her fingers encircling the head loosely each time she slips over the tip. My hand lands on her hip and I dig my nails into her flesh until there's a bite she can't ignore and Amber breaks our kiss to let out a soft whimper. And the sound, the need there, is too much.

I need to stop, but I can't, and suddenly we're devouring each other with openmouthed kisses, tugging and yanking on the few clothes we're wearing until we're both bare and my body is on top of hers. We're both breathing hard when we pause and lock eyes. I smooth a few stands of her hair back from her face, tucking them behind her ears. Amber cups my face in her hands and whispers my name.

Taking myself in hand, my eyes stay on hers. I keep the first few strokes unrushed, deliberately doing what I can to draw this moment out because when I give in to what I want and I know she loves, those hard thrusts will take us too close to the edge.

And when we both come, we're done.

And I don't want this to be over.

Even when I do surrender, it's all I can think about. Amber is close, I can feel it, along with the sound of her soft cries breaking in my ear.

But I don't want this to be over.

Amber's voice disappears and her body goes taut. My body wants more, so I do my best to keep going, wringing everything I can from her until I can't keep up because my own release is too much, emptying myself inside her until my entire body is shaking.

And still, I don't want this to be over.

Amber's arms wind around my neck, pulling me to her so roughly that my arms buckle and I nearly crush her. She wraps her body to mine and for every exhale I take, she inhales; I do the same with hers. Giving and taking, as we say goodbye.

27

(Braden)

"My first love was an angry painful song,
I wanted one so bad I went and did everything wrong."
—Reckless Kelly, "Wicked Twisted Road"

When I cross paths with a black GMC truck on the access road near the Sawtooth trailhead, I notice two things in my rearview mirror.

One, there's a nice mule deer buck loaded into the truck bed.

Two, the truck has Texas plates.

Now, let's be honest, it isn't this guy's fault he's from Texas. But that doesn't change the fact that I'm going to turn around to follow him and have every intention of finding him in violation of some hunting regulation—no matter how obscure or menial. Is it wrong that my shitty outlook on life since returning from his state of residence with nothing but a busted heart is what's spurred this otherwise baseless investigation of mine? Yes. And I know that. Logically.

Too bad logic isn't my forte these days. Instead, it's only cynicism and hostility taking turns at the wheel. And if this poor sap dares question my motivations, I'll be happy to pinpoint the source for him, right down to a small bungalow in the Hyde Park area of Austin.

The driver slows to a stop where the dirt road meets the main county road, signals properly, then turns right. I follow him through Hotchkiss and onto Highway 133, headed out of town. Fifteen minutes later, I've nearly given up this pointless pursuit, only to have him flip on his turn signal and slow his speed to hang another left.

Straight into the parking lot of the Empire Ambassador Motel.

I let out a sigh. This fucking guy. Now I really have to nail him to the wall with something, simply because he was stupid enough to rent a room here, and this place will forever remind me of the moment when Amber texted me a picture of her in one of these shitty rooms.

He pulls into a parking space and shuts off the truck. I hover near the entrance with my truck motor running and watch as a barrel-chested guy in his early forties emerges from the driver side. His clothing is camo from head to toe, in heavier layers than I would have expected given Colorado's temperate fall weather. But he's from Texas, where it's still warm enough for some people to strut around in *rompers*.

A teenager bounds out from the passenger side, dressed in the same gear, all except for his flat-bill hat, from which his floppy brown hair curls out from around the brim. The grin on his face tells the story. The deer in the back of this truck is his, and given that he only looks about thirteen years old, this may be his first Colorado buck with a bow. Well, it better have been with a bow. This is still archery season, and if I find a rifle or a muzzleloader in that truck that will make this easy. Taking a deer with anything other than a bow today would result in losing their future privileges, paying a serious fine, and if I really want to be a dick, they might need to come up with bail money.

I begin a slow creep through the parking lot in my truck and pull in perpendicular behind theirs, blocking them in. Scanning the deer's carcass, I quickly spot a problem: there's no tag on this deer.

Christ, that was almost *too* easy. I didn't even have to break a sweat.

Although some people might claim otherwise, hunting regulations are not only simple, but clear-cut. Some of the most fundamental rules have to do with hunting tags. Each season, once the state draw is complete, hunters who were successful receive a physical tag in the mail. This tag must travel with the hunter, and if he or she fills the tag, three things need to happen.

First, they need to punch their tag by striking a hole through it, effectively destroying it for future use. Second, they need to sign the tag. Third, they need to attach the tag to the animal, prior to moving it anywhere. I happen to know that this deer took a twenty-mile spin around town—all without a tag.

My truck door is barely open before the driver is headed my way, calling out a greeting and extending his hand.

"Morning!"

"Morning." I return his handshake. "Braden Montgomery, CPW unit manager for this area."

"Greg Dunlap. This is my son, Bryce."

I tip my chin toward the truck bed. "Looks like you two had a good day."

Greg chuckles, puffing his chest out a bit. "Yes we *did*. This is Bryce's first archery season, and we're headed home with this guy."

The still-grinning Bryce beams when I give him a nod. "Congratulations."

"Thank you, sir," he breathes, now gawking over the bedside to admire his deer.

I step forward and peer over the tailgate myself, pretending to give the deer an appreciative once-over. Then I shake my head, clicking my tongue a little.

"Man, this sucks. I *hate* casting a cloud over your big Colorado hunt. I mean, you came all the way from *Texas*, after all. Which makes this situation *such* a bummer."

Bryce freezes, darting a glance his dad's way. Greg's head rears back as a puzzled look crosses his face.

"Situation?"

I drop a forearm to the tailgate and lean on it casually, thumbing toward the carcass.

"No tag."

Behind me, Bryce makes a choked-off noise. I hear the sound of his boots shuffling, his hands patting over every pocket on his clothing, followed by the passenger door on the truck opening and a whole host of junk inside rattling about.

Greg shakes his head. "Shit. We have it. I swear. It's just . . . we were . . . *shit*. We never do this, forget to tag out." He flicks a hand toward Bryce. "His first with a bow, you know? I was as excited as he was. But I raised him to know the regs and follow the rules. This was an oversight, nothing else."

"Got it!"

Bryce has his hand thrust in the air, waving the tag about. He slams the truck door shut behind him as he careens our way and looks frantically about for a pen. Greg does the same. Slowly, I pull a pen from the breast pocket on my shirt, stalling long enough to be sure they both have time to note the CPW logo stitched there. I hand the pen to Bryce, watching as he signs it with a shaking hand,

and then uses the tip of the pen to poke a hole in the bottom corner. He hands the pen back to me, the tag along with it. I lift a brow.

"It goes *on* the animal."

His face goes slack. "Crap. Sorry. Yes, sir."

Awkwardly leaning over the bed, Bryce wrestles the deer closer by grabbing on to a hoof and ties the tag to it. He gives me another sheepish apology. I draw in a long breath, as if I'm thinking hard through what to do or say next.

I'm not.

"Improper tagging. Illegal transport," I muse. "I'm well within my rights to assess a hefty fine. If I assess penalty points, you could lose your privileges here in Colorado for a year. Not to mention I could confiscate this deer."

The fines and points seem to the least of Bryce's concerns. Confiscating his deer would mean he can't show off to his friends when he gets home. Or show off right here, via social media—assuming he didn't already do that in the field. So the possibility of losing his deer means his lip is quivering and his eyes are watering. If I weren't such an insufferable asshole these days, I might try to put myself in his shoes, remembering what it was like to be a kid who just shot his first deer with a bow.

"He's *twelve*," Greg sputters. "This was a God's-honest mistake. One that won't happen again. Cut us some slack here. Please."

Greg knows as well as I do that game wardens have plenty of latitude when it comes to lesser violations, which in the grand scheme of things is exactly what I'm dealing with. No one's poaching or trespassing, nor have they cut the head off this animal and left the carcass to rot somewhere in the field.

I could easily send these two on their way with a verbal warning. A few months ago, I'd have done exactly that, mostly because it's nice to meet kids these days who show an interest in anything that doesn't have a touch screen.

But that was a few months ago. Today, things are different.

"Rules are rules. We all have to play by them." I dig out my ticket pad and begin to write without looking up. "I won't confiscate the deer. That's the best I can do."

An hour later, just as I pull into my driveway, my phone rings with a call from Tobias.

I groan. A call from my boss at four in the afternoon on a Saturday cannot be a good thing. Tobias guards his weekends as if they're precious metals, and from Friday at five p.m. to Monday at seven a.m., he's not interested in anything but golf, his grandkids, and working on the '49 Triumph motorcycle he's restoring.

When I answer, I'm prepared for the worst, because I already have a good suspicion what he's calling about. He doesn't offer any greeting—not that I was expecting one.

"Did you just issue a five-hundred-dollar fine and a fifteen-point ticket to some kid who isn't old enough to drive?"

"Yes." I spare him the details because it doesn't sound like he cares. At all.

"*Fifteen* points. Five short of the twenty that would suspend his hunting privileges in the state of Colorado for a year. Similar to what we slapped on that guy who poached an elk on that private ranch outside Delta last year."

"Yes."

"Was this kid carrying a machete? Did he flip you off? Did he kick you with his twelve-year-old feet?"

"He was from Texas."

Tobias curses quietly and grumbles until I'm nearly convinced he has nothing else to say. Finally, he blows out an audible exhale.

"I like you, Montgomery. You're reliable, you give a shit, and I don't have to look over your shoulder every five minutes. And until today, I always trusted you to do your job without any drama. I've never questioned where your head is at. I've certainly never thought it might be up your ass."

He pauses to lower his voice, speaking measuredly so I can't mistake a word.

"I don't know what happened when you took that little unplanned trip to Texas, and I don't care. Get your act together, Montgomery. I won't say it again."

He hangs up. I stare out my windshield, regretting all of what I've done. Jesus. What *have* I done? I must have lost my mind, because this would be one stupid-ass way to find myself on the unemployment line.

Inside my house, I toss my coat on the couch and toe off my boots. Charley skitters around me with her favorite chew toy in her mouth as I cast a look around my place. All my books and my records are in their place; everything is where it should be. All I have to do tonight is crack a beer and heat up some of the leftover soup I made yesterday, slice up some of the soda bread I made to go with it, and call it dinner. After that, I can read for a while or crash into bed or stare at the sunset from my front porch. Life doesn't get any simpler than that.

Garrett may have moved to Kansas, and Cooper may be days away from being a new dad, but they're still my buddies. We'll still hunt turkeys together and drink a few beers when we can. Next year, I'll find myself back in Oregon at the cabin, just like always, trying to track down that buck again—and if my mom happens to be there, we'll share dinner and talk about the same things we always have: books and ferns and politics. And, currently, I still have my job. My dog is still here and is always happy to see me.

My life is just as it was before Amber Regan stormed her way into it and, for a moment, changed everything. She was like an impending flashover in a wildfire, one that after all those years I spent on the front lines, I should have seen coming. The signs were there—the heat, the oxygen, the fuel—but I ignored them. Then boom, it all goes up in flames, my heart and my good judgment along with it.

But it doesn't have to be that way. Not for one more day or one more minute. Not anymore. I can choose to get over this and move on, just the way I did with Laurel. And I will.

28

(Amber)

"Other things being equal, it is the man
who shoots with his heart in his bow that hits the mark."
—Saxton Pope, *Hunting with the Bow and Arrow*

Why I expected that the studio heads of an adventure reality production company would be anything other than walking SoCal clichés, I do not know. And yet, in my mind, they wouldn't be quite this bad. I think it may be the cardigans. Or the porkpie hats.

Either way, Hayes Halston and Vann Newell are *very* Hollywood, in an up-and-comer way—confident but still hungry, desperate but still disaffected—which explains their taking the time to fly to Austin to meet me. Of course, if I were a little less disaffected myself these days, I might be delusional enough to think their trip out here meant I was special. But I've seen exactly how suddenly *special* can lose its luster, so I know that in the end, these guys won't be any different from Smeltzer.

Except for those hats.

Even Jaxon—a full-fledged appreciator of the hipster look when done well—continues to squint at the iridescent peacock feather stuck in the band of Vann's hat, and that's only when he isn't casting a judgmental look at Hayes's puce-colored cardigan.

"Amber, we can't tell you how much we appreciate you taking the time to meet with us. We're hoping by the time we finish these," Hayes says, lifting his beer up, "we can confidently say that we'll see you in Cabo this winter. Cabo for Christmas, right? Come on, nothing beats that."

"Definitely," I answer, giving him a smile before taking a sip of my sparkling ginger lemonade. Jaxon and I both ordered mocktails because we're more interested in staying sober at our business meeting than getting buddy-buddy with these guys. Hayes and Vann each—like the predictably cool out-of-towners they are—ordered Shiner Bocks.

Hayes and Vann booked rooms at a downtown boutique hotel that was once the site of a trailer park but is now home to lodgings with concrete floors and midcentury modern furniture, each accessorized with things like retro Smith Corona typewriters and Polaroid cameras. Just in case Jack Kerouac returns from the dead and needs a place to crash, I suppose. We agreed to meet for a drink at the hotel's outdoor lounge, where a sand-lined courtyard is dotted with gas-operated lava-rock fire pits. We've settled ourselves around one of the fire pits, inexplicably "lit" despite it being the middle of the day.

Surrounding the pit are four leather egg chairs that are both ugly and a little awkward to sit in while hoping to appear confident and tall, especially for someone my size. Hopefully, when it's time to extricate myself from this thing, Jaxon will sidle over here and give me a hand so I don't look like a toddler crawling out of a playpen.

"Cabo beats what I grew up with during the holidays. Too much tinsel draped on cacti in Tucson," Vann mutters drily.

We all give him a courtesy chuckle despite the fact that Vann has spent much of our meeting face-first in his phone. I'm more than used to the way so many of us interact with only half of our attention spans these days, but he's worse than most.

Hayes seizes conversational control again, looking like he's decided that after ten minutes together it's high time we get down to business.

"So, Amber, you checked out our media kit and the links, right? Tell us what questions you have. Tell us what it will take to get you on board."

I do have questions. Lots of them. Half of them, though, they can't answer.

Will I regret this? Is the nonstop ache in my chest due to having a broken heart? Or is that just my soul hardening in anticipation of doing this show? Are you aware I've never guided anyone before? Do you care? Also, can I drink the water there? Because Montezuma's revenge in a house crawling with cameras? No thank you. And, last, do you think Braden misses me?

Jaxon cuts in, saving me with one flap of his manager-lawyer-superhero cape.

"Today is just about Amber getting a feel for how you guys do business. If Amber's going to relocate to another country for six weeks, she needs to know who has her back when she does."

Hayes nods reassuringly before allowing a mischievous expression to cover his face.

"Sure, sure, of course. I get it. It sounds like maybe you're a wild card who's concerned about the *policia*, eh? Are you a rabble-rouser? An agent provocateur?"

Then he *winks*.

And I try not to throw up a little in my mouth.

This show is all I have on the horizon, after all, and I'll be lucky if my pride is the only thing I lose track of over the next few months. But a few years under my belt in this business means I can play along with the best of them.

"Oh, yes," I deadpan, then send him a sly smile. "I'm all sorts of trouble. Gotta be sure I'm covered for the mischief and mayhem I'll inevitably leave in my wake."

Hayes returns my smile with his own, albeit with a lot more teeth showing. If I weren't seriously considering the possibility that my libido has taken leave of my body entirely, I'd think he was saying more with that smile than "please sign our contract." But my man compass is all screwed up, and I wouldn't know what to do with sexual interest if it hit me over the head. My compass guides one route these days—north through Oklahoma and Kansas, then hooks one state over and straight into southwestern Colorado. And given how depressed I've been since Braden left town with nothing but a quiet goodbye in my driveway, I'm not sure I'll ever find a way to recalibrate my man compass.

"Look, Angela . . ."

Vann drains his beer, signaling the bartender across the way to bring another round. Jaxon automatically lurches forward at Vann getting my name wrong, but I shoot him a look to stand down because I'm interested in seeing where this goes. While signing with Bona Fide may be the only option I have right now, deep down, I'm still looking for an out. I have a feeling we're about to enjoy a good cop–bad cop show courtesy of Hayes and Vann.

". . . Let's not play around, OK? We know you're an Afield Channel cast-off."

He levels his beady eyes on mine.

"But luckily for you, rejects are our game. We reboot careers.

If it isn't yours, there are a million other chicks out there with blow-up-doll personalities and good racks that would be happy to take your place."

Jaxon is up and out of his chair before I am, and God bless the man, his hand immediately extends my way. I take it and, despite the way my body is shaking, I rise from the chair like a queen. Jaxon's hand stays in mine. He gives Hayes and Vann a curt nod.

"You've given us a lot to consider. We'll be in touch."

We round the corner out of the courtyard, quick-stepping in silence until we've made it to the lot where Jaxon's car is parked. He moves to open the passenger door for me. I lock my eyes with his.

"No."

He nods. "Obviously. I'll call them tomorrow."

I slide into the black leather seat and Jaxon shuts the door.

Sealed in silence for a moment, Braden is with me. His honest assessment of what I was getting myself into is ringing in my head—and how he was able to predict what just happened here with such eerie accuracy, I'll never know.

⁓〜⁓

"To new beginnings."

I roll my eyes at Teagan's cliché toast, then knock back the shot of whiskey she's poured for me, stopping just shy of slamming the glass on the coffee table in front of me, only because my beer is sitting there and I wouldn't want to knock *that* over. She mirrors my actions, both of us chasing the harsh liquor burn with a gulp of our beers.

I slump into the couch cushions and offer my deep thoughts. "New beginnings suck."

Teagan snorts. "Yes, they do. But this one is happening just the same." I stick my lip out in an exaggerated pout, and she sighs. "You will be *fine*."

My reply is to take a long slug off my beer. This isn't a pity party—it's a suck-it-up-and-move-on party. With boilermakers. Because in my mind, the drink du jour of a pity party is wine, red or white, just so long as it's from a box. But a cheap whiskey shot followed by an even cheaper beer? That is the nectar of someone who might need a goddam break, but doesn't take any shit.

I invited Jaxon, Teagan, and Colin over to "celebrate" the end of *Record Racks*, knowing if I did, none of them would dare bring box wine, so I could safely avoid things devolving into a pity party. Jaxon left a few minutes ago to pick up cheap Mexican food for dinner, and Colin is due here at any moment. For now, it's just Teagan and me.

I cut a look her way. "Have you talked to Colin lately?"

"Colin and I do not talk. You know that. This will be the first time I've seen him since your party when Braden was in town. Even then we didn't *talk*. I mean, we . . ." She circles a hand in the air, aimlessly.

I narrow my eyes to the ceiling with a nod, but it takes me a moment to process what she just said.

"Wait. What? During the party?" I point to the couch. "Here?"

"No, not *there*." Her cheeks redden. "The guest bathroom."

I consider taking her by the shoulders and shaking the hell out of her. Not because I care if she and Colin got it on in my bathroom, but because I'm now intimately acquainted with heartbreak, and therefore, I *really* can't understand why these two stay apart when they don't have to.

Teagan points her beer bottle at me. "Don't start. We've had this conversation before. Colin and me together is like going on vacation. Everyone goes on vacation and thinks they want to move to Paris when they're there on holiday, but then they go home and they realize exactly why they can't live in Paris. Because it's like another world."

"Colin lives in Harper, not Paris. It's, like, two hours away. Not exactly another world."

She snorts. "Don't be so sure. I've seen pictures of his family. They are their own species of Texas tough. Can you picture me there? Colin taking me home to meet his family? *Paris*, Amber. Paris."

I tilt my head, speaking softly. "But he makes you happy."

"Same goes for Voodoo Doughnut. As does a day doing my work with my hands and my fingers doing what they should. A new tattoo. Panda videos. Lots of things make me happy."

Teagan closes any further conversation by tossing a bag of Chex Mix into my lap, then busies herself by peeling the label back on her beer bottle. When I sink my hand into the bag, I think of Braden, the look on his face if he could see me now with my fingers wrapped around a handful of this additive-laden snack mix. It wouldn't make it to my mouth, I'm guessing.

Braden has been on my mind constantly, but no more so than today. Today, he was with me nonstop, which was nice, but made the urge to call him harder to fight. Even after passing on the reality show, I still don't know where I'll go next or if where I end up will be a place that can include Braden. Until I know that, reaching out would merely cause us both more hurt.

Teagan and I both look toward the front door when we hear it open. Colin strides in, takes one look at the dwindling bottle of Bird Dog on the coffee table and the adjacent bucket of beers on ice, then observes Teagan and me in repose holding our beers.

"Boilermakers? You girls are speaking my language today." He pours a shot and clears it, uses the bottle opener on his key chain to crack a beer, and then drops onto the couch between us. I wait until he's midway through his second gulp of beer.

"You had sex in my bathroom."

"Jesus!" Colin sputters through a mouthful of beer, eyes wide. He somehow manages to avoid dribbling any on himself or my couch but wipes his mouth with a shirtsleeve anyway. He sends a beseeching look Teagan's way. "Really?"

She shrugs, a tiny smile playing across her lips and a gleam in her eye that's all for him, one he can't help but give in to.

Oh, man. There it is. The good stuff.

I miss that more than ever now.

⁓

After dinner, we each pour a little more whiskey into our highball glasses and proceed to laze about on the furniture, all of us stuffed with greasy Mexican food. Jaxon returns from the side yard after tossing our takeout containers into the trash.

He closes the slider door behind him, beelines into the living room, and stands in front of the coffee table, eyeing our slothful group before clapping his hands together a few times.

"All right, look alive, you lazy louts. We need to brainstorm."

The sharp sound doesn't particularly rouse any of us, but he does have our attention, so we all send him confused and tipsy looks. He snaps his fingers.

"Amber needs a new thing. What is it? We know her best, so let's throw out ideas. Teagan, what should Amber do next?" He points at Teagan, who is slumped against Colin's shoulder. "Say the first thing that comes to mind. Go!"

"Uh . . ."

"Not an answer," Jaxon snaps. "Colin! Now you."

Colin tips his beer bottle toward Jaxon. "Nurse. Teacher. Doctor. President of the United States. Stripper. Porn—"

Colin squeals like a little girl when I pinch the skin on his forearm, hard enough I nearly break the skin, and we exchange scowls.

"No." Jaxon starts to pace the length of the room. "All require a college degree. Even the stripping would be better served if she at least enrolled in college."

I watch Jaxon dizzily and realize I should have known this was coming. Jaxon is the worst drinker ever, not because he's a mean drunk or a sloppy drunk, but because he's the opposite. If he drinks enough, he goes straight from tipsy to hyperfocused, becoming more driven than he is even when sober—and far more difficult to keep up with.

I raise my hand slowly, waiting until Jaxon pauses pacing long enough to notice me. He sighs. "Yes, Amber."

"Do I get a turn? You didn't call on me, so I'm not sure. It's my life, but maybe I'm just supposed to take orders with my blow-up-doll personality?"

He claps his hands together again. "No time for passive-aggressive bullshit, doll. Do you have an idea or not? What do you want to do?"

I can feel everyone's focus on me, but instead of wilting under the scrutiny, the attention does what it always has. It makes me bolder.

"I want another TV show."

"Good," Jaxon says. "What kind of show?"

Colin pipes up. "The kind she should've had all along. The kind like the one she just filmed and those morons at Afield passed on."

"But something was wrong with it," Jaxon muses. "That's why they passed. We have to come up with a better hook. Maybe the hunting platform isn't enough anymore. Maybe viewers want something else."

We all go silent, lost in our own thoughts, but my heart is beating hard enough to make my hands shake a little. I scan the room around me, taking it all in. Trey's furniture, the mounts on the wall, the fitness supplements piled up on the kitchen counters, and even my talented friends.

Be one hundred percent of who you are.

"A lifestyle show," I say. "*My* lifestyle. All of it. Hunting, working out, staying in shape, the people I know, everything."

My eyes cross the room to Jaxon, who's come to a halt with his back to me. He turns slowly on one heel. A smile crawls across his face.

Teagan fumbles around to drag her phone out of her pocket.

"Make it a Web-based show. Screw trying to find a channel for it. Make your own. That art collective I work with? They just started filming long-form profiles on all of their members." She tosses her phone my way and I scroll through the site, clicking on one of the videos.

Colin cranes to look over my shoulder, eventually pointing at the screen. "These are shot on pretty basic action cams. It wouldn't take much to get you set up to shoot your own show. You did a decent job with your solo hunt footage, so if we spend a little more time together, we can easily get you to where you need to be."

Jaxon hums in thought for a moment. "Endorsers love it when they aren't cluttered in with all the brand noise on TV. Maybe we've been too focused on cable. Maybe the new Amber Regan brand is a little more niche." He sends me a frank look.

"It will take a while to get something like this up to full speed. You'll need another income. We can try to pick up some new endorsements in the meantime, but that will be a long shot right now."

Braden pries his way into my head again, complete with his regular-job-ordinary-life speech. I'd cast it off at the time because anything regular or ordinary felt like failure. Now I can see I don't have to accept it as a failure; I could choose it as a way to have everything I ever wanted. My show, done my way. A full life. One that could include Braden, if I can show him my truth.

I give Jaxon a grin. "I started at Dollar General; I can go back to Dollar General. Lots of people have regular jobs."

29

(Braden)

"Of all the paths you take in life, make sure
a few of them are dirt."
—John Muir

Just before hitting send on my reports to Tobias, I offer up a thank-you to the tech gods. An agreeable, supplicant, polite thank-you that is absent of any cuss words. Because showing up here at four a.m. to bang my reports out at the last minute was a risk, and had anything gone wrong, I would have had to call Tobias and ask for an extension. Since I'm still on thin ice with him, acting like a flake would not be a smart move.

I'd taken this past weekend to make a quick trip out to Kansas so I could help Garrett on his newly purchased farm. After just two days of Garrett running my ass ragged, I was ready to come home to my cushy job. While I always understood that farming is a challenging, backbreaking way of life, just a few days working as Garrett's lowly minion proved that I didn't know the half of it. I rolled into Hotchkiss last night too late and too tired to do anything but eat dinner and crash. But the trip was worth it, no matter how early I had to get up this morning. Garrett is on track for the next phase in his life, he has Cara back, and most important, he's happy. As for me, seeing Garrett settled put a few things into perspective, and my long drive home offered plenty of time to think.

The truth was, I'd fallen for Amber. Hard. Fallen so hard that it was easy to become a vindictive asshole when things ended. Because when you love someone and they choose something or someone else over you, it fucking hurts. When Laurel left, I did the same thing, acted out in the same snarling ways.

But loving and losing Amber was worse. With Laurel, I never once wanted her back, which probably says a lot about how little I had invested in that relationship. Amber, though . . . Amber I wanted back. I *still* want her back. I want to love her and take care of her, have her give the same to me. I want to be there when she eventually does fill a Colorado elk tag, help her pack it out, then take her home and put her in a warm bath like I did a few months ago. I want to do that same thing every single archery season for as long as we can both make it out into the field.

But that isn't going to happen. I'd let her go too easily. Even if we view the idea of what makes for a rewarding life differently, I didn't do enough to see if we could make it work somehow. And finally admitting all that to myself has helped, in almost the same way it did when I was in Oregon and my mom called out my feelings for Amber. In both instances, everything became easier when I owned the truth. The almighty power of acceptance or some shit, I guess, because it's less difficult now to focus on my life and my work, just as I've done this morning.

After sending my reports to the printer, I lean back in my chair and watch the ancient contraption slowly crank out the reports. But they are printing—no error lights, no paper jambs, no ink running low—so I must be doing something right.

A bell dings. It takes me a second to remember the little bell that sits on the reception station, there for those days when there are public hours but I also have work to do in my office. That way anyone who comes in to find an empty front desk can feel as if help is just a bell ring away. Today, though, I do not have public office hours. But since I arrived at the crack of dawn, I didn't think to lock the front door behind me.

The bell dings again.

I cast a look down at my clothes, the ones I wore all day yesterday and put back on this morning after dragging my ass out of bed. My ancient Oregon Ducks tee isn't exactly work wear, but I have an extra uniform shirt stashed in a desk drawer, so I dig it out and start to put it on over my T-shirt. Per our employee manual, we're required to wear uniform shirts tucked in, so I unbuckle my belt and open my pants up to tuck it in.

Ding.

Jesus.

Ding-ding-ding.

"Be right there!" I call out, biting my tongue to keep from saying anything more colorful. The bell then starts to ding nonstop.

Fucking hell. My pants are only half-closed, but I manage to get my zipper up just as I storm into the main office.

Where Amber is standing, continuing to ding the fucking bell with a goofy grin on her face. Her eyes then dart to where my hands are on my still-undone belt. The grin fades from her face, and she stares at my hands.

"Please tell me you were back there polishing your crystal ball.

Because if I interrupted another woman doing the polishing, that's going to make my trip out here a real bust."

"Neither," I manage, croaking until I clear my throat. "I was working. Alone. The office isn't open today, so I just had a T-shirt on. I had to put on a uniform shirt."

Amber's features relax. She's dressed in a black hoodie and some faded jeans with a hole in one knee that looks earned instead of designed, and a pair of brown lace-up work boots. Her hair is in a loose side braid, and she's tugged on an obviously well-loved Rangers ball cap. A white three-ring binder is in her hand, which she now holds up.

"I need to show you something."

Before I can say "what?" or, you know, ask what the hell it is she's doing here, Amber is headed down the hall and into my office.

Christ. I know how this scene ends because this is where we started. Been there and done that. And even if my heart believes going there again sounds like a good way to make it stop hurting, my brain knows that won't help me move on. Even so, I follow her anyway.

My stupid heart sinks when I don't find her sitting on my desk, but standing awkwardly against the wall across from my desk. I clear her without pausing and sit down in my desk chair. Amber clasps the binder to her chest but doesn't say anything—she simply stares at me. I raise my brows. She blinks and smiles sheepishly.

"Sorry. Seeing you again distracted me for a second. I missed looking at you."

Fuck *me*. I'm unable to come up with even a smart-ass remark because all I want is to tell her how much I missed everything about her. Amber thrusts her binder forward.

"I'm here because I want to show you this."

My brow furrows up. "You came here from Texas to show me a binder? You could have mailed it. Saved yourself the travel money. And the time."

The dynamic that's always defined us creeps up with my dry sarcasm and her responding smirk, and it feels like whatever time was lost between us is nothing but old news. Once again, I'm the big oaf who likes telling her how it is, and she's the beautiful woman who loves pushing my buttons. Amber lurches up from the wall and begins my way. My heart starts to pound, and when she's near enough that a rush of strawberry hits my nose, I close my eyes and take a deep breath, reopening them just as Amber hops up on my desk. She shimmies around a bit to get comfortable, and all I want to do is grab her by the hips and make her stop.

She flips open the binder, shielding the contents from my view. "I'm not going to do the reality show."

Relief rushes through me, hard and fast, replaced by hope that I know I shouldn't latch on to. "Good. I know it's not my business, but I'm glad."

She shakes her head. "It *is* your business. Or at least I want it to be."

Amber sighs. "You were right about everything. The two clowns who run the studio came to Austin and implied I have the personality of a blow-up doll . . . but with a good rack. And this was their approach to get me to sign with them. I'd hate to know what they'd say if they *didn't* want me."

"They *what*?" My body rises up from the chair a few inches as if these pricks are in the room with us and I can take them by the throat the way I want to. Amber waves a hand in the air.

"Don't make me repeat it. All that matters is that I passed, and they, along with their porkpie hats, are back in LA."

She takes a deep breath and turns her binder around. My eyes drop and zero in on a picture of Amber standing in her backyard, looking pared down but more beautiful than ever.

"I have a new plan. This"—she points toward the photo—"is a working pitch book for the new Web-based show I want to create. One that reflects my lifestyle and my perspective, but updated. I'll still focus on outdoor sports, hunting and shooting mostly, but I want to branch out from there."

She starts to flip through each page. First to a picture of her in a wintering cornfield, clad in a traditional olive-green shooting jacket with a twelve-gauge in her arms. The next is a shot of her and Trey out on his boat, lines cast, while they laugh their asses off. She turns another page. Amber and Trey again, but this time it looks like they're at his furniture business, because industrial lathes and saws are in the background and Amber is watching Trey work on a sketch.

"I want to include segments on all the cool people I know, or the artists that hang out with Trey and Teagan." Another page flip to a picture of Amber standing in a pigpen surrounded by piglets with Colin grinning side frame. "Even guys like Colin. Ranchers and farmers. Their stories, my stories, all through the filter of my brand."

The next picture gets all of my attention. Along with my dick's attention. She's out for a trail run, dressed in skimpy workout gear, with sweat trailing down her neck and disappearing into the cleavage I missed more than I can stand at the moment. I must have let out a noise of some sort because Amber chuckles.

"Glad to hear I look good enough to sell the fitness segments I have in mind."

"Damn good," I choke out, dragging my eyes away from the photo to look at the real-life Amber in front of me. Her cheeks are flushed bright pink and her eyes are lit up with excitement and focus. She's proud of this—and she should be.

"This is amazing. This is the kind of show you deserve to have. This is *you.*"

Amber's cheeks flare a shade darker and she averts her eyes from mine by looking at the wall behind me. "You told me not to settle, to be a hundred percent of who I am. That's what this is."

"I'm so fucking excited for you, sweetheart," I whisper.

I spot a few tears brimming in the corners of her eyes, but she blinks them away before returning her gaze to me.

"I have one area I'm still struggling with." She turns to the last page.

It's a photo of her standing in her kitchen, flour dusted on her cheeks and her hair a little mussed as she pretends to look frazzled while reading a cookbook. She's wearing a 1950s-housewife dress that's so short her garter is visible, with red heels so high they make my mouth go dry.

"I want to do some cooking and food segments. While I'm not *this* bad in the kitchen, I could use someone to help me learn about, oh, I don't know, making sauerkraut. Or energy bars. Or snack mix. Someone like you." She grasps her binder to her chest. "Tell me what you think."

I swallow thickly. "I think I was trying to get over you. And I think you're making that impossible."

"Good. Because I'm not over you. I don't want to be. I want *us.*"

My heart starts to stagger about in my rib cage, like it wants to bust out of my chest and flop itself right at Amber's feet. My brain, though, knows there are still valid reasons why we can't be together. One of them is glaringly obvious.

"But you live in *Texas,*" I murmur.

"I'm also in between fixed gigs right now. So I could get a job at the Cabela's in Grand Junction and work on the first few episodes around here so we can be together. That's the beauty of what I want to create. It doesn't have an address."

My face furrows as I take in all that she's offering. To leave her home, her friends, and her family, relocate to Colorado and get a real job here—just to be where I am. It would sound awesome if I didn't know what it's like to be on the other side of a sacrifice like that. And even though I didn't ask Amber to do this, I hate the idea that she would forfeit parts of her life to be with me.

There's another solution though, one where it doesn't seem like anyone would have to sacrifice anything.

"Or I could move to Austin."

Amber sucks in a harsh breath. "You would do that?"

I shrug. "Garrett's in Kansas now; Cooper's busy with babies. My family doesn't live here. I like my job, but it's not my life, so I can find another one. And since going to Austin ruined me with real barbeque, now I can't eat at True Grit and enjoy it."

Amber grins. I tilt my head, pausing to be sure I'm ready to tell her the real reason why, whether it's Texas or Tennessee, *where* I end up doesn't much matter.

"I once moved across four states because a woman broke my heart. So I can certainly move three states to be with the woman who can help me make it whole again. Because she's the one I want to give it to."

We stare at each other for what feels like days. Two people so different, and so alike at the same time. Amber crawls off of my desk and into my lap.

"Do you remember that day we said goodbye outside your house? When we talked about no promises but made one anyway?" she asks.

I nod. Amber's eyes go soft, lost in what looks like sentimentality. A feeling that I know she's fighting hard to avoid running from, because she forces a long breath before saying more.

"We said we would forget all the reasons this shouldn't work and try to find just one reason it would. I found that reason,

Braden. It's an easy one, too." Amber gives me a weary smile. "Because I love you. That's my reason."

I swallow the rise of emotion that threatens to turn me into a blubbering fool, answering her with the only words I can manage.

"I love *you*."

Amber lets her eyes drop closed, obviously working to keep her own blubbering at bay. She sighs and opens her eyes again.

"But we should keep discussing this. My life's changing in big, scary ways. Now you're talking about doing the same thing to your life. So we shouldn't rush into this. We don't have to decide anything today, or tonight. We can talk it out. Grown-up and mature-like."

I put my arms around her, pulling her close and brushing my lips across hers.

"Sure. We'll talk it out. All night or for as long as we need to. We have our one good reason, so all we have to do is start there and we'll be fine." I kiss her once, murmuring my next words against her lips. "Now. When you talk about being grown-up and mature, you mean *naked*, right?"

Amber laughs, relieved and relaxed. "Yes. Naked is very grown-up. And very mature."

I lean back, look at her for a beat. "I missed you. Losing you turned me into a real asshole."

Amber crooks a skeptical brow.

"Fine. It turned me into a *bigger* asshole." I shake my head. "It's possible I ruined some poor kid's first deer hunt with a bow, that's how much of a jerk I became. You make me happy. You keep me from acting like a selfish ass all of the time. And I need you to keep doing that so I can become the guy worthy of loving you."

She wraps her body to mine as tight as she can, arms around my neck, legs around my waist, and her face tucked into my neck.

"You already are that guy. But I need you to have me one hundred percent; a full life, no compromises. Without you . . . I'd always come up short."

Those words become everything. Filling in every scar in my heart and each empty space in my world. Amber made my once-simple existence so fucking complicated that I can't imagine it without her again, and I don't want to. She is the untamed, uncontrollable force I needed in my life more than I could have ever understood.

And I'm ready for her now. Ready for what makes her wild and wonderful, for the way I know she'll always make every steep and muddy trail worth the climb—season after season.

Acknowledgments

Many thanks to the amazing team at Pocket Books for all their efforts to ensure that the final installment of the Grand Valley series is the best it can be and finds its way into readers' hands. Thank you also to my agent, Victoria Cappello, for her ongoing guidance and expertise.

Thank you, as always, to Warren. *Ready for Wild* demanded a fact-checker such as yourself. A check is in the mail for your services—in the meantime, go show those mountains who's boss.